A REIGN SO RUINOUS

FATES SO FATAL, BOOK 2

RACHEL TORK

For anyone who struggles under the weight of their past. We may not be able to choose our beginnings, but cycles of trauma can be broken. I promise, there is light in you.

TRIGGER WARNINGS

Explicit sex scenes, suicidal ideation and mentions of past attempts, conversations about infant loss (not involving the main character), recollections of child abuse, mentions of rape (not involving the main character).

CHAPTER
ONE

June tells me someone must keep a record. That if I do not, the true story will be forgotten. I do not want to remember, but I cannot forget either. I fear the sound of their screams will forever echo in my mind.
—Lady Anabeth, Royal Scribe's Apprentice, D'anna

EVERY SINGLE CITY bell in D'anna clanged insistently, the shrill echoes a clear warning to the mountain capital's residents: take cover, hide, and gather any weapons you have.

The bells only rang in dire circumstances.

In the year she had been living at the Sisters of Arcane's newest temple outpost perched on a mountainside at the edge of the city, Nya Evva hadn't heard them. In fact, she had been told many times by the sisters that they hadn't rang once in her lifetime.

The capital, ruled by the aged mortal queen, Cion Livii, had been a center of trade and knowledge for many years now. The queen was beloved, the Kingdom of Aren a peaceful place, though Nya understood it hadn't always been that way. Her parents had foregone telling her the details of just what the cost of that peace had been, but she filled in some of the blanks from others since arriving here.

"We need to go below," Sister Jada insisted, tugging on Nya's hand. The priestess' hazel-gold eyes were wide, shining with a terror that contrasted sharply with her typical calm, no-nonsense demeanor. "Hurry."

"But how do we even know if—"

"Nya, it's for your safety." Jada's complexion, though usually fair, was now completely devoid of color. "We need to run *now*."

"What about the others? There isn't room for all the sisters and apprentices below. And what of the citizens, especially the ones without magic? I could help—"

"No," Jada said sharply, her gaze swinging around the airy meditation room, as if afraid danger was already lurking nearby.

It was empty, aside from the two of them, but Nya could hear footsteps pounding on the roof garden above, in the hallways beyond. Past the smooth, bone-white pillars, open to the cool mountain air, she heard screams echoing from the city. The fine hairs on the back of her neck rose.

Dark hair had come loose from Jada's intricate braids, framing her flushed, frenzied face as she scanned the horizon. "Nya, I promised your mother I would keep you safe. And if this is what I fear it is…" She trailed off, her hand tightening around Nya's. "You cannot be seen."

"What *do* you fear it is?"

Jada's throat bobbed, and she looked back at Nya as she whispered, "Rumors have begun to drift from Arcadia of a new god. Someone the principals were unaware of. Someone who would be very interested in you."

"Why?" Nya asked, her jaw trembling, just as the roar of a dragon echoed through the slopes. The sound rattled down to her bones, striking a chord deep within the frantic pounding of her blood.

Jada shook her head and a tear fell down her cheek. "Gods forgive me. I thought the rumors were just that."

"What do you—"

Jada leapt in front of Nya abruptly, and the entire temple trembled and shook. They both crashed to the ground as stone and debris rained down around them. Pain lanced up Nya's left leg, but she could not see what had happened, could not understand how one moment, they had been standing in the untouched study room and now were buried under rubble, screams echoing somewhere nearby.

"J–Jada?"

The priestess had covered Nya's body with her own, protecting her from the worst of the sudden blow. The dust cleared just enough to see again, and a choked gasp escaped Nya as she saw Jada's empty, wide eyes above her. Something was impaled in her abdomen, warm blood leaking from the wound and covering the turquoise wrap dress Nya wore, staining the fabric a deep crimson.

The dragon roared again, much closer this time— maybe even directly above her.

Nya reached blindly for a thread of the web connecting her parents, their dragons, and her. Her mother had always insisted she work harder at strengthening her ability to reach them down their mental pathway, but she had never taken it seriously. All three of the mortal kingdoms and Arcadia, the land of the gods, were at peace and had been since before her birth. Besides, she knew her parent's dragons only ever let her in as a courtesy. She was not truly bound to that place, and it often felt odd to intrude.

Still, she tried, gasping for air under the crushing press of the wreckage and the weight of Jada's still body.

Heles. Thessilnn.

The dragons did not respond.

Mamma. Papa. Please.

Nothing.

She started to sob in broken, hitching gasps, wishing she had listened to their warnings to be careful and aware, wishing she had hugged them one last time before leaving the safety of her childhood home. Her parents had not stopped her, but she'd seen the fear in her father's eyes when she had left astride Heles all those months ago.

She had been so insistent she needed to go, claiming she was sick of the cloistered embrace of the quiet forest in Mise where she was raised. Her true reasons for leaving them behind, for apprenticing with the sisters in order to take their sacred vows of chastity and service, were her own secret—her own *shame.*

She supposed it did not matter now.

She had bluffed to Jada. She had heard the rumors slipping over the border these past months but had willfully cast them aside as gossip. People grew bored in times of peace, and what the whispers claimed was impossible. It had to be. She *needed* it to be.

There had been a slew of horrible storms sweeping across Aren this past year, brought over on howling winds from Arcadia and leaving destruction in their wake. An unusual number of earthquakes had caused widespread avalanches in the more remote mountain districts to the east, some of them large enough to level entire small villages. Nya had reasoned with herself again and again that the strange weather was not caused by what everyone said it was.

That somehow, there was still a piece of the once-mighty god king, Kronos, out there.

Not his own soul, of course. *That* had been destroyed in dragon fire decades before her birth, marked and banished forever with the same symbol Nya had once seen flicker across her father's forehead on an unusually cold winter night, the same day Nya's little brother had been born still and quiet.

The mark of a goddess.

Two moon cycles ago, she had finally asked for the truth. According to Jada, the mark that destroyed Kronos was that of the Nyx's heir, a goddess reborn twice over, who had been killed by Kronos and returned the favor in her second life. The one who had fallen for a demi-god, the lost heir to the fire god, Vulcan, who himself had paid a steep price for taking a god king's promised bride.

It made sense, she supposed, as hot tears streamed down her blood-stained cheeks where she lay beneath the rubble, that he would seek her. Maybe it was for the best that she died here before they could find her. That way, her parents would be safe—forever broken by her death, but safe. Then again, maybe they didn't fear the void that came after this world, but rather lives that offered much worse fates.

"I'm sorry," she mouthed silently, her eyes landing on the slate-hued sky above her.

Her chest was beginning to cave under the stone and

debris above Jada's body. She closed her eyes, her body still trying to fight for oxygen, for life. But her mind was made up. She would let herself fade. Within some small, dark place in her mind, letting herself die felt right.

"There, underneath the rubble."

The voice was deep and masculine, a little grating at the end of each word, almost as if it hurt to force them out. She knew it was familiar, but for a moment, lost in the haze of pain and looming death, she did not understand why.

"Are you sure, Morgen? No mortal could survive beneath all that pressure, much less live past the initial blow. Which was a bit dramatic, if you ask me. Varax is too damn big for this place."

"We are not looking for a mortal."

She did not recognize the other voice, but…

Morgen.

Morgen.

She hardly had the ability to draw air now, between the pressure of Jada's body and the debris covering them, so when she gasped the words, they were nearly soundless.

"No. Please, no."

She willed her body to give in faster. Now, before they found her. She would rather die than realize the undeniable truth she had long suspected. She did not want to see his face when he realized it too.

In the end, her body's will to survive betrayed her. The broken chunks of the temple and debris above her was cleared, and she saw two towering male forms, backlit in the stark light of the cloudy afternoon.

"Move the body, will you, Carus?"

She reached for Jada a moment too late. The priestess'

limp form was already being tossed aside like it was nothing more than a sack of grain. A whimper slipped past Nya's lips, and the taller of the two men sighed as he kneeled.

She saw it, the moment he truly understood what was happening. She knew he was aware of who she was, so perhaps it was just the shock of seeing her after a year of utter silence.

His entire body froze, his golden-tan complexion paling. Long, dark hair—not black, but a deep shade of brick-red—fell down his back, half of it carelessly knotted into a bun. His jaw flexed, tugging on the faded scar that ran across his slightly hooked nose and down to the top of his upper lip. Their eyes met, and she wanted to scream as the truth she had so naively denied to herself was made painfully obvious.

She had always known he was not mortal, so it was no surprise to see the silver flickers of ether cutting through the brown of his irises. But the bright gold veins lighting them up, the ones she had tried again and again to tell herself were just a deep amber…

There was no denying it now, just as she couldn't before.

"Problem?" the other man, the one Morgen had called Carus, asked, as if they had not just destroyed an entire holy temple and tossed Jada's body aside so casually.

Morgen's throat worked, the faint, white scar there bobbing. "We're looking for a goddess."

Carus snorted softly. "And it looks like we found one. You're right, there's no way a mortal would have survived under all that. Though…" His head tilted, light-blond waves falling in his brown eyes. "She's injured badly. You should probably heal her before we go."

Morgen lifted a hand, long fingers outstretched towards

her. The gold flaring in his irises brightened, and she flinched away, even as copper filled her mouth. "Don't. *Please*. Don't."

He could heal her. He'd done it before, but she didn't want to be fixed now.

Morgen's lips parted, and Carus laughed again. "You do know you're going to die if we don't help you, right?"

Please. Please, just let me go. It's better this way.

He ignored Carus, a shadow passing over Morgen's face, his mouth tightening as Nya accessed the pathway for the first time in a year. He didn't reply, though; he just pressed his hand firmly over her torn skin, just above her collarbone. Unable to move or stop him, she just let the tears roll down her cheeks as she felt the essence of Life itself push into her body, healing her, forcing her to keep breathing. She didn't scream, even when the magic began to burn her insides to the point of agony. But when he finished and she could breathe again without feeling like her lungs were going to collapse, she looked directly into his still-aglow eyes.

Morgen. Please.

He ignored her, and she died a little more inside, the same part of her that had been withering away since she'd first suspected who he truly was.

In the distance, another dragon roared, though not the enormous crimson beast perched on the edge of the cliff the temple jutted out onto.

Varax, she tried. The dragon's amber eyes met hers, blinking slowly. *Help me.*

She merely rustled her enormous wings. *Don't complain to me about truths you both denied. For far too long, I might add.*

"We need to go," Carus said. "There are riders

approaching, and it's probable the mortal queen will send them here first, given her history with the girl's mother." He glanced at Nya, still on the ground. "It is her, isn't it?"

Morgen's jaw twitched. "It's her."

Nya knew he had just heard her speaking to Varax. Unless the dragon actively closed the pathway, all three of them were connected, had been since Nya first saw blinking amber in her dreams four years ago. At least, they were, until Nya had run and shut both of them out.

Years ago, when she had casually floated the notion of one dragon with two riders to her father, he'd frowned and said he had never heard of such a thing. She had never brought it up again.

A mistake. All of it.

Morgen's eyes flashed to hers, and she wondered if Varax had ferried the thought to him.

Good.

"We're leaving," he said shortly, tugging Nya up. "Now."

"Where?" she challenged, jaw clenched tight to keep it from chattering.

Carus paused and looked between the two of them, brow furrowed. "Do you two——"

"*Now*," Morgen snarled, the ground trembling beneath them as his power rose. He dragged her over to Varax, long fingers wrapped around her wrist. "Get on the saddle."

Her nostrils flared. "And if I say no? Are you going to force me? Sounds familiar."

Fury flashed in his eyes, the gold veins brightening again. He knew exactly what she was trying to do, and she was sure he regretted telling her about his past now. She had too much leverage over his emotions.

"Morgen! They're getting closer. If you want to avoid a confrontation, I suggest we move, *quickly*."

"Nya. *Now*," Morgen growled.

She could try to run. The single advantage she had was that Varax wouldn't hurt her. But Morgen knew how untrained she was in her magic, and she was fully aware he knew just how to use his.

They knew everything about each other except the things that truly mattered.

He held her hard gaze for a few moments, not backing down. Finally, she gave a mocking bow of her head. "As you wish, my *king*."

Before either he or Carus could react, she climbed atop Varax, ignoring Morgen as he followed, settling into the saddle behind her. She glanced at the ruined temple below, hating herself and hating him. She had come here to run from the truth, to take vows of holy devotion and celibacy in an attempt to save herself. She had only ended up damning others.

Today would be a good day, Varax, Morgen said into the pathway.

Even there, his voice was edged with tension; his body was so stiff behind her, she felt his muscles *must* hurt. She told herself didn't care what he was feeling.

The dragon roared and then abruptly dove off the cliffside. Nya leaned low into the saddle to avoid flying off, Morgen doing the same behind her. To their left, Carus rode a tan Fesper dragon, about half the size of Varax, and in the distance, she caught a glimpse of the queen's fleet approaching.

They left the capital and the fleet behind quickly, and

Nya knew in her heart where they were headed. It wasn't far to Arcadia's border with D'anna, and, too soon, the shimmering veil she had never seen but heard about countless times appeared ahead.

"Brace yourself," Morgen said gruffly in her ear. "It might feel as if you can't breathe for a moment."

She ignored him. The barrier approached, and she closed her eyes. When the heavy, sticky feeling of magic enveloped her, stealing the air from her lungs, she leaned into it.

Take me, she pleaded, perhaps to the magic itself, or even to the gods beyond, the ones she shared blood and power with. *End this before it can begin.*

Neither listened.

They broke the barrier, and the smell of honeytwine trees and fresh water surrounded her. A lush, broad valley caged them on either side, but she knew in her heart they weren't close yet. A usurper didn't hide in a sunlit field. Wherever they were going, wherever he had been hiding all these years, would not be pleasant.

Neither would her role.

CHAPTER 2

FOUR YEARS PRIOR

I saw her again in my dreams, the child, now laughing. It is a mockery, I fear, not a true vision of Fate. Even if Sora were to return, I do not think it will be for long. The world is in such a state of unrest, and Kronos is still watching closely. Vane never asks about the dreams, but I think he knows. After all, he was the only one I told. I abhor the false hope it gives him.
—Lady Anabeth, Royal Scribe's Apprentice, D'anna

IT WAS BARELY dawn when she crept out of the house. She was sure one of her parents sensed her leaving, but they didn't wake to ask where she was going. She was grown at twenty and two, after all, and there was little danger here in the vast, secluded forest in Mise. They didn't cloister her, never had, though she could tell it wasn't always easy, especially for her father.

When she was a child, he'd been constantly on edge. He always tried to hide it, but there had been many occasions when a twig had snapped outside or something had rustled in the brush, and the silver of ether had brightened in his eyes, the air warming with the inferno of his magic. She wasn't entirely sure the reasons, but once, when she'd asked her mother why he was always so afraid, she had told her: *"He tries not to show it, Nya. But neither of us are used to safety, not for long, and you are precious to him, to both of us. The thought of watching someone hurt you terrifies him."*

Her mother had said it as if he'd watched before, unable to do anything.

Her parents had always appeared young and never aged. She knew they were not mortal—always had, since she first understood what that meant—but she had an inkling they were much older than they let on. She knew they had been a part of the downfall of the tyrant god-king of Arcadia, Kronos, over half a century ago now. Kronos, who, she learned in a record keeping text, had died in dragon fire, marked, damned, and destroyed by a new god who had gone into the blaze with him.

She had only ever heard of Nyx's mark damning souls. Nyx, the goddess of night, who she was named for and whose midnight magic mingled in her veins alongside a rising inferno she had never understood.

She had long suspected who her parents were, who *she* was. It was precisely why she did not tell them when she started to remember pieces of her dreams two seasons ago. They feared Arcadia, and rightfully so, but she did not want them to worry. She didn't truly think she was in danger.

Heles snorted as Nya skirted past her enormous, dark-scaled body, curled in the shadows of the long-limbed trees just behind the house.

You are going somewhere.

The voice was not Heles', but Thessilnn's, who was

much more awake, staring at Nya knowingly with opaque silver eyes.

"Yes," Nya whispered. "It's fine. I'll be safe. Just tell them…tell them I'll be hiking until later."

Thessilnn huffed. *They will be angry if they find out we lied.*

"Then don't let them find out."

Heles yawned, but her raspy voice filled Nya's mind next. *Will you at least reassure us you can actually use the pathway we so kindly opened for you, little one?*

Nya sighed. *I will signal if I need something.*

Thessilnn huffed, her breath stirring the leaves before she lowered her head to the ground. She shut her eyes, but as Nya walked past her, she spoke once more.

Just try *not to ferry the other dragon down this pathway once you get there. I am trying to sleep for once, and it will put an end to your sneaking before it even begins if your parents hear her.*

Nya stopped short, looking back at Thessilnn, the moon to Heles' night sky, but she was already feigning sleep, and Heles was actually snoring.

So, it was real. The dreams of the amber eyes…*real.* And the rest of it?

She sucked in a sharp breath. She would see once she arrived if the impossibility the dragon had claimed was true.

About three miles away, a creek bed that ran through much of the forest opened into a waterfall. At the bottom, there was a large outcropping of stone; a clearing big enough for even dragons as large as Thessilnn and Heles to land.

Nya reached the waterfall just as the sun crested the horizon, bathing the world in a red-orange glow. The only problem was, skirting around the falls and down the hill would take at least another half hour. She didn't see anyone below, but she *had* promised sunrise. What if she missed the window?

She never remembered her dreams when she awoke, not before this. Even so, these dreams felt more like an echo reaching her in the hazy moments before waking. The dragon, who called herself Varax, never showed herself in the visions. Perhaps she could not. Nya was fairly sure Varax was reaching her on some kind of mental pathway, similar to how her parents communicated with Thessilnn and Heles. She had never heard of a pathway working at such a long distance, though, to be fair, she had no idea where Varax actually was. Halfway through the last moon cycle, the dragon informed Nya they would meet. It was not only two nights ago that she told her of the other rider. No name was given, but Varax referred to the rider as a 'he.'

It was ultimately stupid, but in her anxiety and flustered anticipation, Nya attempted to scale the side of the damp stone beside the falls. About halfway down, her foot slipped, and despite scrambling to grab a nearby notch in the stone, it was too slick, and she plummeted into the churning water.

She could swim just fine, but fear tore at her senses as the undertow beneath the falls caught her. She tried to kick away from the violent pull of the water, but it was in vain, her lungs already seizing from the panic and lack of oxygen. She was just about to reach down the mental pathway to her parents' dragons when strong arms pulled her up, away from the undertow and out of the water.

Palms flat against the cool, coal-hued stone beside the falls, she gasped for air, coughing. Next to her, someone did the same before reaching towards her.

She reared back on instinct but froze when she saw his face.

He *looked* young, perhaps a few years older than her, with a golden-tan complexion, high, pronounced cheekbones, and a strong nose. Dark hair that fell somewhere halfway down his back was plastered to his face, and he shoved it back with one of his hands. But what really gave her pause were his eyes.

His brown irises were intersected with a shocking shade of amber-gold. The fact that they were rimmed with silver was the first thing that made her reconsider his true age. He was clearly not mortal. There was something else there too, a sort of haunted cast that reminded her of the way her parents sometimes looked at each other; a pain that never quite left and spoke of much endured. But where their pain was always softened by love, this man's was…cold. Empty.

Her gaze wandered behind him, searching, and the man said, "Varax is down creek…frolicking, I believe."

I do not frolic. I am cooling off my scales.

The man's mouth twitched, just barely. *Sure.*

Nya's lips' parted in disbelief. She could hear the dragon *and* the man in the same way she could hear Heles and Thessilnn. The dragon, Varax, had not lied or bluffed about coming here, nor about the other rider, if this was indeed him. She should probably clarify that, but—

"Are you alright?"

She took a slow, shuddering breath, trying to wrap her mind around what this meant. "I'm fine."

"It's just… The near drowning. It couldn't have been pleasant."

Her brow creased, and she studied him. Even just

sitting next to her, waves of magic ebbed from him like a pulsing aura, energy shifting almost visibly in the air around him. Whoever he was, he had come from some powerful bloodline. Perhaps he was even a full godling, given the visible ether in his eyes and the noticeable breadth of his magic. Presumably, he had come here with Varax, which meant…

Ask him the question, Nya, the dragon urged.

The man's eyes widened incrementally. "So, it's true," he said quietly.

Nya worried her bottom lip between her teeth. "You're her rider?"

He gave a shallow nod. "And now it seems you are too."

"You didn't connect us on purpose, did you?" she asked, curling her hands into fists. Despite the warm morning, she was starting to shiver, water still dripping from her water-logged shirt and pants. "It's just…you're not mortal. You could have devious reasons."

His lips curved. His upper lip was thinner than his bottom, just barely caught by a faint scar that ran the length of most of his face. "Neither are you. Although, if you think gods can bridge minds, I'm going to venture out on a wild guess and say you don't know much about Arcadia or the gods who live there."

She looked away, feeling a little stupid. The dragon had been so insistent they finally meet after nearly a year of the dreams. Looking back on it now, Nya thought she might have always been aware of another presence lingering nearby, perhaps not even aware of its proximity. When Varax had finally revealed it was her rider, that was when Nya's curiosity had peaked. She had been *excited* to come here today, hardly thinking about the dangers a meeting such as this might pose.

But this man…this god, or whoever he was, was right. She knew almost nothing about Arcadia beyond a few passages in books and her parents' fear. Given how powerful they were, that alone probably should have warned her off, but perhaps the need to know who she truly was pulled stronger.

She had hoped this meeting today would begin to make the truth clearer.

"Hmm," the man hummed. "You don't know much at all of it, do you? And now…" He tilted his head to the side, gaze sliding over her. His eyes no longer appeared so bright. "Now, you're regretting coming here. Maybe you're even afraid."

"Should I be?"

He shrugged as if it did not matter, laying back on the stone and throwing a forearm over his eyes to block out the sunlight. "My name is Morgen. Figured we should at least know that much about each other, since Varax insists on collecting us both."

She blinked a few times. After a few short moments of initial shock, he was being oddly casual about this. It was probably a bad sign.

She had never heard of one dragon with two riders. Technically, Heles and Thessilnn had both claimed her parents, even letting her into the mental pathway when necessary. So perhaps this wasn't as unusual as she assumed. Maybe lots of dragons had two riders in Arcadia.

"No, they definitely don't," Morgen said, voice muffled.

"I wouldn't have come all the way out here if this was a normal occurrence, even with Varax's constant insistence."

She stiffened. "You can hear me?"

He lifted his arm, squinting at her. "I don't think I always can. Just when Varax leaves the pathway open. For example, just now, I only heard that last bit of what I assume was a lot of spiraling. "

This notion, she was familiar with. Her parents were constantly speaking silently, enough to the point it sometimes irritated her, because their dragons always allowed for it. Letting *her* into the connection only occurred when necessary, usually when Thessilnn wanted to scold her.

"So, just to clarify, this is not a common occurrence?"

Morgen propped himself on his elbows. He was wearing a sleeveless leather tunic, and she tried to ignore the muscles straining in his biceps.

"Dragons don't typically have more than one rider at a time," he said, brow raised. "Ever, actually, as I understand it. But you don't seem as shocked as I would have expected. Have you never studied dragonlore?"

She probably should have said yes. It would look far less suspicious. Instead, she shook her head. "No, I have. I…just thought I read something about this once."

"Mhm."

She looked away, twisting her fingers in her lap. He obviously didn't believe her, though he didn't push either.

"Where did you come from?" she asked, clearing her throat in an effort to break up the nervous tension in her body.

"Somewhere you've never been."

She surprised herself when she snorted loudly and replied, "That's presumptuous."

"Fine, then. Arcadia."

Now, she looked at him sharply, lips parting. He really had been to the land of the gods, a place she had only ever been able to conjure up weakly in her imagination. She wondered if he'd ever met any of the principals. Maybe someday, if he kept coming back, he could tell her what they were like.

"That's…far," she settled on after a few moments of silence he hadn't bothered to break. "You must have been traveling for days."

He laughed, the sound so rough, it almost seemed like it hurt. She noticed he had another scar, this one cutting across his throat.

It looked like someone had tried to slit it.

He must've noticed her looking, because he raised a hand to his neck, ghosting the scar. "Ah. That is a story for another time."

She found it odd he planned to tell her at all. They had just met, after all.

"What was funny?" she asked instead of inquiring about his scars like she wanted to.

He tipped his head back, throat working. "Sorry, inside joke."

She looked away but pressed, "Between you and…?"

"Me and myself, mostly."

Turning to him again, she frowned at the odd answer. "Uh-huh."

"But to answer your question about my journey here—

Varax and I took a shortcut of sorts. She's not a fan of long flights."

Nya nodded slowly, wracking her brain for what he could possibly mean. She remembered reading once that ether could be used to create shorter pathways between places; powerful gods, usually the eight principals, could tug on the invisible strands of silver matter that made up the universe, creating a portal. But did Morgen actually mean he had portalled himself and an entire *dragon* here all the way from somewhere in Arcadia?

"Who exactly are you?" she whispered, slowly shaking her head.

He caught her eyes, the only feature that differed from a face that was almost entirely identical to her mother's. She had her father's dark, hooded eyes.

"Who are you?" Morgen replied softly; a challenge she didn't actually think he wanted her to take.

Neither of them answered the other's question, nor did they look away, in some sort of silent agreement. She solidified it when she said, "My name is Nya, if you didn't catch that from Varax."

His mouth twitched, lowering his chin in a shallow nod. They understood each other; they would not share their true identities and would not ask for explanation.

"Alright, Nya. What would you like to do today?" he asked, tilting his head to the side. "We should figure something out, since I have an inkling Varax is going to insist on semi-regular visits now that she finally convinced you to meet us."

She forced herself to relax into the agreement between them, to bite back her questions about who he was, his true reason for coming here, and how in the gods' names he had so much power. Instead, she quieted her curious nature for once and laid back on the stone with him, letting her clothes dry and accepting this for what it was for now.

She'd never had a friend, not unless she counted her parent's dragons. Perhaps, for now, this strange understanding brought about by even stranger circumstances could be just that. Morgen didn't seem inclined to make it anything else either.

"We could join Varax in her frolicking."

He chuckled—again, with that rough, grating sound that made her wonder just what had been done to him—and warned, "I'd be careful. She's a very proud creature."

I will forgive this first offense, Varax grumbled, and Nya and Morgen shared an amused look as she added, *Though the water is pleasant.*

Nya laughed, eyes on the hazy morning sky above.

CHAPTER

THREE

I am constantly reminded that there are much worse things than death. Sometimes, one of the servant girls will look at me, and for a flash, all I see is her. I cannot properly communicate the pain it brings me. I will never say it aloud, but sometimes, I envy her, my friend who was torn from this cruel world too soon. At least, for a time, she has a chance at peace.

—Lady Anabeth, Royal Scribe's Apprentice, D'anna

STEEP, craggy peaks the color of obsidian rose from above the cloud line. The air had grown much cooler in the last hour, and it smelled vaguely of smoke and sulfur. Below, the land was rocky and barren. Nya craned her neck, palms flat against the warmth of Varax's smooth, crimson scales as the wind tore her hair free of the braids she had pulled it into this morning. When she saw the first bursting plume of sparking-red lava, she bit the inside of her cheek, unease stirring her stomach.

Something about this place felt oddly familiar.

The wind.

The smell.

Even the way the air almost seemed to shimmer and shift at the edges…

Her pulse quickened. There was a thrumming deep in her chest, and she had to wonder: Had she been here before?

It was completely impossible, given she had never before stepped foot in Arcadia in all her twenty-six years. But as they dropped altitude, nearing the side of one of the larger peaks, she couldn't deny the strange, pulsing feeling of familiarity. Perhaps she had dreamt of it once?

Eyes still on the barren landscape, she asked Varax, *What is this place?*

"It's called the Gods' Aisle," Morgen said in her ear, his voice low and nearly lost to the frigid, rushing gales around them.

She tightened her jaw, suppressing a shiver of heat at his closeness, despite the cold air. "I wasn't talking to you."

Varax huffed, a small burst of fire escaping from her open maw and momentarily blasting heat and smoke in their faces.

To their right, astride his ash-toned dragon, Carus called, "Problem?"

Morgen waved his concern off with one hand, the other still wrapped around Nya's waist. She had been fighting to ignore his touch for hours now. She wasn't sure why he hadn't just portalled them here, even as much as the idea of doing *that* unnerved her. Still, it would be better than the infuriating, shameful heat she had been constantly tamping down during their long flight.

It had been over a year since she had last seen Morgen.

She had fled Mise and traveled to Aren within days. She ignored both Varax and Morgen's voices until they stopped trying altogether. Or so she had thought. Her traitorous body still remembered his touch. She could only hope he was too distracted to notice the insistent pounding of her pulse that had too little to do with fear she *should* be feeling.

They landed with a sudden jolt, snapping Nya out of her haze. The entrance to what appeared to be some sort of underground cave system yawned open wide just ahead, like the snapping jaws of some enormous beast. She wished it really was some living creature, ready to swallow her up and make her disappear forever. Maybe she had always wanted that, even before Morgen had come into her life. Perhaps, torn apart in the teeth of a predator, she would at least feel some sort of purpose.

The cliff that the dragons idled atop it jutted out just enough to fit them both, surrounded on all sides by thin chasms filled with red-hot lava bubbling a short way below. Every few seconds, the molten, burning substance rose nearly to the top, though it didn't ever spill over.

Next to them, Carus' dragon practically threw him off its back and then flew off, shrieking.

"The impatient bastard couldn't wait an extra minute," Carus said, shaking his head at the disappearing form as he got to his feet, dusting off his pants. "I'm hungry too, but that doesn't mean I go around flinging people off my back and giving them sprained ankles."

You should tell your idiot friend to be careful—again. Veeron tells me he only let slip the insults because he needed to hunt more than he needed to bite his human.

Nya ignored Varax, heart in her throat as she observed

all around her, trying to catalog it quickly. She was quickly beginning to understand what was happening; this was the cold place Morgen had often described, and Carus must be the 'friend' he had once briefly spoken of.

Though Varax had just called Carus an idiot, she didn't make the mistake of assuming he was weak. He was broad and obviously trained physically. He could probably kill her in a dozen different ways if he wanted. According to the books she had studied with her mother as a child, very few in Arcadia were not trained with a blade or bow. When everyone else could also use magic, it was useful to have other ways to kill, or at least maim, your opponents.

He had the same shade of tawny skin as her, but his mop of light hair was more blonde than silver. She was sure he had some sort of magic, though she couldn't quite tell which bloodline just from the energy surrounding him. Almost all with magic—mortals and gods alike—gave off a similar vibration. The intensity depended on the breadth of their magic, and the few people Nya had encountered with some distant relation to one of the principals tended to exude a lower, more resonant vibration.

Carus' magic felt like that.

It was the most powerful resonance she had felt from anyone, aside from her parents or Morgen. Perhaps it meant one of his parents was a demi-god. The power would be slightly diluted but still stronger than most. She had learned from the sisters at the temple that demi-gods weren't actually all that common, and only a handful of the principals *actually* had the large number of children mortals assumed all of them did. The term had evidently become more of an exaggeration than a true indicator of parentage in the past century. Who knew how many demi-gods actually existed anymore, as bloodlines diluted and mixed?

"Like what you see, sweetheart?" Carus quipped, and she cursed herself silently for staring at him for too long as she'd been thinking. "I'll have to turn you down. You're very pretty, but you're not my type, and besides, I know better by now than to touch Morgen's things…or soon to be things? Not sure on that one yet, but let's just say, I like my eyes where they are."

She ground her teeth but ignored him, jumping smoothly off Varax. Carus watched her dust off her hands, head tilted to the side.

"Morgen?" Carus was staring at her as he said it, his brow furrowed.

"*What.*"

He was right behind her, and she could feel the irritation emanating from him, mingling with his magic and mani-festing so strongly, the vibration pitched her ears and shim-mered in the air.

"She's ridden on dragon-back before, hasn't she?"

Morgen made some noncommittal noise in the back of his throat. "I'm sure she has. Her parents have two of them, evidently."

Carus looked past her, holding Morgen's gaze, a brow raised. It was obvious Morgen hadn't told Carus of their meetings, though she wasn't sure why.

After a moment, Carus gave up, throwing his hands in the air and sighing dramatically. "Fine, fine. Let's just get inside before the storm starts."

Nya glanced at the sky. Though it was gray and cloudy,

the atmosphere appeared mostly calm, aside from the cold breeze.

She stiffened when Morgen grabbed her arm. "We're going inside."

She held firm where she was, knowing if he was anywhere near the same person she had once thought he was, he wasn't about to drag her inside, not by force. Tilting her head back so she looked him directly in the eye, she demanded, "Where. Are. We."

His nostrils flared, and she felt a tiny shock of electricity where his skin met hers. "I told you. It's called the Gods' Aisle."

"I've never heard of it."

"You've never been to Arcadia."

"I've seen maps. This is not on any of them."

Carus coughed loudly. "*Ah*, have you considered, sweetheart, that it might not be in our best interest to tell you exactly where you are?"

She tore her arm from Morgen's grasp, narrowing her eyes at Carus. "What, afraid I'm going to summon Thessilnn and Heles here? They're very big and *very* protective of me. I also understand they haven't had a good fight in nearly a century."

Carus thinned his lips, unnerved, but Morgen only said flatly, "Except you couldn't reach them, could you? And on the off chance you manage to at this distance, it won't matter. I will not be divulging the exact details of our location to you, and it's not common knowledge, even to your parents. We are going inside. *Now.*"

A few flashes of bright crimson lightning in the distance suddenly cut across the sky, and the low rumble of thunder vibrated the stone. The quiet was all at once disturbed, and the smell of rain hit her nose. It was as if one moment, the valley was gray and still, and the next, it was seconds away from chaos. Carus rubbed at his forehead, surveying the coming storm, then shrugged once and headed for the cave entrance.

Morgen glanced at her, but this time, she looked away immediately, following Carus. They appeared to be right about the storm, and as much as she didn't want to do anything either of them said, this was Arcadia. Perhaps they weren't bluffing when they insisted they needed to take shelter.

As they ducked into the dark, cool tunnel, Morgen murmured in a low voice, "I will say this only once, Nya: do not try to run. You won't make it far, not alive."

Her breath caught at the delicate feel of his breath brushing against the shell of her ear. "Is that a threat?"

"It's a warning. We are in a dangerous place. There's a reason even the principals do not come here. Not anymore."

"And yet, *you* are here."

Ahead, Carus yawned. "Not much choice when you don't want to be skewered, or burned alive, or eaten up by an endless night. Though," he glanced back at her, expression thoughtful, "I suppose you can probably do at least two of those things."

"Did I make myself clear about running?" Morgen pushed, ignoring Carus.

She swallowed against the tightness in her throat. "Quite." Then, quieter, she added, "Why am I here, Morgen?"

He didn't reply, and she cursed herself for expecting him

to just be honest with her. She didn't want to accept that the years between them were just a falsity and a clever ploy on his end, but that kind of ignorant thinking had gotten her into this mess in the first place.

The narrow, damp tunnel soon opened into a large cavern that appeared to be functioning as some sort of mess hall. Nya stiffened, her steps slowing as she saw the sheer number of mortals, demi-gods, and godlings gathered there, eating and drinking at rows of roughly hewn wooden tables that lined the floor. There were…so many. They were all wearing variations of leather or metal armor, and weapons seemed to be in abundance as well, slung over their backs or lying atop the tables next to their plates of food. Even from a distance, it wasn't difficult to notice most were physically strong. She might have been sheltered from the realities of war, but not so much that she couldn't recognize this for what it was.

An army.

Heads turned their way within seconds, and a hush fell over the expansive space, only broken by the occasional dripping of water from stalactites above and a few waves of low whispers across the long tables. As eyes slipped over her, a tremble ran up her spine, and she curled her hands into tight fists to keep her body from shaking too visibly. Some of them merely looked curious, but others—mostly the men— were already exchanging obviously interested glances and grinning at each other.

Morgen sighed, rolling his jaw. "As you were," he said, raising his voice as he swept his gaze around the room.

Throats cleared, and for a moment, the entire room

relaxed, everyone tucking back into their drinks and settling once more against the benches.

"But be aware." Morgen paused, sweeping his burning amber eyes over the entirety of the room. "If anyone decides to try and lay a finger on my betrothed, I will take your hand. If, of course, I'm feeling forgiving. If not…" He shrugged. "Well, you know me. Dislocating a spine will do on most days."

Nya's breath caught loudly before she could stop it, and not from the threat of violence he had just promised.

Betrothed.

Her mind emptied out. The tense silence turned into a roar in her ears, and she could not stop herself from looking at Morgen with wide eyes.

Why would he want to marry her? Why now, when for all the years they met in the vast, empty forests in Mise, he had been so insistent on not touching her? Until he *had*, and she'd left without a trace. He hadn't sought her out, not after what had happened, what they had both realized that day.

Perhaps that was it, though. He knew who she was: the daughter of two heirs to principal gods. Seeing the army before her, it suddenly clicked, what he wanted.

In all technicality, as Kronos' only living child, the throne of Arcadia was his birthright.

The room fell into a tense silence for a moment, and then Carus bellowed, "You heard your king! Leave the girl alone, and get on with your night. *Fates!* You'd think he just threatened to de-spine you or something."

It took half a second before chuckles began to drift around the room, and then everyone was roaring with laughter and banging their mugs on the tables. Her stomach turned as she stared at the sudden shift in mood. These soldiers might fear Morgen to an extent, but they quite obviously also respected him. This wasn't an army created with threats or even payment. They were here out of choice.

"What?" Morgen said, leaning down to her. "Did you expect them to be afraid of me? You might not believe me, but I don't make a habit of threatening them unless necessary."

She stepped away from him. Fates damn her for being so short and him so tall. "Who are they?"

"Demi-gods and their children, mostly, and a handful of mortals and godlings."

"I can *see* that."

He snorted, his head tilting to the side. His hair had come loose, the deep-red strands now falling down his back, and since they had walked into the cavern, he had visibly started to relax. Not wholly, but she knew his tells well enough to know he wasn't about to snap anymore.

"They support my claim," he told her. "Arcadia currently has no official king, so it's only a matter of time."

"But I thought Sol—"

"Is not a particularly popular choice here, as you will soon discover. None of the other principals have even attempted to step up, though."

Nya scowled. "Have you *ever* considered that perhaps a monarchy is not the answer? I thought you hated Kronos."

"I do. But you're preaching to the wrong crowd when it comes to the way Arcadia's government should be structured," he said, brow furrowing as he looked at her intently. "You need to bathe. You're covered in blood and dust, and I'd prefer you not to be so haggard during our wedding."

"You're delusional," she snapped, earning a few looks from the crowd just beyond them. "I'm not marrying someone like you. Not now, not ever."

He dipped his head once more, nose-to-nose with her as he said, "Someone 'like me'? And what am I, Nya?"

"A monster," she hissed, a wave of burning darkness rising in her throat.

He chuckled darkly, though his smile was empty and cold. "I know what I am. At least I don't try to deny it to myself. I think if you knew what was at stake here, you might be a bit more willing."

"Morgen." Carus stepped between them, his back to her. "Perhaps we should take this little lovers' spat somewhere…not here? Someplace more private, don't you think?"

Nya flared her nostrils, looking between the two of them. "We are not lovers. And there is no fucking way I am marrying a demi-god who thinks he's king just because he has the right blood and a few armed friends in a volcano."

Incorrect, and also incorrect. Or am I to really believe you forgot what we did?

She flushed, and she hated herself for it, though she hated him more for bringing it up.

When Carus cocked his head to the side, an obvious request to follow, she didn't hesitate this time, if only to get some distance from Morgen. Even so, he followed a few paces behind. Perhaps he had seen the looks on the faces of the men they were leaving behind in the mess hall. She didn't understand why he cared, given *he* was the one who had just kidnapped her.

Neither he nor Carus spoke as she was led into another

tunnel that branched off from the mess hall cavern, this one dryer and wider than the one at the entrance. The light was dim, illuminated by burning torches mounted every few paces on the stone walls, and the floor was a mix of packed dirt and stones. Both the walls and floor sparkled strangely, perhaps with some mineral or geode.

They hadn't been walking for long when Carus turned abruptly to the left, leading her into a warm, slightly humid cavern, though this one was much smaller than the mess hall. In the center lay a pool, the water a deep shade of turquoise from whatever sediment lay within it. A young woman with short, dark hair and a sharp, pale face was sitting against the wall, cross-legged and reading a leather-bound book. She hardly looked up when they entered.

"This is her, I presume?" she drawled, her voice low and flat.

Carus coughed, shifting on his booted feet, but Nya caught the small, incredulous smile he tried and failed to suppress at the woman's demeanor. Perhaps they were friends. Nya could not imagine having more than one. It had always just been her parents and then, eventually, Morgen. There was a reason she had always dreamed of having a large family, even if such a thing was foolish.

She supposed it did not matter now, just like any other dreams of the future she'd had before today.

"Nya, this is Imeria," Carus said, gesturing at the woman. "She'll help you get ready."

"I am perfectly capable of bathing myself, and I do not need to get ready for anything," she snarked, crossing her arms over her chest.

Carus glanced at Morgen but he was already looking at her, jaw set. In the corner, Imeria snorted softly, but no one acknowledged it.

"What you saw in the mess hall just now," Morgen said with a deadly softness, "is barely a quarter of our forces. Perhaps you think them fools, but all of them possess magic and are viciously trained. I am not above sending them to the Elysian Valley, where most of the principals—including your grandparents—play house. But I'd prefer to try other tactics first. Think what you want about me, but I would prefer not to incite violence unless necessary."

She held his gaze. Veins of amber-gold flared as she asked, "How does marrying me help you with that?"

"You're not stupid, Nya. I'm sure you've already figured it out."

Her jaw trembled, but she ground her teeth to still it. "You're using me as a bargaining chip…perhaps even a way to strengthen your claim too, given who my parents are."

Morgen's lips twitched, but he only said, "I'll let you bathe."

He turned to leave, but his steps faltered as she called, "Do you think you're better than him just because you won't kill without reason?"

He said nothing, and even as her stomach twisted with the words, she added bitterly, "Using me like this… presuming you have the ability to *own* me—it makes you just as corrupt."

A droning buzz disturbed every invisible thread of ether in the air, the embers of life itself that he had inherited from Kronos twisting around each drum of her pulse. Carus made a choked sound as the air thickened, sparking visibly with energy, like tiny bursts of lightning, but Nya only scowled. There was a slumbering beast inside her, one with cold, burning eyes and a thirst for the emptiness of death. She never let it free because she did not understand its moral-less, wild nature. But for a moment, as Morgen filled every inch of the air with his power, she had the sudden urge to take it all away, to create a void of endless, unforgiving darkness before she burned every inch of the room, the realm, the entire world, to ashes—

Pure light flared, abrupt and blinding, as it flooded the cavern. She did not know which of them it had come from, but it cleared within seconds, and Nya found Morgen staring at her with wide eyes, his irises dull. For just a moment, he looked like the man she remembered from their meetings in Mise. It didn't last long; when he blinked, silver and gold settled once more as a strange cast behind his eyes.

"Have her ready within an hour," he snapped, but she caught the catch in his voice, and as he left, he rubbed his fingertips across the jagged scar on his throat.

The humming air settled and stilled in his absence. Carus watched him go, shaking his head. "You two do know each other, don't you?" he said, brow furrowed, though he didn't acknowledge the odd burst of magic.

Imeria, who was closer now, sighed, rolling her eyes. "Carus, sometimes, I think you can't possibly get any dumber, and then you blow all my expectations out of the water."

"*Hey—*"

"Of course they know each other. She can lie about it all

she wants, and Morgen can try to deny it, but I've met old married couples with less history."

Nya hissed out a breath. "Stop talking about me as if I'm not in the room."

Imeria's striking green eyes swung to her, hands on her narrow hips as she mused, "Oh, so you'll speak to us then? No strike of silence to protest the marriage ceremony you insist won't be happening within the hour?"

Nya looked away, her pulse fluttering in her throat. She didn't think Morgen was bluffing when he said he would send his armies if she didn't go through with this. Perhaps it wouldn't happen right away, given she was fairly certain this place was not close to the Elysian Valley or the mortal border, but did that matter? She could refuse and try to escape, but even if she made it out of this barren mountain range alive, it wouldn't stop violence from ensuing. Surely, the principals banded together could defeat Morgen, but given his power and his army, it wouldn't be pretty.

Her parents were probably looking for her now too. Perhaps they would even return to Arcadia for her. They had suffered through enough war and death for the peace of both realms, and if she didn't agree to this, all their pain could be for nothing.

"I will bathe," she said after a moment, then glanced at Carus and added, "But he leaves."

Carus chuckled. "Don't worry, I wasn't planning on peeping. I'll be right outside if you need anything, though."

Nya had the distinct feeling the words were meant for Imeria. They might be treating her like a 'guest', but the truth no one said aloud was that she was a prisoner.

Once he was gone, Imeria motioned to the pool. "In. I have soap for you, and while you wash, I'll try to detangle the blood and gods-know what else from your hair."

Nya hesitated, and Imeria groaned. "Please don't tell me you're a prude. I don't have the mental energy to convince you I couldn't give a damn about any nudity, much less yours."

"I was actually more worried about being in a vulnerable state around you," Nya said flatly. "Given the fact that I was nearly killed and then brought here against my will."

Imeria barked out a laugh and pulled a small dagger off the belt slung over her hips, extending it to Nya handle first. "If it makes you feel better, here."

She took it, unsure of whether this was some trap. "Ah… Thank you."

"You wouldn't be able to kill me," Imeria said, as if it was an indisputable piece of common knowledge. "Perhaps if you actually learned how to use all that power eating you from the inside out…then, I think even Morgen would have to be careful." She shrugged. "It's a shame your parents kept you so sheltered."

Nya didn't acknowledge the words, despite knowing, deep down, they were all true. She could understand why her parents did not want her to be a part of the world that had caused them so much pain, and yet, here she was, completely and utterly unprepared.

She pulled off the shapeless robes she had worn during the duration of her time as an apprentice in the temple. The fabric was now torn and stained with blood. As it fell, she tamped down the sudden urge to set it aflame, instead slipping quickly into the warm water, the lapping turquoise coming up to her chest as she leaned back against the stone edge.

"Well, Morgen might hate *you*, but he won't hate your body."

She whipped her head around. "Excuse me?"

Imeria shrugged, though her lips were titled in a wry smirk. "I said I didn't care about nudity, not that I wouldn't make comments."

Nya rolled her eyes twisting to face away from Imeria again. She held back a flinch as Imeria ran her hands gently through her matted tangles of her silver hair, long ripped free of the braid she'd put it back in this morning…or was it yesterday?

"He likes some curves, you know," Imeria said matter-of-factly. "That's why he's never been interested in me. I am tragically twig-like."

Nya bit back a yelp as Imeria pulled at another tangle then cleared her throat and said, "Am I to assume he's been with many women?"

Imeria's hands paused, cool fingertips brushing against the back of Nya's neck. "Carus is probably a better person to ask if you want a true answer. But the girls around here talk sometimes about what he likes and *how* he likes it. Many claim to have been with him, but I'd say at least half of them are lying. They probably won't like you."

"Why? Because I 'stole' their lover?"

Imeria began running her fingers gently through Nya's hair to comb it before starting on what she assumed were braids.

"No. Because you will be queen. I'm sure some of them were hoping for the title, and then he brings you here, a complete stranger, and marries you on the same day."

Nya suppressed a shiver at the words, forcing herself to sound as if she didn't feel the weight of them, asking with a put-on scowl, "Are they really so stupid to think he's doing any of this because he *cares* about me? He and Carus destroyed a holy temple, murdered my mentor, and now, I'm being forced into a marriage I don't want because of threats I'm sure are very real."

Imeria sighed and tapped her shoulder. "All done. Dry off, and then we'll get you dressed."

She handed Nya a threadbare towel and stood, striding purposefully to a corner of the cavern, where she retrieved a deep red garment. Warily, Nya did as she said before letting her pull the dress over her head and fasten the strategically placed swaths of fabric, wrapping around her chest and partially over her middle before falling into a light, silky skirt reaching just below her ankles. Clearly, the dress was not made for someone as short as she was.

"Now for the veil," Imeria murmured.

Nya's stomach turned when she saw the sheer white piece of fabric in Imeria's hand. "I don't want to wear it."

Imeria held it out. "Well, Morgen wants you to. Besides, it's traditional."

Nya scowled. "Do you just follow everything he says blindly because he claims to be a king?"

"No," Imeria said, her voice softer now. "There is little you understand about Arcadia, Nya. Most of us owe Morgen even more than our lives. No one follows him blindly and certainly not without reason. He may be called a usurper by the principals, but I'd much rather have a usurper than a liar like Sol. And the realm *needs* a king."

She opened her mouth, but Imeria shook her head as she fastened the veil over Nya's head, securing it with small chains at her crown.

When she stepped back and surveyed her work, her smile was tight. "It's time. Follow me."

CHAPTER 4
THREE YEARS AND SEVEN SEVEN MONTHS PRIOR

The mortal war keeps Vane away from the palace most years. It is for the best. I do not know what he would do if he knew she was here, amongst the eldest princess' handmaidens, of all places. She does not remember, though June assures me the dreams will begin soon, if they have not already. It's only a matter of time.
—Lady Anabeth, Royal Scribe's Apprentice, D'anna

THE AIR WAS COOLER NOW, but even in the dead of winter, it wasn't frigid. This part of Mise was far enough south that the snow and ice rarely touched it. Still, when she started to shiver, Morgen slung off his heavy cloak and tugged it over her shoulders.

She was beginning to lose track of how many times they had met here now. Mostly, he listened to her talk, sharing little about himself. It was a bit irritating, given her life wasn't exciting in the least. But she didn't like the way he disappeared into his own mind when the forest grew too still, so she spoke of anything and everything she could think of.

The only things she knew of him so far were that he was a demi-god who had grown up in Arcadia, that he had bonded with Varax when he was seventeen, and that had happened a long time ago. Beyond that, he was a mystery.

"Is it cold right now?" she asked as he adjusted the cloak. "In Arcadia? There are seasons there, right?"

He cleared his throat. His long hair was half pulled back, as usual, but a few wayward strands fell in his face as he dipped his head to meet her eyes. She ignored the small urge to tuck his hair back, to linger maybe, her hand pressed to his cheek.

"Where I am now, it's cold most of the time."

She bit the inside of her cheek, not wanting to push him too far too soon. But curiosity and the burning need to know more about him got the better of her.

"What about where you grew up? It was different from where you are now, wasn't it?"

His hands stilled, hovering just above the clasp by her throat. He was trying to look away, but she sought out his gaze, a brow raised. His expression was closed off, and she had the distinct feeling he was about to shut down.

"Morgen," she said softly. "I'm not going to judge you."

His jaw tightened, fingers brushing her neck. She started to arch it but stopped herself the moment she realized what her body was doing. Thankfully, he didn't appear to notice.

"You might. You know a few things about Arcadia, don't you?"

She shrugged. "I know some. If you'd rather not tell me names or places, I don't mind. I just want to know you better."

He looked away, dropping his hands. "It's not a pleasant story, nor is it a short one."

With a sigh, she plopped down next to Varax, who was curled into as small of a ball a Vemon dragon *could* manage. Nya patted the space next to her.

"We have time."

Morgen's mouth twitched, and his eyes were still wary, but he joined her on the forest floor, facing her cross-legged. She didn't say anything, giving him space to figure out how he was going to begin.

Finally, he said, "I lived in my father's house as a child, but I never had parents. My mother died in childbirth, and the wet nurse was gone by the time I was four. Mostly, I was shut in my room, and I preferred it that way. It was safer."

She furrowed her brow. "Safer?"

"My father…he was not fond of me."

Her stomach dipped. His body was covered in scars. Could someone really do that to their own child?

"Whatever you are imagining," Morgen said quietly, "it was much, much worse."

"But *why?*"

It was perhaps a silly question to ask. Why did anyone hurt an innocent? But she chased a selfish need to understand, because she was reeling with such an overwhelming wave of confusion and anger.

Morgen sighed and lifted a long-fingered hand, brushing calloused fingers against her cheekbone. She stared at him, her lips parting to say what she did not know, but then, he murmured, "I don't see ether in your eyes often."

She blinked a few times. He was close to her now and

still hadn't moved his hand from her face when she realized…

Oh gods.

He was beautiful. There was something raw and wild about his features that made her both sure he was not merely mortal but also not just a god. The more time they'd spent together, the more she had come to like being around him. He was closed off, so their friendship had been slow blooming, but now, she found herself terrified. Quite suddenly, she *wanted,* and she did not know what to do with it.

He started to move away, almost as if he sensed it, but on instinct, she grabbed his hand, holding it to her face. His expression shuttered, but not before she saw the flash of heat in his eyes.

"Nya." He was shaking his head. "We cannot go there."

Her cheeks warmed, and she let go of his hand. He didn't move it again right away, even as she asked, "Will you tell me why?"

His throat bobbed, his eyes lingering somewhere near her shoulder. "If I say it's because I don't want to, will you stop asking?"

"Of course," she whispered. "I would never force you to do something. I just thought… Well, it doesn't matter now."

Now, his hands dropped, and he shut his eyes, jaw tight as he sat back. He almost looked like he was in pain.

"Morgen?"

He took an abrupt, sharp breath then got to his feet, speaking with his back to her.

"I should probably go."

She stood, chewing anxiously on her lip. "Alright. Will you come back?"

His shoulders rose and fell a few times, and then he turned. She couldn't quite read his expression as he said, "Of course. Before the moon cycle ends. Varax will check in with you as well."

She nodded, unsure what to say. Finally, she settled on, "Okay. Be safe."

"Mm."

"And Morgen?"

He turned from where he'd been about to climb onto Varax's back.

"I want you to come back, alright? I'm not upset… A little embarrassed, but I'm not angry with you." She grimaced. "I am sorry if I made you uncomfortable at all."

He froze, eyes widening. For the first time since he had rescued her from the undertow, she swore, she saw the amber in his eyes flare almost to gold.

Before she could register what he was doing, he was in front of her, a hand gently cupping the back of her neck and his lips pressing to her forehead. It was her turn to freeze, entirely unsure of how to react. But after a moment, she leaned into his touch. It felt natural to be like this with him.

After a long moment, he pulled back but didn't move away, resting his brow on hers. She dared a glance at him, finding his eyes closed.

"It's not because I don't want…" He shuddered, and she shivered as his thumb brushed against the side of her ear, the touch delicate. "But nothing about this is simple, nor is it safe, even if we just remain friends. I'm selfish enough that I will keep coming back, but things need to remain as they are."

She shut her eyes too, lifting her hand and ghosting her fingers across the curve of his high cheekbones, relishing the small catch of his breath. "I understand you want to protect me, but who looks after you?"

He didn't respond, and she opened her eyes to find him looking at her, the amber-gold soft, but there all the same. His nose nudged against hers, and she hardly dared to breathe when he brushed his lips over hers.

"No one," he whispered against her mouth before pulling away.

She felt immediately unbalanced at the loss of his presence. It was as if her whole life had been lived in halves, and she just hadn't realized it until this moment.

By the time she had recovered, he was already atop Varax, readying to take off. He always flew away, out of her sight, before he conjured up the portal.

"Why don't you just portal from right here?" she called.

Even from atop Varax's enormous back, she could see his lips curve. *Perhaps someday, I will show you.*

It wasn't until after they were gone that she realized how sad his smile had been.

FIVE

This gift is a curse. I am constantly in a room made of mirrors, and I do not know which reflection is showing me the truth. Ghosts haunt my dreams, taunting me. I think I will be a ghost too. I see her, Sora, my lost friend, drifting empty-eyed down the palace halls after the princess. I do not call her name. I do not even catch her eye. Perhaps I will only watch now. Fate may use me, but I will never again intervene.

—Lady Anabeth, Royal Scribe's Apprentice, D'anna

IMERIA LED Nya through the dim tunnels, her hand lightly atop Nya's forearm to keep her from tripping, given her vision was slightly warped from the veil.

"Just a little further," she murmured.

Nya ignored the way her throat closed at the words, instead forcing herself to strangle out, "Who exactly will be performing the rites?"

"We have a handful of priestesses who defected here," Imeria said. "Aside from the principals themselves, they most understand the importance of Morgen taking the throne.

But many of them fear Sol, so only the bravest of them left."

Nya didn't ask about what this 'importance' meant. Both Morgen and Imeria had alluded to it several times in the mere hours she had been here, but it was obvious neither were going to tell her just because she asked. Information was clearly doled out based on importance and trust here, and, evidently, she was given neither of those things beyond her place as a pawn.

She tried not to let that sting. Once, in all her naivety, she had assumed she knew more about Morgen than most did. Perhaps she'd even thought that she knew him the best of anyone.

Those were the assumptions of a cloistered child.

Imeria halted suddenly, and Nya stumbled, nearly falling on her face before a strong hand caught her arm. Even without seeing him clearly, she knew immediately it was Morgen. He had a presence that was far too charged with magic to be anyone else.

When she did look at him, she set her jaw, an attempted block against her own feelings that mostly failed.

His hair was completely unbound now, falling into his kohl-lined eyes, and he wore what she thought might've been some sort of ceremonial robe that left his chest bare. She had seen him without a shirt a handful of times before, and though it had always elicited a reaction, she had never *hated* the way her body responded to it as much as she did now.

Especially as she saw the simple iron-hued circlet resting at the crown of his head.

He truly thought he was a king.

"You don't need to do this," she said in a low voice, the smell of incense and smoke permeating her nostrils.

His jaw flexed, and for a moment, he said nothing, simply holding her hard gaze. A tiny spark of hope lit inside her, but it was smothered the second he let go of her arm and said, "Follow me."

She took a deep, steadying breath. They were really doing this then.

She wasn't exactly sure what marriage entailed in Arcadia. In the mortal realm, it meant different things to different people. To much of the wealthy class, it was simply used to elevate status or strengthen a bloodline. Though, she had acted as an apprentice during a handful of ceremonies during her time with the sisters and had observed some she had been sure were love matches. Still, even then, to legally bind yourself to someone else came with risks she had never quite understood. Even her parents, who she was sure loved each other more than most could even comprehend, had suffered unimaginable pain, and all because they had wed each other.

Now, she was marrying the son of the god-king responsible for the pain that never quite left their eyes.

Morgen led her to a small, raised basin, made of the same dark stone as the walls around them. Crystal clear water made a shallow pool in it, two slim silver daggers resting on the edge. A woman hovered nearby, wearing red robes and a veil over her face that made it impossible to tell her age. It probably wouldn't have helped if Nya could see her features anyway. She understood many of the demi-gods and godlings in Arcadia were decades, if not centuries, old and still never aged.

The priestess approached, silent and on whispering feet. When she stopped just in front of the basin, she tilted her head, her eyes presumably on Nya. "Pull back your veil, Nya Evva."

She did as the priestess requested, though the fact that the woman knew her full name unnerved her. Morgen had probably told her, but the way she said it was too knowing, as if the priestess was aware of something Nya was not.

As soon as the sheer fabric was gone from her face, the woman sucked in a short breath. "Fates, you look just like them," she whispered.

Nya narrowed her eyes. "Who are you?"

The priestess shrugged, the small movement barely visible beneath the heavy robes. "I am but a whisper of Fate, and you are a ghost to me."

Nya's breath was shallow. "What is your name?"

The priestess sighed softly, her breath gently disturbing the veil over her face. "My name is Ana." She lifted a slim, pale hand and added, "Palms up, both of you."

Morgen was looking at the priestess, his brow creased but his eyes unreadable. He only moved when Nya held up her hands as Ana had instructed. When he did the same, Ana murmured something Nya did not understand then flipped his hands, placing his palms atop hers.

The torches extinguished and then flared back to life in a flash. Ana's grip tightened momentarily before she let them both go, ordering, "Remain as you are until I say."

She began to speak again, and after a moment, Nya realized the foreign words were in the Old Language of the gods, though she had no idea what any of it meant.

Her chant-like monologuing went on for far longer than

Nya had anticipated, and the more time that passed, the harder it became to hide her trembling hands and her racing pulse. When she took an audibly shaking breath, Morgen's thumb brushed over her palm. Her gaze shot to his.

It's almost over.

She swallowed tightly. *How do you know?*

His eyes flicked to Ana. *I can understand what she's saying.*

She didn't ask how he knew the Old Language, or how he could tell Ana was almost done just by understanding the words. It was painful enough to send her thoughts purposefully down the pathway once. She didn't need to keep chafing the wound of betrayal she felt each time he used it to speak to her.

Ana stopped speaking abruptly and picked up the daggers, holding them out. "Cut your palms directly under your left pointer finger, then clasp your hands again."

Nya's hand shook as she took the dagger.

A weapon.

A weapon she had never been trained to use in a room full of people who could probably kill her within seconds if they wanted to. She had no choice but to comply.

Morgen waited to make the cut in his palm until she pressed the sharp blade to her skin. She flinched at the bright shock of pain, but he didn't even wince. Their blood dripped into the pool of water and sizzled as it hit the surface, causing Ana to jump.

"Was that not supposed to happen?" Nya heard herself say. Her own voice sounded tinny and wrong in her ears.

Ana cleared her throat but didn't answer the question, instead ordering, "Clasp your hands. Now."

Nya took a deep breath and obeyed, but as soon as her bloody skin met Morgen's, the entire room plunged into a thick darkness. Whispers floated around them, voices that the small mortal portion of Nya instinctively knew were *not* human.

A shiver crawled up her spine as the pool sizzled once more, and Ana said in a hushed voice, "*Diombach rìogna.* Fate is not yet sated."

In an instant, the torches flared, and Nya swore that, for a moment, the fire was not flickering orange and red, but a cold, sparkling obsidian. Her attention was quickly drawn to Morgen, though, as he demanded gruffly, "What do you mean by that?"

Ana took a deep breath and lifted her veil, revealing a face that was young only in appearance. Nya wasn't fool enough to believe Ana was truly her own age, even if she appeared in her twenties.

"Nearing a century ago," Ana said softly, "two heirs returned to Arcadia after over a hundred years of exile. Fated to meet, fated to rule, doomed to die." She paused, silver ether flickering faintly in her light brown eyes. "Vulcan realized the tragic vision Juno had seen was true first. Then, Thanatos, and finally, Nyx, who only accepted Fate for what it was when they both took each other's last breaths with blades to the heart, and then were consumed by dragon fire in front of me. But I...I had always seen you, Nya. Again and again, haunting my dreams so often, I was convinced, until the moment they were gone, that Fate was somehow wrong."

"You knew my parents, didn't you?" Nya said, her voice nothing more than a hoarse whisper.

Ana searched her eyes, and instead of answering, she said, "I am a daughter of Juno. My dreams are never just dreams, and my feelings are always omens. But I was mistaken to believe that just because you became true, Fate was finished."

Morgen's grip on Nya's hand tightened. "What are you saying—"

"It is done," Ana said sharply. "If you wish to complete what we discussed, it must be done before sunrise."

Without another word, she turned and strode quickly out of the cavern. Imeria stepped aside to avoid getting barreled over, and Nya tugged her hand away from Morgen's to step back from the pool.

"What did she mean, just now?"

Morgen shook his head. "Let me heal your hand."

"*What did she mean?*"

A tremble went through the cavern; Morgen, presumably. Nya didn't care if she was making him angry. She was confused and enraged and terrified of what all this meant.

"Imeria, leave us," Morgen said.

Nya glanced back to see Imeria raise a brow. "You're sure?"

"Go," he ordered shortly.

She huffed, muttering under her breath, but Morgen ignored her as she left. Once they were alone, Nya ripped the veil off, throwing it to the floor.

"If what Ana just said to you refers to consummating the marriage, you'll be consummating it alone. I'm not touching you."

His expression darkened, jaw tightening. "It did not. I would never force you to do that."

"Oh, but the line stops…where? Murdering my mentors? Kidnapping me? Forcing me into a marriage with threats against my family? You know, for all your talk of morals and honor, you only seem to adhere to those things when it suits you."

He took a step towards her, then another until he was close. Too close. But she refused to back away, or to admit she was afraid of his proximity. Not because she was afraid of *him*, but of herself. If she ignored her stubborn feelings that still lingered, perhaps they would just go away.

"There is so much you—"

"Don't understand? Yes, I picked up on that, actually. I haven't been here a day, and everyone has been constantly reminding me of that."

"Because it is true."

She flared her nostrils. "Then why don't you tell me? Or do you not trust me enough for that?"

His eyes flickered. "You hate me. Why would I trust you with important information?"

Her quiet laugh was cold. "I do. But it does seem to be common knowledge. If everyone knows, why bother keeping me in the dark? I suppose I could just…oh, I don't know, flirt my way to some answers? Your men seemed interested enough. Perhaps I'd even let them touch me for information. I know you threatened them, but I can be very persuasive—"

His hands slammed into the stone on either side of her, and his eyes sparked with bright amber. She was playing with fire here, but she needed to understand what was happening, and he wouldn't hurt her.

"I meant what I said," he said, breath ragged. "No one will touch you."

Her gaze drifted to his throat. She didn't mean to, but it was habit when he was this close, and, like always, it elicited such a wave of rage in her that she didn't know what to do with it. She hated that most of all, perhaps, that she still cared.

"Hardly seems fair," she whispered. "Since you seem to have your share of lovers here."

The thick hum in the air shifted. Changed. The amber in his eyes did not disappear but deepened, and he laughed softly, though the sound was still cold and humorless.

"Jealous, are we?" he murmured, leaning in, his breath caressing the shell of her ear.

"I just said I hate you." Gods, her voice sounded all breathy and wrong. She was supposed to be angry. And she *was*, but…

"Oh, I know, and I believe it. But you also want me."

He pulled back slightly, looking her directly in the eye. She squared her jaw. "I don't. I never did."

The last words were a mistake, because they both knew they were a lie.

"Say that again," he said softly. "And I will leave right now. Imeria can take you to a bedroom of your own, and I will see you in the morning to discuss the political merits of this arrangement."

She opened her mouth, but even as her lips parted, nothing came out. All she had to do was lie but—

Her breath hitched as his thumb traced her bottom lip. "I thought so," he said in a low, rough voice.

His voice didn't sound like this often. Only certain

pitches and volumes made the never-quite-healed wound at his throat so painfully apparent when he spoke. But she had heard this voice before, in a damp alcove behind a waterfall. The memory was the source of all her shame, but even so, at the reminder of it, her traitorous body did not push him away when he dipped his head to the curve of her neck.

Her back arched into his touch, and in that moment, she hated herself much more than she hated him. Teeth grazed the skin just above her collarbone, and a frustrated growl tore from his throat. He fisted one hand in her hair, breathing hard, his entire body trembling with restraint. She didn't understand why he was holding back now, given that, moments before, he had been taunting her.

Tell me to stop. His lips parted against her heated skin, and he added, this time aloud in a hoarse whisper, "Please."

That word was what ruined everything. It reminded her of all the times he had given her power over him, despite the fact that he was clearly stronger than her in every way. For just a few seconds, she forgot the past few hours, the past day, the past *year*.

Don't stop.

She couldn't make herself say it out loud, but perhaps it had been a mistake not to try. Using the pathway always made them both more vulnerable. It was much more difficult to hide the emotions laced within each thought.

Morgen froze against her, and for a thick, tense pause, the only sound in the cavern was the catching of their heavy breaths. She sought the clarity and resolve to push him away, but every thought of doing so dissolved as he bit into the soft skin at the juncture of her throat and shoulder. She gasped at the sharp spike of pain, though it quickly melded into something else entirely as his tongue swirled over the hurt. Through half-lidded eyes, she saw the water in the basin spark again.

Morgen let out a low, "*Fuck*," and then tore away from her abruptly, taking a few stumbling steps back.

She stared at him, eyes wide and heart hammering. His lips were swollen and stained deep red—the color was from her blood, she realized, once her mind caught up to what had just occurred. She lifted a shaking hand to her throat, and he was close again in an instant, muttering, "Let me heal it."

She was too stunned to protest, feeling the brief burn of his magic—Life magic, laced with the essence of Pure Light and Deep Night, of Fate and Duality, of Death, and Fire, and War.

The magic of all the principal gods—the universe itself—lay within him, the same as it had in Kronos. It had been why the god-king had been so impossible to defeat.

She should have let herself die rather than help Morgen on his quest to achieve the same level of power Kronos had. Her life would have been a small sacrifice for peace, maybe even a chance at democracy. Her parents had given theirs and more to ensure those things, and here she was, betraying them.

He pulled his hand away, and she slipped past him, trembling from head to toe and heading for the hall. She had no idea how to navigate these tunnels. All she knew was that she needed to get out and never return.

Morgen didn't even try to stop her.

It unnerved her, how easily he let her go now, but she

didn't care enough at the moment to ponder further as to why.

Varax!

She also knew Morgen would hear her calling for the dragon, but Varax was her only way out of here. Nya supposed she was about to see if the dragon's loyalty was truly to her too.

I am sleeping. A pause, then, *You wish to leave.*

Yes.

An emotion that felt like a long-suffering sigh flashed through the bond. *Fine. Follow the tunnel until you reach an opening in the caves. There is not an outcropping, so you will have to jump straight onto my back.*

Nya didn't waste time after that, the torchlight blurring as she ran. True to her word, Varax was circling below when Nya skidded to a stop at the opening in the tunnel.

Are you ready?

Nya took a deep breath. It truly was a cliff, the drop falling hundreds of feet below into stone threaded with thin streams of lava.

I'm ready.

She reared back and jumped onto the dragon's back, clinging to the saddle as Varax screeched and took off into the stormy sky.

CHAPTER
SIX

HOURS LATER, Varax landed in a field surrounding a small lake. Night had fallen, and Nya was shivering violently, had been for some time now. She hadn't thought to change into something warmer before fleeing and was now regretting it, even if she'd had no idea where to find more well-suited clothing for flying. Besides, if she'd looked, someone might have stopped her.

Her vision blurred as she slid off Varax's back, landing in a heap. She pushed up to her hands and knees, the dirt rough against her skin. The air smelled sweeter here, free of the heavy scent of smoke and sulfur that permeated the

Gods' Aisle. She curled around herself in the tall, swaying grass, feeling her consciousness begin to slip away.

Someone is coming. Varax was rustling her wings. *He will help you. I must go.*

Nya half-heartedly reached for the dragon as she took off, a wave of panic overcoming her. Varax wouldn't leave her if she was truly in danger, but…

Footsteps crunched in the grass nearby, and Nya stiffened when a smooth, masculine voice mused, "Why am I not surprised a Vemon dragon managed to seek you out too?"

She tried to open her eyes as he knelt next to her. A familiar chill crawled up her spine; a beckoning whisper laced with the promise of an endless fall into the void. It was a feeling she often felt around her mother—and within herself.

He came into focus for a moment, and as she saw the moon-pale skin, dark hair, and ether-laced black eyes, she whispered, "Thanatos."

His smile was hard to read. "Hello, granddaughter. I'm glad I found you. They were hours away from ripping apart the entirety of the realm to find you, and that would have created quite the mess."

"Wha—"

Her vision tilted.

Thanatos was no longer a man, but a creature of night and lightless stars she could not see but *feel* in the echo of her own soul…

In a flash, he returned. Cold fingers skirted just above her collarbone, and he frowned. Just before she faded completely, she heard him mutter, "Fucking Fates."

When she came to, Nya was wrapped in several blankets, a large fire roaring in the nearby hearth. She blinked a few times, trying to orient herself but not recognizing the room.

The decor was simple, mostly consisting of a few ornate mirrors on the walls and two woven rugs covering the dark hardwood floor. Thick curtains were pulled over the only window in the room, and she was lying on one of two large couches that took up most of the space. It appeared to be some sort of sitting room.

She swallowed, her throat dry, and pushed herself into a sitting position. Her limbs were sore from riding two days in a row. The hum of low voices filtered into the room from the hallway; she wrapped one of the blankets around herself and crept towards the door, her feet faltering when she heard her mother's voice.

"—not going back. He doesn't *own* her just because he married her."

Someone cleared their throat. "Not technically, but it appears the situation is more complicated."

"What the fuck is that supposed to mean?"

Nya's lips trembled. That was her father. They had both come for her, all the way to this place they feared and hated.

"Yes, what *do* you mean?" That voice, a woman's voice, Nya did not recognize.

"I mean…" He—Thanatos, she realized—sighed heavily. "It appears Kronos' son is much smarter than his father ever was. He did his research. He's aware of the ancient traditions, Nya."

Nya. Another of Nyx's name.

The goddess who she was named for, who had created this world with her twin brother, Sol, born alone in darkness before he had lit it up. After hearing and wondering about the principals her whole life, it felt odd to hear two of them speaking just beyond the door. They were her mother's true parents, after all.

"Do you mean…?" Nyx trailed off quietly.

"Yes."

"Would either of you like to explain what you are talking about?" her mother asked sharply.

"Marriage would not usually hold much sway when it comes to leverage in a situation such as this. You were correct when you said he doesn't have ownership over her because of it—we weren't *that* archaic, even in the early days." Thanatos cleared his throat. "At least… Well, we learned our lesson. But there was a tradition, mostly used amongst demi-gods, that fell out of fashion rather quickly. Even Kronos didn't think of it when he tried to force you into marriage, Sora. He never had any interest in remembering our histories, especially if they involved anyone he thought beneath him."

Thanatos paused, and her father snarled, "Out with it."

Nya bit her lip, the wild urge to laugh suddenly overcoming her. There were two principals in the other room. Night and Death were mere feet away, and her kind, grumpy father had just demanded an explanation from them, no reverence or fear to be found in his voice.

It took her a moment to remember all the reasons why he might not be on the best terms with Nyx and Thanatos, mainly the one that involved them selling her mother to a marriage with Kronos.

"There was a mark on her throat," Thanatos said, and Nya's heart nearly stopped. "It was newly healed, probably by him, given that few gods have that ability to project healing to others. But…it will never truly go away, nor will the pull that comes with it."

"Fucking Fates," Nyx said, softly enough that Nya barely heard it.

"*That* is exactly what I said," Thanatos agreed. Then, before either of her parents could interject again, he explained, "In the early days of this world, a handful of idiot demi-gods had the bright idea to introduce blood bonding into betrothal ceremonies. When done correctly, it makes it very difficult to be far from one's partner for long— bordering on painful. It's like opening a window in your soul and letting a small part of someone else in. Effectively, the two souls are forever tied by an unbreakable thread."

"And if either were to die?" her mother asked, and Nya's stomach dipped at the horror in her voice.

"You know how our souls are," Thanatos said quietly. "Few have the power to destroy them completely. *But* if someone did manage to do such a thing…the other would be ripped irreparably. *Anabás Caegal.*"

Nya took a step back into the sitting room, her hand at her throat, feeling the erratic flutter of her own pulse beneath her skin.

"You saw Ana there, didn't you?"

Nya jolted, whirling to find a woman perched on the edge of a chair in a shadowed corner of the room. Had she been there the entire time?

The woman smiled, though it did not quite reach her eyes, then stood. She was much taller than Nya, though that wasn't a difficult feat to achieve. Silky dark hair fell nearly all the way down her back, and her hooded eyes were a striking shade of jade-green laced with silver. She smoothed delicate hands over the front of her azure dress, waiting.

Nya's lips parted, realizing there was an odd, restless feeling in the air. It made her think there was something on the tip of her tongue, similar to what she had felt during the ceremony, when Anabeth had revealed herself. Anabeth, who was a daughter of—

"Juno," Nya whispered, warily eyeing the Goddess of Fate standing before her. "Why didn't you say anything when I woke?"

Juno raised a dark brow. "If you had seen me, I presume you would have gone to the hall immediately, and I figured you might want to hear the truth on your own before you saw them."

"And what truth is that?" she dared, already knowing the answer. Not just because of what she had overheard, but because the truth of it was undeniable in the pull now thrumming in her blood.

Go back. Go back. Go back, it urged.

As if Varax hadn't tied them closely enough. Now, fighting the gravity she had already been pushing against for years felt like a nearly impossible feat.

"You and Morgen are tied by the very threads of Fate," Juno said, her gaze unflinching. "But what Nyx, Thanatos, and your parents do not understand is that this has been true for a long time. He only made it more obvious to everyone else when he sealed the betrothal with your blood."

"I didn't drink his blood, though."

Silver glinted in Juno's eyes. "No. You did not. A purposeful self-protection measure on his end, I believe."

"I'm going to assume this 'bond' is supposed to work both ways, but it won't now."

"Mhm," Juno hummed, wearing the same knowing expression her daughter had. Nya did not like it. "It will be a useless block for him, though. I imagine he's already realized that."

"What do you—"

"She's awake?"

Nya whirled at the sound of her mother's voice, her breath catching in her throat as she saw both her parents in the open doorway. She had not seen them since she had left for D'anna a year ago to apprentice at the temple. Naturally, they looked exactly the same—her mother a near-copy of her, except with wide, icy-blue eyes instead of hooded brown ones, and her father still ridiculously tall. His dark facial hair was a bit more grown out than he usually wore it, and both of them had smudges of purple under their eyes, as if they hadn't been sleeping.

She stared at them, twisting her hands and trying to hold back tears of shame, unsure of what to say. Eventually, she hung her head and choked out, "I'm so sorry."

Seconds later, it was like being hit with a battering ram as both crowded her, familiar waves of magic wrapping around her as they held her close.

"You have nothing to be sorry for," her mother whispered, stroking her hair. "*Nothing*, Nya."

When they pulled away and gave her some space to breathe, she met her father's eyes—*her* eyes—and felt her heart sink at the terror reflected there.

I'm sorry.

His brow creased, and he shook his head slightly.

Your mother is right. You have nothing to apologize for.

Yes, she is right. And perhaps, for once, you should have listened to her, Thessilnn grumbled down the pathway. *You made us lie for you, and look where that got you, little one.*

Her father's mouth twitched, and her mother muttered, "Yes, well, if you two lazy beasts had better counseled her, perhaps this wouldn't have happened either."

Heles is lazy. I am merely tired after cleaning up all your messes for nearly two-hundred years.

Heles didn't say anything down the pathway, but Nya heard the snapping of enormous jaws just outside the window. From the corner, Juno cleared her throat amidst the chaos and said, "Ana was the one who performed the betrothal ceremony. Nya just confirmed it."

Nya's mother looked at the Goddess of Fate sharply. "I thought she was still in D'anna, with Cion?"

Juno shrugged. "Perhaps the queen sent her away. She is near to the end of her mortal life now, and Ana will always maintain her youth. Humans can be very vain about age."

"I doubt it," Nya's father muttered. "If she left D'anna, it was for a reason."

"I just gave one," Juno pointed out.

Nya worried her bottom lip between her teeth and glanced between her parents. "You both knew her—Ana—from before?"

Her mother took a deep breath, her thumb brushing over her wedding band. It was a nervous tick both her parents had done without realizing it for as long as Nya could remember.

"We did," her mother said. "I'm sorry, Nya, love, we should have told you much more than we did, especially before you left home."

Juno laughed softly. "I fear you were several years too late with any warnings, Sora."

Nya tried to school her expression into confusion at Juno's words, even as her palms turned clammy and cold. Her mother glanced at her, brow furrowed.

"What does she mean, Nya?" But before she had to try and think of how to reply, her mother's expression became faraway. Silver flooded her eyes for a flash, and her throat worked. "Your hikes. Of course... You were meeting someone."

She glanced at Nya's father, and he let out a tight laugh, running a hand over his face. "Yeah...a *field*. They were meeting in a 'field.'"

Nya said nothing, a little unnerved by how quickly they'd figured it out, by how much she now realized her afternoons spent with Morgen had resembled her parent's first meetings. She hadn't known many details about their past before leaving Mise last year, but as a child, whenever she'd asked her mother how she had met her father, she had always been given the same answer: on a warm, late summer day, in a field of wheat. They weren't supposed to meet, but her mother kept returning, despite the danger. Because sometimes, you loved someone more than you cared about duty or honor. Because sometimes, love superseded those things.

Nyx rose from where she'd perched on the arm of one of the couches. "Would you mind explaining to the rest of us?"

Nya's mother turned to the Goddess of Night. "I'm surprised you haven't caught on. We're referring to the circumstances that led to your former king tearing my heart out with his bare hands."

Out of the corner of her eye, Nya noticed both her father and Thanatos flinched at the words. Nyx remained completely still, but the shadows at the corners of the room deepened, stirring as they swirled across the hardwood.

Nya's head felt light. Too much was happening, and she didn't—*couldn't* think or even breathe…

"Out. Everyone," her father barked suddenly.

Nyx's brow furrowed. "We are not finished discussing—"

"We'll finish talking once my daughter can stand for more than a few minutes without fainting. *Out.*"

His tone brooked no argument, and maybe Nya was a bit delirious, because she couldn't hold back a laugh, covering her mouth with her hand to stifle it. It was just too much, to see her *father* order around a bunch of principals. He was technically one of them, she supposed. If Vulcan ever fell, as heir, his place would be in Arcadia, on the council.

Juno brushed past her, and the mark Morgen had left on her tingled slightly. Nya ignored it, watching Nyx and Thanatos leave, whispering amongst themselves. Once she was alone with her parents, her mother gently lowered Nya's hand from her face.

Nya hadn't even realized the laughter had turned to tears.

"Shh, love."

"Mama, I—" Her voice broke off. "Do you hate me for

it? I swear, I didn't know, not for most of it, and then I just—"

"Nya," her mother cut in gently, a hand cupping Nya's cheek. "You are one of the few things in this godsforsaken world I could never hate. I know you think you've done something terrible. I do not think so—but even if you had, it wouldn't matter to me. Do you understand?"

Nya's throat was tight with unshed tears, so she merely nodded. Her mother tucked a loose strand of silvery hair behind her ear and said quietly, "Good. I'm going to go talk to the others, but your father will sit with you, alright?"

Nya took a deep breath. "Okay."

Her mother squeezed her shoulder before glancing at her father, who gave a shallow nod. Nya sank onto the couch by the hearth, and once her mother was gone, her father joined her. For a few minutes, they just sat in silence.

Nya knew her mother loved her fiercely, but she had always felt closer to her father. Perhaps it was the hint of mortal blood they shared that allowed for a sort of understanding even her mother could not claim.

Eventually he spoke, asking, "Did you hear what we said, in the other room?"

She glanced at him, brow furrowed. "How did you know?"

His lips twitched. "Because I've caught you trying to stay up and listen past your bedtime one too many times. I can usually sense when you're nearby. You're my daughter, and I would have done the same."

She smiled despite herself, but it quickly slipped away. "I didn't realize Juno was in the room... She didn't say anything because she thought I needed a moment to hear the truth alone."

"Juno isn't usually wrong."

"You know all of them—the principals," Nya pushed, watching silver flicker in his eyes as she said it. "And they know you. Respect you, even. Why did you stay away from Arcadia for so long?"

He laughed tightly. "I don't know how much they respect me. They just know I have plenty to hang over their heads if they tried to insult or threaten me."

Her next words were quiet. "Because you died for them? For the realms?"

"I wish I could say I was that noble, Nya," he said, meeting her eyes with a sad smile. "But only your mother can truly claim that honor. I was just happy to finally follow her into the void that day."

Nya frowned. "You were happy to die?"

His throat worked. "We should have told you all of this. I'm sorry we didn't and that you've had to make sense of the past in pieces."

She dropped her gaze to her hands, twisted in her lap. "I don't know if it would have made a difference, but you could tell me now."

When she looked at him again, his eyes were on the fire and filled with enough pain, she almost took the request back. But then, in a quiet voice, he said, "There are many, many things worse than death. I didn't realize that when I was young and still in my first life. Some of it probably had to do with being raised in the mortal realm, where death is feared above all else. But Arcadia is different, and my mother had ill-prepared me to face it. I think she hoped I would never venture across the border, perhaps never really even realize the truth about who I was." He laughed, a soft, sad sound. "She didn't live long enough to understand how impossible that was."

"Because Vulcan is your true father."

He nodded slowly. "Yes."

"And what is worse than death?" she dared, her heart beating too fast and her stomach already turning in anticipation.

Her father looked her directly in the eye as he said, "Watching the one person you swore to protect destroyed in front of you while you are helpless to stop it. Living with the memory of it and being forced to exist, decade after decade, in an empty world you both created. Kronos murdered your mother simply because he could not have her, Nya, and then, when he exiled me to the mortal realm, he took magic from it too."

A shiver raced up her spine, and he took her hand, adding in a low, insistent voice, "I am not telling you this to scare you. Your mother and I wish we did not keep so much from you, but I will *never* regret keeping you from this place for as long as I could. Fate is at its cruelest in Arcadia, and to immortal souls, death only holds meaning when it is wielded as a punishment in the worst of ways."

She nodded, unsure of what to say. What could she say? All throughout her childhood, she had imagined Arcadia through rose-tinted lenses. She had assumed her parents were exaggerating the true danger of the realm of the gods, but over the years, she had slowly learned that perhaps that wasn't the case at all.

"Do you ever regret meeting Mama?" she whispered

after a long stretch of silence, only broken by the popping of embers.

A huff of air escaped him. "No."

"Even with everything that happened? You wouldn't go back and—"

"No, Nya, love. Never. Some love is worth the pain that comes with it."

An unwelcome flash of Morgen's face flitted through her mind, and she didn't know why. She didn't love him. She had simply been infatuated with the first friend she ever had, and now, that person was gone, leaving behind only someone she hated.

"Would you like to talk about what's happened?" her father asked.

She sighed, looking away. As usual, he was unnervingly good at reading her.

She didn't want to talk about Morgen, not ever again. But perhaps that was childish; this problem was not going to just disappear, and the least she could do was try to help find a way to fix it.

"I have to go back," she said, her fingers twitching. "I assume… What Thanatos said about the blood bond means staying here could mean war."

Her father stiffened, and the dying flames in the hearth abruptly flared. "You don't have to go anywhere. Not if you don't want to."

"He has an army, Papa," she whispered. "Supposedly more than what I even saw, which wasn't a small number, and they are all loyal to him, not to mention Varax."

"Ah, the dragon?"

"Yes. She's just as large as Thessilnn and Heles."

He cleared his throat, eyes drifting from her and landing on the flames. "She's bonded to both of you?"

Nya took a deep breath. "Yes, but I don't think she would betray Morgen any more than she would betray me."

"So that is his name?"

She shut her eyes briefly, steeling herself. And though she hated defending him in any way, she needed to explain.

"It's wrong, what he's doing, but his life has not been easy."

Her father didn't immediately react with anger or protectiveness as she expected. Instead, he sighed heavily and patted her hand before resting it atop hers. He was warm and steady, just as he'd always been, but still, she shivered when he said, "No, with Kronos as a father...I cannot imagine his life has been anything but cruel to the extreme."

Her gaze wandered back to the dying hearth, watching the flame spark midnight for half a second as she whispered, "You have no idea."

CHAPTER 7
TWO YEARS PRIOR

Certain days hold weight. I can feel Fate pressing in on me from all sides. For the first time in one-hundred-and-four years, my friend is alive. I fear her heart will not beat long, and this time, I do not think Vane will allow himself to live once she is gone.
—Lady Anabeth, Royal Scribe's Apprentice, Royal Rider's Training Camp

SUMMER HAD RETURNED in full swing, bringing with it wave after wave of oppressive heat. Nya had slipped out of the house early this morning to try and avoid walking in the worst of it, having told her parents she was going on another 'hike' last night at dinner. They hadn't questioned it, even as she'd started to go more often, and she was grateful for it, even if she felt a bit guilty for lying to them.

Down creek, Varax was splashing in the clear water, terrifying small fish and creating waves as she slapped her enormous tail. Morgen was laying on his back next to Nya, a broad arm slung over his eyes. She could see the smile he was trying to suppress as Varax made a noise Nya had once quietly penned as 'excited crowing.'

Earlier, they'd all flown together for the second time, and though it was exhilarating for more than one reason, it had left Nya overheated and sticky. They were lounging halfway in the shade, but it did little to keep the heat of the sun from reaching them.

She turned her head to face Morgen, squinting against the sunlight filtering in through the branches. "We should go for a swim."

He lifted his arm, glancing at her. "A swim?"

"Yes, a swim. In the water. Is that a foreign concept to you?"

He snorted and flicked her nose lightly. "No. I know how to swim. Why, though?"

She scowled, batting his hand away. "It's hot out. It will help cool us down, and it can be fun, if you can find it in yourself to conceptualize that."

"Am I boring you, Nya?" He rolled onto his stomach, chin resting on his hand. "I would say I could leave, but I'm going to guess Varax would throw a fit if I suggested it so soon."

She pushed playfully at his bicep, ignoring the hard tension of the muscles beneath her palm. "No, I never said that. You've just been quiet today."

"Hm, have I?"

"*Morgen.*"

He didn't like it when she pushed like this, but she couldn't help it. She had tried to talk to him plenty, but he'd barely said anything until now. He became closed off and quiet like this when he was in pain. Which, to be fair, she was realizing was the case most of the time, but she had begun to be able to read him well enough to know when it was worse.

He sighed softly, sitting up, palms pressed against the dirt behind him. He was wearing a sleeveless tunic that was halfway undone at the top, revealing the sculpted planes of his chest. She pretended she didn't notice and that looking at him didn't make her feel like she was halfway on fire most of the time. If she wasn't such a coward, she would ask if it was the same for him.

"It's my birthday today," he said after a moment, still not looking at her.

Her lips parted, and she exhaled slowly. She understood enough to know this was not a happy day for him. Not in the slightest.

His fingertips brushed against the scar at his throat. "When I was ten years old, as a birthday 'gift,' my father decided to test how well my superior healing abilities would work on myself."

"Are you saying he…he was the one who did—"

"Yes, he slit my throat. I left my room that morning because I was a child and an idiot, and I thought, *surely, he won't torture me today.*" He laughed bitterly. "I choked on my own blood for nearly an hour before I could breathe normally, and I didn't make the mistake of thinking he gave a damn about what day it was ever again."

"Why are you telling me this?" she whispered. Her face felt cold, and barely suppressed rage was making her shiver.

His jaw rolled. "You look at the scar a lot. I figured today was as good of a day as any to tell you how I got it."

Her breath caught. "I'm sorry, I didn't mean to stare, I just—"

"I don't mind," he cut in abruptly. "I never have. You don't look at me with pity…more like you want to hurt whoever did it." He chuckled dryly. "Perhaps I like it when I see a little violence in your eyes."

Her stomach dipped at the words, at the low tone of his voice, at the heat she swore was suddenly simmering in his eyes, despite what he'd just told her. They stared at each other for a little too long, until Morgen inhaled sharply and got to his feet, offering her his hand.

"Alright, a swim it is."

She took it, the familiar callouses on his palm and fingers scraping against her skin. He let go once she was on her feet and they meandered over to the creek. When they reached the smooth, gray stone at the edge of the water, she paused, glancing down at herself.

She was wearing light canvas pants and a woven shirt. Not really the best clothing for swimming, though she did have a shift and shorts beneath the clothes. They were technically undergarments, but if she didn't want to swim in her clothes, she had no other options.

Morgen was already pulling off his tunic, though he left his pants on. She tugged her clothing off too before she could think twice about it again. Except that he had definitely not been expecting her to do it, because as soon as he turned back and saw her, he froze.

"You…" His throat worked. "Won't you get cold?"

She shook her head. She was trembling again, but this time, it wasn't from anger. Still, she kept her voice level, almost bored, when she replied, "It's boiling out, and we're swimming. Besides, I didn't want to get my clothes wet."

"Right." He turned away from her for a moment, his hand on the back of his neck. "Right," she heard him mutter again, so low, she nearly couldn't hear it.

She wasn't completely naive and had an inkling as to why he might be acting like this. If he was feeling anything like what she was right now, she understood.

"Doubtful," he said under his breath, back still to her.

Her cheeks warmed, and she glanced over to where Varax was still splashing around, seemingly ignorant of their conversation. Except that the damn dragon was the one who had just strategically opened the pathway at the worst moment possible, ferrying Nya's silent pining over to Morgen.

She scowled at her and didn't wait to see the dragon's reaction before reaching out to touch Morgen's arm.

"Morgen—"

"*Don't.*"

A sudden wave of energy slammed into her, and she stumbled back, nearly falling on her ass. She knew without even asking that it was a manifestation of his magic. He grabbed her arm just before she completely lost balance and then let go abruptly as if he'd been burned, his expression horrified.

Once the shock of what had just happened registered and passed, she reached out again. "Hey, it's alright—"

"No...*no*, it's not." His breath was ragged, each word rushed and panicked, and his eyes were wide and shining with a strange light. "You should be running. Why are you not running?"

Her brow creased. "You didn't hurt me, Morgen. And you're surely not the first person with magic to accidentally release too much power when your emotions are running high."

"I lost control," he was saying, over and over again, shaking his head.

She didn't know what to do. He appeared to be on the verge of some sort of panic attack, perhaps already there. Touching him would probably just make things worse, so instead, she reached out in another way.

A wave of fire, so cold it burned, blasted through the air, shimmering with midnight. He stumbled as it flashed and faded just shy of his body, the panicked words stopping and his eyes widening for a different reason.

The icy-hot feeling of the magic left her quickly. It always did, but it had been just enough to bring him back to the present moment—and to make her point.

"See?" she said, fighting to keep her voice level. Her heart was beating too fast for comfort, though she didn't know why she was so nervous. "It happens, and I didn't hurt you."

"Your magic," he murmured, not looking at her yet. "That was it."

She tentatively took a step closer to him. "I'm not afraid of you," she whispered.

"You should be."

She shrugged, forcing herself to appear as apathetic as possible. "What, because you had the equivalent of a magical temper tantrum?"

He shook his head, and every inch of her came alive as he traced his long fingers lightly over her collarbone. "No.

Because I *never* lose control. But when I'm around you…" He shook his head slightly. "I can't make sense of it."

Her breath grew shallow and uneven as he traced his thumb up the curve of her jaw. He wasn't looking her in the eye, but when she brushed her fingers over his bare chest, his gaze shot to hers.

"Maybe it's good to lose a little control sometimes," she whispered.

He muttered a low, "*Fuck*" and dipped his head—not to kiss her like she wanted, but instead resting his brow on her shoulder. Her breath hitched, and she knotted her fingers in his hair. One of his hands was resting behind her neck, the other gripping her hip, his fingers twitching against the fabric of her undershorts. She shivered when he spoke, his lips moving against a sensitive spot just below her throat.

"Losing control is never good. Not for anyone like you or me."

"Because our magic could hurt someone?" Her voice sounded strange; breathy and low.

His breath fanned across her skin as he laughed roughly, his voice still muffled when he replied, "Because a lack of control and an excess of power always ends poorly."

"Do you never let go? Even just for a moment?"

He lifted his head slowly, and she found his expression had evened out again. "No," he said softly. "Not even for you, *oíche ríonn*."

He pulled away and headed for the water before she could register what he'd just said. She was certain the words were in the Old Language of the gods and filed them away so she could figure out their meaning later.

Once she was in the water too, they fell back into their

usual routine. She talked, he listened, only occasionally interjecting. She stuck to safe topics, things that didn't matter, like her opinions on types of tea, her favorite star, asking what the worst weather was for flying…

But something had shifted, and they both knew it. She just wondered how long she would have to live with him pretending it hadn't.

~

Hours later, when she returned home, she asked Heles, *What does 'oíche rionn' mean in the Old Language?*

Heles blinked at her slowly, eyes shining in the dim light of dusk. She nudged Nya's shoulder with her gigantic snout. *It means you, little one. Night, speckled with the ever-burning fire of dying stars.*

CHAPTER

EIGHT

I was wrong. I knew I was, and yet…even as they are gone forever, the child still mocks me in my dreams. She runs away when I reach for her.
—Lady Anabeth, Consort to Her Majesty Cion Livii, Queen of Aren, D'anna

JUST BEFORE SUNRISE, Nya slipped quietly out of Nyx's house. No one had awoken, not even the dragons. But just as she made it to a packed dirt road past the garden full of night-blooming florals, a vaguely familiar voice mused, "I thought I might see you out here."

She jerked then whirled to see Thanatos leaning casually against a tree. He was wearing a black turtleneck and a silk bathrobe, of all things, and his jet-black hair stuck up in a way that made him look distinctly mischievous.

She didn't trust him for a second.

"What do you want?" she asked sharply.

He chuckled under his breath, shaking his head. "You know, you look just like Sora, but everything else…all that fire and reckless determination; that is all your father."

"You're not the first to make such an observation," she said stiffly, unsure what his intentions were. To make her go back, she assumed, which she couldn't do.

Except, he surprised her when he waved a dismissive hand and said, "You can relax. I'm not going to wake them, nor will I stop you."

The smart thing to do would have been to leave then, but curiosity got the better of her. "But why?"

He sighed heavily, glancing back at the house, hands shoved deep in the pockets of the pants he wore beneath the robe. "You can't stay here, for several reasons. I understand your parents' wish to deny that, but they cannot protect you. This thread of fate is yours alone to follow."

"I know," she whispered. Then, after a beat, she added, "You didn't want to do it, did you? Sell my mother to Kronos, I mean?"

She wasn't exactly sure why she asked the question. Perhaps it was a burning need to understand why such a thing had happened in the first place, to make sense of the decisions that had led to so much pain for both her parents. For *all* of them.

Slowly, Thanatos shook his head, the silver in his eyes dimming so much, she could no longer see the outline of his irises. "Of course I didn't. I would have rather died than let him keep summoning her to that godsforsaken palace. But when the decision was made, it wasn't my soul on the line. Nyx was supposed to marry Kronos, and when she didn't, he was enraged. Then, Sora was born, and he gave us two options: bind her soul to his and sign her away to a betrothal as soon as she came of age, or allow us to *watch* as he destroyed her before she'd barely had a chance to exist.

Because of the embers, Kronos was more powerful than any of us, so we could not fight him." He looked away, mouth downturned. "It was foolish of Sol to ever grant him such power in the first place."

A shiver raced down Nya's spine. They could say what they liked about Morgen, but she knew he would never hurt an innocent child.

She turned, readying to leave, but then glanced back one last time. "My father told me last night that in Arcadia, there are many things worse than death."

A shadow passed over Thanatos' face. "Indeed. He learned that when he took on the burden of watching exactly what I thought I had prevented. Death *always* finds a way, Nya. Fate ensures that, and even I am powerless to stop it."

This time, she didn't reply, and he didn't stop her as she left, but his words haunted her as she walked, turning over and over again in her mind. She couldn't shake the feeling that the phrase was familiar to her.

When she reached an open field somewhat shielded by a forest on one side, she sat in the tall grass and closed her eyes.

Varax?

It took a moment, but as always, the dragon answered, and her voice filled Nya's mind. *I presume you would like me to collect you.*

I need to go back.

You know, I could have told you this would happen. It would have saved me all the flying.

Nya opened her eyes, resting her chin atop her knees. *Apologies.*

Ah, yes. You sound very *sorry.*

The pathway quieted after that, and she curled her arms around herself to try and shield against the cold wind. Nyx had given her a small pile of clothing that had been her mother's, and before she'd left, Nya had tugged on a thick sweater and fleece-lined pants. Still, the sun was just starting to crest over the horizon, not yet warming the ground.

She wasn't sure if Morgen would risk coming with Varax through a portal. If not, it would take her at least a few hours to get here. But perhaps, after Nya had fled so suddenly, he would make her wait as a sort of punishment.

Would he be angry? He hadn't made any moves to stop her, so he had to know she would have no choice to go back. She had never seen Morgen get truly angry. She wasn't even sure he was capable of such an emotion. Anger required letting go, and he never let himself do that.

She was just about to stand and stretch when she saw a slight shimmer in the air at the edge of the clearing, so subtle, she doubted it was actually there. But then, quickly, it spread and thickened, a large portion of the empty air solidifying into what looked like an opaque mirror. Before her mind really had a chance to catch up, Varax materialized, shaking her head and slapping her tail against the dirt as she landed.

Morgen's voice echoed down the pathway. *Varax. I'd appreciate it if you* try *to be quiet.*

You know how portaling makes me feel.

Nya's throat tightened, both hearing and seeing Morgen atop Varax, but it wasn't just that causing a sudden wave of sadness through her.

She had never seen him portal before. He had promised she would someday, but she had never really believed him.

Now, she wasn't sure what to believe anymore.

He didn't dismount, and she took a deep breath, approaching Varax with slow steps, giving herself time to try and tamp down the tidal wave of emotions rising within her. Seeing him brought far too much relief that she wanted to blame on the new bond between them. Deep down, in a place she would not admit to, she knew this was the same feeling she had experienced each time he'd come back to her in the years before.

"We need to go quickly," he said quietly, extending a hand. "Before they realize I'm here."

She had wondered that—if the principals could sense a presence like his.

Begrudgingly, she took his hand, but as their palms brushed, his touch sent a spark of something electric up her arm. He must have felt it too, because his fingers twitched against hers. She forced herself to meet his eyes, aglow with amber-gold. He didn't even bother to hide the embers around her anymore.

That's new. You don't usually shock me when we touch.

His eyes widened slightly before he corrected himself and his expression flattened again. Probably because she'd just willingly used the pathway. But he didn't address her words, merely muttering, "Hold on."

She did as he said, wrapping her arms around his torso. For just a moment, before she went back to hating him, before she accused him of deceiving and betraying her, she let herself lean into his solid frame. Once, flying had been one of the few times he allowed her so close, and she had relished every second of it. Now, every time she felt him breathe against her, it was bittersweet.

Varax shook her head, obviously agitated as Morgen reached out a hand, the other still resting on the saddle. Nya watched the air around his fingertips begin to warp and glisten, turning the same shade of silver as ether before it spread wide.

Now, Varax. His voice sounded slightly strained, and she tightened her arms in anticipation as the dragon spread her wings and took off.

It was over in the blink of an eye, but in that breath of a second, she swore she saw a thousand blinking stars strung with silver.

She opened her mouth to ask about it as they slammed onto a slab of rock that jutted off the mountain, but she stopped short as Morgen's entire body shuddered and then went completely limp behind her.

"Morgen?"

She tried again.

Morgen?

Her pulse skyrocketed. A sharp pain started at the center of her chest and spread, racing down her body with frightening speed. It felt like she was being ripped apart from the inside, and she almost expected to see blood when she pressed her hand to skin. Something was *very* wrong, but she couldn't make sense of it.

"I told him not to do it!" a familiar voice called over the wind around them. "The bastard can be really stupid sometimes, *especially* when it comes to you."

Nya took a short, pained breath. Carus was waiting just below, his hands on his hips, as if he'd been expecting them.

"Let go of him," Carus said, scowling. "He deserves to hit the ground in a heap and wake up with a sore head, but I'm a good friend."

She didn't move or let go of Morgen's arm, which she had grabbed without realizing. Carus glared at her, and despite the pain and panic, she narrowed her eyes.

Carus groaned, throwing his hands up in the air. "Oh, relax, sweetheart, I'll catch him." He shook his head, adding more quietly, "Fates, there's two of you now."

The pain peaked, and Nya forced herself to let go of Morgen, her heart in her throat. Despite the fact that Morgen was a few inches taller than him, Carus caught his limp body without much struggle, and when Nya practically fell off Varax's back too, Morgen opened his eyes, muttering, "The fuck are you looking at me like that for, Carus?"

Suddenly and all at once, the unexplainable pain disappeared.

Carus snorted obnoxiously. "Oh, good morning to you too."

"And why are you hugging me?"

With a long-suffering sigh, Carus rolled his eyes. "First of all, you're welcome. I really wanted to drop you. Second of all, you are an idiot. And if you're wondering exactly how you fell into my arms—ask your wife."

It took Morgen a moment to make sense of those last words, and Nya understood why. Their marriage didn't feel real, and for Carus to reference it so casually was a harsh slap of reality.

Morgen blinked a few times, evidently still regaining a grasp on his surroundings. When he saw her standing over him, scowling, he *grinned*.

Gods, he was really smiling at her, broadly and unrestrained.

Despite her anger at him and the fact that she had every intention of finding a way out of all of this and leaving him behind, his expression hit her like a punch to the gut. She had never seen him smile like that, without any check on his emotions. Without *control.*

"Riiight," he said, the expression holding even as his eyes fluttered shut. "I married you, and now you're *really* mad at me." He sighed, the sound oddly contented. "But you came back. I knew you would, *oíche rionn.*"

Nya opened her mouth and shut it twice before she actually spoke, trying and failing to make sense of the way he was acting. "Carus? What…what is happening?"

Carus rubbed at his temple. "Thanks to you, he is drunk off his ass, and now I will have to deal with his caterwauling until he hopefully passes out."

"I didn't give him anything—"

"Not on wine. On his own magic."

"I don't understand—"

"Carus!" Morgen groaned, slapping Carus in the face. "You should kick me in the head again before it explodes like last time."

"Nope," Carus said, attempting to drag him towards the tunnel entrance as lightning cracked across the sky in the distance. "Not this time. I told you not to do this again, and you are going to live with the consequences, migraine included."

Nya watched, unsure of how to make sense of the strange scene. She followed Carus, and as soon as they were inside, Imeria appeared, laughing softly.

"Gods, really?" She sighed. "I thought he learned his lesson last time."

Morgen was muttering something now, over and over again, his voice slurred but insistent. It took Nya a moment to realize it was her name.

"Look, Ima, can you just take care of Nya while I get *His Majesty* to bed before he causes too much of a scene?"

Imeria rolled her eyes. "Fine."

Carus nodded and turned his attention back to Morgen. "Alright, you big, dumb fucker, let's go."

Morgen opened his eyes, still saying her name. His irises were completely flooded with both silver ether and the bright gold of the embers, the strange light broken only by pupils that were dilated a concerning amount.

"He's really just…drunk?" Nya ventured, glancing at Imeria.

Imeria snorted. "Essentially. When he uses too much magic too fast, the strain of it nearly kills the part of him that's mortal, and then the embers come to the rescue to keep him from dying. But his internal magic tends to overdo it, and it goes to his head. Don't worry, he'll be back to his normal, broody self within a couple of hours."

"Does this happen often?" Nya asked, her eyes on Morgen, who appeared to be trying to crawl away from a very irritated looking Carus.

Imeria shook her head. "No, only a handful of times. He knows his limits and doesn't usually push them like this. It leaves him far too vulnerable." She raised a brow, watching as Carus fought off Morgen's haphazard slaps. "*Obviously.*"

"Nya!" Carus called. "Will you please come over here

and assure Morgen you are still breathing, have not fallen off a cliff, and are not going to hate him forever—all things he will not shut up about, by the way."

She bit her lip, and Imeria nudged her arm. "If you want some peace today, you'd better do as Carus says. Take my word for it."

"Right," she muttered before approaching tentatively and kneeling on the floor where Morgen was half-propped up against the damp tunnel wall. As soon as he saw her, he stopped flailing and trying to hit Carus in the face.

"Nya?"

Oh gods. He sounded so…scared, almost boy-like in a way she was sure he really never had the safety to be.

"Carus said you were worried," she said softly. "But I'm fine. You should probably try to go and sleep this off."

His brow creased. "Everyone is angry with me."

"Damn straight," Carus muttered.

But Morgen didn't look away from her. She was caught, trapped by his wide-eyed gaze.

"I'm used to it," he whispered. He still wore a crooked smile, though it was sad now. "No one has ever loved me, not even you." His eyes fluttered shut. "I just don't like it when you look at me like you *hate* me."

She didn't look away from him. Couldn't. "Carus, can you help me carry him to bed?"

Carus cleared his throat, and his gruff voice was softer when he replied, "Yeah, let's go."

Morgen didn't protest this time, slinging one arm over Carus' shoulder and wrapping the other around her. Imeria watched them go, a slant to her brow Nya couldn't quite read. She would deal with figuring Imeria out later.

She would deal with *all* of this later, because that pain in her chest she had felt earlier, when they'd just emerged from the portal—that had been because Morgen was dying. She didn't want to think about what it would feel like if he was actually gone.

"Alright," Carus said under his breath as they rounded a corner, revealing a hammered metal door that had been constructed to fit the dimensions of the cavern entrance. "Here we are."

He kicked it open with his foot, and they shuffled into a hollowed-out space containing a large bed, a desk covered in neat stacks of parchment and a few daggers, and a weapons rack in the corner. Very little about the room felt personal. Perhaps nothing, if it hadn't been for the small wooden rack hanging just to the right of the desk.

From small hooks, mementos that would be meaningless to anyone else but her had been hung: a small leather pouch that contained river stones she had carefully selected, a string tied to the end of a long, blue-black feather, a page from a book folded to look like a dragon, and a woven crown of long-dried wildflowers that had sat atop her head on her twenty-fourth birthday.

Her chest tightened, and she blinked away the burning in her eyes, re-focusing on the task of helping Morgen onto the bed. Once he was flopped haphazardly across the mattress, Carus sat back against the wooden headboard with a sigh.

"Go on," he said, adding with a wink. "I'll make sure he doesn't accidentally smother himself."

But she didn't smile, instead glancing at the rack of mementos again. Still, she stood, forcing herself to start walking to the door, but Morgen caught her wrist before she could get far.

Eyes half shut, he muttered, "Don't go."

She froze, blinking rapidly. It made her head spin, trying to reconcile the ruthless god who had forced her into a marriage and tricked her into an unbreakable bond with the man lying on the bed, begging her to stay with him. In the end, she couldn't. But she couldn't leave him like this either. So, she glanced at Carus and said, "Ah, I should probably stay. Just in case he freaks out again."

Carus tilted his head. "Can I trust you not to attempt to murder him, or shall I remain here?"

She shrugged. "Even if I tried, he could easily stop me."

"And if you managed to get the knife in him while he was asleep?"

Her lips twitched. "I doubt I could injure him in a way that was too fatal for his body to heal."

Carus' eyes flicked to Morgen's throat for a split second and then back to her. "I doubt so too." He scooted off the bed and strode to the door, stopping short just before he left. "Nya."

She bit her cheek, flooding her mouth with the taste of copper. "What?"

Carus tipped his head back and let out a long breath. "Once he's back to normal and you go back to lying to yourself and pretending you hate him, perhaps at least attempt to understand he has very little idea of how to properly treat someone he cares for. He's balancing a lot right now—more than you know or could even understand—and he's still trying."

"Trying?"

"Not to let it go to his head. Not to be like his father."

Her laugh was little more than a harsh puff of air. "He doesn't have to *try*, because he's never been anything like Kronos. I've never doubted that. I just hate that he lied to me."

Carus stared at her for a long moment, his jaw working, but he didn't say anything else about it. He just turned and left, the door closing quietly behind him. She sat on the edge of the bed, taking deep breaths, until her pulse slowed and her anger faded.

"You don't have to do that, you know."

She twisted, finding Morgen looking at her with half-lidded eyes. His words were still slightly slurred, his voice unguarded, so he clearly wasn't himself yet. Still, she asked, "Do what?"

He shrugged, closing his eyes. "Lie to him. Carus has known me long enough that he understands the truth."

"The truth?" Her voice was barely more than a hoarse whisper, but he heard it.

"My own mother didn't even want me, up until the day I killed her by coming into this wretched world. I was born wrong, and nothing can fix that. Even as a child, I knew it."

His voice was fading as he slipped closer to sleep. Nya took a deep breath and shook her head before curling into his chest and whispering, "No one chooses their life, not at first. The only thing that matters, the thing that makes us who we are, are the choices we make. I am very angry at you, Morgen, but…if you were anything like Kronos, you would have done much worse than use marriage to me as a political pawn. Men less evil than Kronos would have probably done unspeakable things to me the other night simply because they could."

She was sure he was almost asleep, but he shuddered, his arms wrapping around her. This close, he smelled the same as she remembered and was just as warm. She could almost pretend nothing had changed between them.

Tomorrow, she decided, she would hate him. Tomorrow, she would use threats and ultimatums and call his claim to the throne false. But for now, she let herself love this idea of him for the last time.

When she was sure he wasn't awake any longer, she pressed a hand to his chest, feeling every steady beat of his heart. Tears dampened his shirt when she shut her eyes, and, silently, she confessed the one truth she would never speak aloud.

You were wrong to say you have never been loved. I love you. I love you so much, it's destroying me.

CHAPTER

NINE

Peace. Cion loves to use that word. Some of it is her pride, I think, to remind me she was the one who created it. Certainly, she shares the credit, but the true burden was borne by two gods, heirs who looked like newborn stars as they disappeared in fire before my eyes all those years ago.
—Lady Anabeth, Consort to Her Majesty Cion Livii, Queen of Aren, D'anna

Nya.

The voice floated to her across a void filled with sparkling constellations. Every single burning, dying star was tended to by her. The light they were formed of was not warm, rather, so cold, it hurt as she cradled one against her chest. Someday, she would take a single breath, and when she blew it out, all of them would extinguish in a silent, empty supernova.

Vaguely, she knew she was dreaming, because this place was familiar. It was where she had gone nearly every night of her childhood, and it was where Varax had found her four years ago, staring at the deepest, darkest part of the void for just a little too long, wondering what would happen if she reached for it, just as she was doing now.

Perhaps it would be for the best if she let go, emptied out the magic she had been granted by the gods who had made her, and just disappeared as it returned to the night sky where it belonged.

A quiet death, wreathed in fire.

Nya. Nya. Nya*!*

The voice was more insistent now, almost irritating in its repetition. She sighed softly, her fingertips dancing over velveteen darkness. A slip of fate; that was all she was. Death was her destiny, and it would be the finale in a circle that had been *turning, turning, turning* ever since Nyx had refused to marry the king.

Nya, please.

Oh, but that voice…

It made her hesitate, caused her to cling to another thread of fate, this one still wound tightly within the circle of tragedy and loss but steeped in the promise that she was not alone in her destiny. She *could* ignore it. She could have ignored it many times now, but, just like all the times before, she caved, allowing the fear of loneliness to weaken her.

All she had to do, all she *ever* had to do, was turn around, and he was there, pulling her away from the void that might save him, if he only let her go.

∼

Her eyes flew open, and she heard someone very close to her murmur, "Shh…I know, I know. You're alright."

She touched her own face to find her cheeks damp with unnaturally cold tears. Her body was trembling and aching, as if she had just run a long distance, and her heart was racing, the uneven, harried beats making her breath catch.

Waking up like this was not unfamiliar. She'd had nightmares since childhood, had often woken in a panic, though she never remembered what they were about. When she was small, her parents would rush in and soothe her, but as she grew, she learned to deal with the aftermath alone. Except she he wasn't alone now, and it took her a moment to remember why.

"I'm still here," she muttered, sweeping her gaze around Morgen's room before sitting straight in the bed. *His* bed, where she had slept next to him all night, while he was drunk off his own magic.

"It's alright," he said, and she finally faced him as he scrubbed a hand over her jaw. "My mind is sane again."

She glanced at him, remembering all the times she had wondered what it would be like to wake up with him.

"You were acting like you smoked a *lot* of gardroot," she finally settled on.

She had once tried to convince him to try the plant with her, which he had blatantly refused. She had smoked it only once, just before she left Mise for D'anna, and had cried for hours straight in a mind-haze and then fallen asleep on the floor.

He lifted a shoulder, his shrug nonchalant and his voice flat when he said, "I'm sure I was. And I'm going to assume Carus explained why?"

"He did."

"Good, then. You need to—"

"Why?"

He paused, tilting his head to the side. "Why what?"

"Why did you portal twice in a row like that if you knew it would do that to you? I called for Varax, not you, and I was perfectly fine waiting for her to fly to me."

A muscle in his jaw twitched, and he looked away. "I needed you here. We have to get started with negotiations, and that requires your presence."

"Well, you lost just as much time as it would've taken Varax to fly to me and back flopping around drunk and sleeping off the effects of what you did instead. I'm going to venture to guess you knew that would happen, though." She squared her jaw, seeking out his eyes. "So, try again. Why did you do it, Morgen?"

He shook his head and muttered, "I don't have time for this," before rolling off the bed.

She scowled, watching as he pulled off his shirt and traded it for a fresh one then knotted half of his hair back. He was moving too fast to feign being relaxed or uncaring now.

"You need me to cooperate, right?"

He turned, his expression flat, though the embers were bright in his eyes. "You know I do."

"Fine, then. Answer my question, and consider it your ticket to me shutting up today while you use me for your plans."

He scoffed. "You never shut up, Nya. I don't expect that to stop just because I indulge your curiosities."

The words hit her like a slap in the face. She *was* talkative, especially around him, and she had always assumed he liked listening. But maybe he had just been tolerating her all those years, biding his time until the moment was right.

"Right, of course," she said quietly. "It doesn't matter anyways. I'm at your disposal no matter what. You made sure of that."

His expression clouded slightly. "You know I didn't mean—"

"I know *exactly* what you meant. Let's just get on with the manipulation for today. I'm too tired to play games."

He didn't reply this time, turning and walking to the door. She assumed he wanted her to follow and had just forced herself to get off the bed when he paused, a hand braced against the cavern wall.

"I did it because I was worried. Blood binding is old magic, and there isn't much information on how it works or what the toll can be at a distance. You were far away and had been gone for more than a day…" He sighed sharply. "I didn't do it with the intention of hurting you."

"Why *did* you do it?" she dared to whisper.

But apparently, she had pushed too far for now, because he didn't respond, pushing the door open and striding into the hallway.

She caught up to him, and they walked side by side, neither of them deigning to speak to each other as he led her gods knew where. When they entered the cavernous dining hall, full of soldiers talking and eating breakfast, her steps slowed. He was heading for one of the tables in the center, and nearly every pair of eyes in the room were drifting to her—and not all of them appeared friendly. Morgen was obviously respected, but she hadn't expected him to eat in the mess hall, nor did she like the visibility.

"Go on and sit," Imeria said in her ear, causing her to jump. "They all know you're married to him, and even if some of them aren't happy about it, none of them would dare lay a finger on you."

Nya would have rather run the other way, but she appeared to have little choice in the matter, so she gingerly slid into the spot next to Morgen. He'd already filled her plate with food, and she ate quickly, ignoring the openly hostile stares of two soldiers across from her at the table over. Morgen talked quietly to Carus, who sat on his left, Imeria occasionally interjecting from her spot across the table.

When Nya finished eating, Morgen said in her ear, "Done?"

She nodded, keeping one eye on the soldiers whispering amongst themselves as they glared at her.

"Good," Morgen said.

She hardly had time to register what he was doing before he'd portaled behind the soldiers, punched one of them in the face, and shoved a dagger in the other's belly in quick succession.

All at once, the dining hall fell into complete silence. Morgen snatched one of the soldier's napkins off the table and wiped the blood from his knuckles while the soldiers groaned in pain below him.

"Anyone else whispering about secret plots to murder my wife?" Morgen's voice boomed through the hall. "If you are, congratulations: you are at least less of an idiot than these two." He glanced down at them, his expression twisted in disgust. "If I catch wind of *anything*, you'll both be implicated immediately, since you had the gall to think I wouldn't hear you from a single table away. You know I value all of you, but…" He looked back at Nya and lifted a brow. "Your lives become void if you threaten hers."

He returned to their table, this time without the portal, and offered her his hand. She took it, telling herself again and again the whole display had just been for show. It would make sense why he did it; if he allowed insubordination amongst his ranks, it would only cause larger issues down the line. He obviously understood how to gather not just an army, but loyal fighters she didn't doubt would die for him and whatever it was they all believed in.

When they left the cavern, Carus followed them, keeping a few paces behind until Morgen led her into what appeared to be some sort of war council room. A large, circular table took up the center of the space, its surface filled with carved indents and overflowing with maps and charts, most of them unfamiliar to Nya upon first glance.

Morgen let go of her hand, and Carus sat in one of the numerous chairs scattered around the table, leaning back as he twirled a small dagger in his hands.

"You really shouldn't have portaled so soon after what happened yesterday," he said, gaze flicking between her and Morgen.

Morgen strode over to the table and placed his palms flat against the surface. Nya watched, eyes widening as the grooves in the table lit up, flowing with tiny rivulets of what appeared to be some sort of liquid gold. That was when she realized the table *itself* was a map too. She saw the words

Gods' Aisle carved near the edge and noticed the word 'veil' in several places. The table must be a map of Arcadia.

"I don't recall asking for your opinion," Morgen said flatly to Carus.

Carus leaned forward. "Yes, well, I don't recall requesting to babysit your magic-drunk ass."

"You were not there when I woke up," Morgen said, tilting his head to where Nya still stood near the entrance. "She was. So, I presume you were not burdened with the task for too long."

"Yes, I left. After I caught you when you fell off Varax then dragged you through the halls while you whined and flopped about like an overgrown child having a tantrum."

Nya's lips twitched, unable to stop the small laugh that escaped her even as Morgen scowled.

Carus grinned, pointing at her. "See? She thinks I'm funny."

"Incredible. You've finally found yourself a captive audience."

Carus burst out laughing, slapping a hand against his knee, and Nya pinched her lips together. She should *not* laugh. The joke was made at her own expense, and it was true, after all. She was trapped here. Maybe her mind was becoming a bit loopy with the confusing whiplash of emotions.

"So," Carus said, clearing his throat and placing a folded piece of parchment on the table. "The letter was drafted while you were having your sleepover. The other generals and I settled on three days."

Morgen gave a short nod. "Fine."

Nya glanced at the letter, already having a feeling what it was, but still, she asked, "Three days for what?"

This time, when Carus smiled, though it was not kind or amused but calculating. "Three days for the principals to meet our terms and accept Morgen as king. Otherwise, we're ready to send our armies."

CHAPTER 10

ONE YEAR AND SIX MONTHS PRIOR

*My hand is shaking, so I apologize if this is illegible. I was wrong.
Their souls were not destroyed but guarded from Fate itself by the
dragons. Cion fears the power she felt when she touched their child, but
I cannot bring myself to care.*
—*Lady Anabeth, Consort to Her Majesty Cion Livii, Queen of Aren,
D'anna*

"You look tired."

Across from her, leaning against a fallen tree, Morgen made a noncommittal noise in the back of his throat. The truth was, he'd looked tired for a while now. She had been holding back the need to make a comment about it on a hunch he wouldn't want to talk about it, which was probably true. It usually was.

"Have you been sleeping?"

He sighed. "I sleep."

She bit her lip. "Well, I just—"She cut herself off when he leaned forward, brushing his fingertips to her mouth.

"Don't do that," he murmured. They were close, closer

than he usually let them get, and she could see the silver-bright strands of ether pulsing in his irises. "You don't need to worry. I'm fine."

"Who will worry," she whispered, "if I don't?"

He didn't move away like she expected; instead, he tucked a strand of hair behind her ear and said with a sort of irritated fondness, "I have a few friends who fuss. Or at least they would call themselves my friends."

Her brow creased. "Do you not think of them as friends?"

"I do, but…" He glanced away. "I've known them for too long. I would never want a friendship formed of pity."

She understood immediately. "You knew them when you were young."

He looked back at her. "Some of them, yes."

"And they didn't do anything to stop it? What your father did to you?"

His low laugh was bitter. "They would have been killed for it. Besides, even if they were not children, they were quite young."

"I don't think I could have done nothing," she whispered.

He slid his palm up her cheek, cradling her face. "I know. Which is why I am very glad you were not there."

Her breath caught when he leaned forward, but, as always, he did not kiss her. Still, with his forehead pressed against hers, it was the closest she had been to him in a while.

Varax.

Yes, Nya?

Is it just us here?

The dragon paused. *Yes. Say what you need to. He will not hear.*

She closed her eyes, fingers curling in the fabric of Morgen's shirt as she felt the rise and fall of his chest. In the safety of her own mind, she whispered a truth she was sure he would never accept.

I love you.

There, in the sanctity of her thoughts, she pretended she heard him whisper it back.

ELEVEN

'Twin soul'. The phrase haunts me. June dismissed it as impossible when I brought the concern to him, but I could tell he was unsettled.
—Lady Anabeth, Consort to Her Majesty Cion Livii, Queen of Aren, D'anna

NYA WATCHED the lava spark and bubble below her, legs curled to her chest against the biting chill of the wind. The tears on her cheeks had long dried, but still, she remained on the ledge, where she had been for hours after walking out of the war room. No one had followed her. They all knew she wouldn't leave again, and there wasn't anywhere to run to beyond the cave systems of this mountain.

The principals would not accept the terms, whatever they were, she was sure of that. There would be war in Arcadia, one that would surely impact the mortal realm. Her parents would be involved because of her role in all of this; if anyone was hurt or died, their blood was on her hands.

She heard footsteps behind her but did not move or even

turn to see who it was. If one of Morgen's soldiers wanted to murder her, so be it. At least then, it would cause mutiny within his forces, perhaps even enough to stop all of this.

But then, Imeria said, "Did you know the Gods' Aisle is at the very edge of the realm?"

Nya didn't reply, eyes still on the molten fire below.

"That's why the land is so uneven. It moves, and when it does, we get a lot of that bubbling up," she added, pointing at the lava. "But it isn't always like this, with the lava and the lack of plant or animal life. In fact, the Gods' Aisle is sometimes one of the most beautiful places in Arcadia."

Nya glanced sidelong at her, a brow raised. "I don't know if I believe that."

"It's hard to see it right now, I know," Imeria said, her eyes sharp as they slid across the barren landscape. "This is where the principals first woke. However they came to be, this place was their passage into this world, and whenever the realm is unstable, this is the first place it becomes obvious."

"Unstable?" Nya echoed, eyes narrowing.

Imeria nodded. "I'm sure you heard of the storms. I don't think the bad ones were as far as D'anna, but that will change soon."

"I thought the storms were because of him?"

Imeria laughed. "Morgen?" She shook her head. "No. He's powerful, but not so much that he can idly keep storms like that raging for days. I mean, you saw what happened when he moved Varax through a portal twice in a row. He's an heir, but he is still half-mortal."

"If it's not Morgen, then what's causing the storms?" Nya pushed.

"He should probably be the one to explain it to you," Imeria said with a grim smile. "But I meant what I said, Nya. We do not follow him blindly or without reason. I care about Arcadia, and the mortal realm, believe it or not. Bad things are beginning to happen, and it will get much worse."

Nya chewed on her lip. "Why haven't the principals done anything? They must know."

Imeria expression darkened. "Our guess is that Sol still has an iron grip on the council. Kronos may have been king, but Sol was the one who gave him power in the first place—and that choice was not made on a whim. Kronos was all powerful, but in many ways, Sol was his puppeteer. Not to mention, when Kronos was destroyed, the council was already so divided, they practically rallied around Sol just to maintain some semblance of peace."

"I thought they were only divided because of Kronos?"

"Some of them." Imeria snorted. "But Bella has *always* hated Nyx, ever since she married Thanatos. The rumor, which I'm sure Bella herself has been tirelessly facilitating for the last several centuries, is that Nyx stole Thanatos from her. Vulcan sided with them, especially after he became convinced Sol had his mortal lover killed."

Without thinking, Nya said, "She died of illness."

"Ah," Imeria said with a nod. "I forgot. Your father's mother, right?"

Nya blinked away the burning in her eyes. She would not think of her parents right now. It would destroy her to think of what they must be feeling.

"Yes," she forced out.

"I'd venture to guess Sol orchestrated something there,"

Imeria said. "I'd also bet if Sol knew about your father at the time, he would have been killed too."

"But…why?"

"Who knows for sure. Juno, Janis, Bella, and Sol himself all have had plenty of mortal lovers, and hundreds, if not thousands, of demi-god bastards to account for the affairs. But I do know Vulcan never took on another lover after her, and he never had any other children. Perhaps Sol did not like that a god as powerful as Vulcan had that kind of devotion to a mortal."

"But Sol never went after my parents after they destroyed Kronos," Nya said quietly, glancing at Imeria. "Why?"

Imeria sighed heavily. "I think…I *know* Kronos was becoming harder for Sol to control. Sora and Vane did him a favor, though I'm sure he would never admit it. The principals love letting others clean up their messes for them."

Nya let the words sink in for a long moment, thinking of Juno's cryptic words and the way Nyx and Thanatos practically waited for her parents to come up with a solution to the mess they were in. The principals were the most powerful beings in this world, and yet…yet Kronos, who was now thought of by most as a tyrant, had not been defeated until Nya's parents stepped in. And that was *after* they had already suffered greatly at the hands of the god-king.

"Perhaps you're right," Nya murmured, eyes on the horizon.

Imeria lifted a shoulder. "I am. The more you keep your eyes open here, the more you'll realize the truth is not simple, nor does it paint a very pretty picture of the council."

Nya swallowed against the tightness in her throat, though the feeling of panic returned almost immediately as she saw a flicker of movement cresting over one of the faraway peaks. Then, there came another, just before the horizon shimmered, thickened, and turned the same opaque shade of silver as Morgen's portal had yesterday.

"Imeria?" Nya whispered, eyes wide.

The demi-god was already to her feet, grabbing her wrist and dragging her back in through the tunnel as she bellowed, "Storm approaching!"

Nya's breath was uneven, but she forced herself to say, "I don't think it's a—"

"Get her below."

Nya whirled, finding Morgen a few paces away, calmly strapping on dark armor. The material of the metal almost looked burned; forged by dragon fire, she realized.

"What's happening?" Nya asked, her heart pounding as the hallway suddenly flooded with soldiers. It had taken all of a minute for them to mobilize, half of them already in armor and carrying heavy spears and swords, as well as huge crossbows.

Carus appeared behind Morgen, flashing her a grim smirk. "They rejected our terms, apparently, and now, they're here for you."

Her stomach dipped, and she shook her head. "No… You can't—my parents will be with them."

"I'm sure," Morgen said, flexing his left hand.

"Morgen. *Please*, don't—"

But he swept past her, ignoring her plea and ordering in a short voice, "Do *not* let her leave, Imeria."

He didn't wait to see what Imeria said. Nya set her jaw,

gaze flicking back to the demi-god, who was still trying to pull her away from the tunnel entrance.

"Nya, you need to come with me," she urged.

Nya swept her gaze around the tunnel, which was growing emptier by the second. A feeling was rising in the back of her throat, a fire so cold, it burned as it fought its way to the surface.

He thought he could tell her what to do? That *any* of them could?

A low laugh escaped her, her own voice nearly unrecognizable to her own ears as the sound slipped past her tingling, numb lips. They should *all* be afraid, even him. She had a raging inferno in the empty space inside her, where her heart supposedly lay—perhaps it was time to stop smothering it.

"Nya?" Imeria's voice was smaller now. Perhaps she was scared. Perhaps she should be.

Slowly, Nya tilted her head to the side. "If I were you, I wouldn't try to stop me."

Imeria's brow creased, and she reached out a hand, though her fingers trembled. "It's alright. We just need to—"

"*No.*"

The word exploded through the hallway with physical force, a blast of ichor-stained fire flaring in its wake. Imeria flew back, her body smacking against the stone wall and landing in a limp heap on the floor.

Nya cocked her head, staring at her for a moment. Once she sensed a heartbeat, she turned and followed the sound of the battle already underway outside.

CHAPTER

TWELVE

The Sisters requested a meeting. Many years ago, there was a disturbance amongst the dragons, some disagreement within their ranks leading to the disappearance of a young Vemon dragon. They tell me she was related to Thessilnn and Heles, though not directly, just shared blood a few generations back. When I asked why she left the keep, no one would give me a clear answer. It unsettles me. Why invite me here, only to withhold the truth?
—*Lady Anabeth, Consort to Her Majesty Cion Livii, Queen of Aren, D'anna*

NYA STEPPED out onto the same jagged cliff where she had been sitting with Imeria just a few minutes ago. She realized what she had done at the same moment her mind made sense of the scene unfolding in front of her.

Because of her, Imeria was hurt, maybe even badly. What unsettled her the most was that she hardly remembered doing it. It was as if a thick veil had settled over those moments, twisting and distorting the memory until it didn't even feel like her own. She didn't have time to examine the fear that made her feel, though, because her attention quickly turned to the battle beyond.

On the ground, Morgen's foot soldiers held the line easily. They were no match for whatever small forces the principals and her parents had managed to gather. But in the sky…

Four Vemon dragons circled Varax, three with riders and one without. Lightning cut across the sky, and she saw Heles swerve to avoid it, a trail of fire flaring in her wake. It took Nya a moment to realize there was no thunderstorm at all this time, but that the lightning was Morgen's.

It made sense, she supposed, with the amount of energy she felt every time he walked into a room. As he wielded bursts of it, exploding violently from his hands in shades of crimson and blinding-white, he looked every bit the avenging god.

From behind her, another dragon emerged from the side of the mountain: Carus' Fesper, Nya realized. Her mother and Thessilnn were further down the barren valley, followed by who must be Vulcan atop a deep-blue dragon. The rider-less dragon coasted directly above Nya, leaving Heles and her father open, too focused on avoiding Morgen and Varax to notice Carus' dragon was diving right towards them.

VANE.

Her mother screamed, both down the pathway and aloud, the sound cutting through the raging battle in the mountains and echoing shrilly in Nya's thoughts.

Nya's eyes widened, a scream tearing from her throat, because her father had noticed the approaching dragon's wide-open mouth a second too late——

The air shimmered, and before her mind could fully comprehend what had happened, Heles and Varax collided, their screeches ear splitting. Carus' dragon swerved and barely avoided the full brunt of the blow. All three dragons landed in a heap, the sound of the hard landing resounding. She was fairly sure both Morgen and her father were unconscious, but she couldn't tell, and she couldn't get down off this damn cliff. Her mother was frantically calling her father's name as she and Thessilnn raced down the valley, but there was no response, not even from Heles.

Nya's chest constricted to the point of pain as panic overwhelmed her, and she shut her eyes, willing her body to somehow just *move*.

When she opened her eyes again, she was a few feet away from Morgen and Carus, who was at his side. For a few seconds, the shock of what she had just done rooted her to the ground, before she decided that right now, she didn't care how she had portaled. Her feet were moving before she even knew where she was going, her vision flashing red with rage as she approached Morgen, Varax curled protectively behind him.

When she got close enough to understand what was happening, she froze.

There was a deep wound in Morgen's chest in the small gap between plates of armor, and he was coughing up blood, each breath causing his entire body to spasm. Carus knelt next to him, a firm hand on his shoulder.

"You idiot," he was saying, but he didn't sound angry, merely worried. "Just hang on a second. It'll be over soon."

Morgen tried to respond, but instead, he coughed up more blood, his hand shaking as he brought it to his lips.

When he saw Nya, his brow creased, confusion clouding his eyes. Carus noticed her a second later, and his nostrils flared.

"Figure out your way down, did you?" His voice was so cold. Gone was any semblance of teasing or kindness.

She set her jaw, ignoring him. Her mother was still speaking down the pathway, but the sound was muffled to Nya. She would face that reality in a moment.

"You—" Her breath caught, eyes on Morgen. "You are dead to me if my father doesn't live."

Morgen tried to speak again but only coughed up more blood. Carus shook his head and snapped, "Relax, sweetheart, and direct your death threats my way. *I* went for Heles, and I would've had a straight shot, but Morgen stopped me. Demi-god or not, your father would have been dead on impact if Morgen hadn't interrupted."

Nya blinked a few times, shaking her head. "I don't... I—"

"Go," Morgen choked out, a trembling hand pointing behind her.

She glanced back to where her mother knelt next to her father, who was still unconscious. The battle had halted too, she realized, half of Morgen's army nowhere to be seen and the other half holding a line of defense around them.

She didn't move right away, torn. Morgen was still bleeding and drawing in those horrible, rattling breaths. If what Carus said was true, Morgen had just saved her father's life. But...*why?* Why, when, mere moments earlier, the battle had been raging, and Morgen had been aiming for Heles too?

"N-Nya, g—" Morgen tried, his expression twisting with

pain as his lungs rattled and the wound on his chest bled freely.

Go. You don't need to pretend you care.

That was the problem, though, wasn't it? She did care, more than she wanted to. She wished she could tell herself it was just the blood bond, but she couldn't deny this was more than that. Still, in a last-ditch effort to prove herself wrong, she turned and hurried over to where her mother had both hands pressed to her father's chest, her eyes shut and her entire body trembling.

When Nya stopped short just behind them, her mother said in a strained voice, "Nya, love, come here."

Nya took a shallow breath, kneeling with her. There was a large gash across her father's torso, and his eyes were still closed. Something else was lingering with him too, some *feeling…* A shadow reaching for him, one she sensed her mother was trying to keep at bay.

"You feel it, yes?" her mother whispered in a hoarse voice, looking at Nya with silver-bright eyes.

Nya bit her lip. "What is it?"

A dark shadow passed over her mother's face. "Death." She took Nya's hand, a silent tear slipping down her cheek. "Fate is unhappy with me. I've tricked it too many times on your father's behalf."

Nya glanced at him, unmoving, and with that cloud of darkness looming closer, she suddenly understood what her mother was asking of her.

"There is a place somewhere inside you, Nya," her mother whispered. "A dark place, where the very essence of Death lives. Perhaps, like I did once, you have hidden it, locked it away. I need you to reach for that place—welcome it. And then, I want you to take that shadow lingering over your father and shove it as far into that place as you can, drown it in darkness as you lock it away."

Nya nodded, not wasting time to argue or ask further questions. The shadow was close.

She shut her eyes, hovering a hand over her father's chest as she looked inside herself. She was no stranger to the place her mother described. It had always beckoned to her with cold seduction, biding its time and waiting for the moment she finally gave in. Now, she reached freely for those dark stars, guttering with lifeless, midnight fire. For a moment, she lingered, breathing in the void, ignoring the call to exhale, because if she did—

It didn't matter. That wasn't what she was here for.

She snatched Death's shadow before he even realized she was there, and instead of hiding him as her mother had, she let the frigid fire within her chest rise to the surface, engulfing the cloak of darkness until it crumbled to ash, the echo of a far-off scream lost to the swirling wind of the void as it was swept away forever.

Just before she left that place, ignoring the aching need to follow into that chasm of nothingness, she sensed Death —not his cloak nor his hands, but the full force of his presence, and when she turned, she saw his true form before her. The small drop of her blood that was mortal shied away at the sight of the utter nothingness taken form, only broken by the blinking of two, silver-laced eyes.

Be careful, he whispered, his voice hardly more than an echo. *This is a place few have been. It holds great temptation and danger.*

She smiled. The stars flickered with a single thought

from her, the void roaring in her ears as she held one in her hand. *Do not worry. I have been here many times before.*

For a brief flash, fear crossed Death's faint features. It was the last thing she saw before he reached for her, and she was pulled away from the void, the stars and the fire in her hands.

CHAPTER 13

ONE YEAR AND ONE WEEK PRIOR

There are 'new' gods born often. Even I am considered one of them. But few of us are whispered about with such feared reverence as this usurper who is stirring trouble across the border. They even say he is responsible for the storms. Cion has urged me to travel to Arcadia and investigate. While the stories are troublesome, I do not think the storms are a result of a god. Even Kronos could not send such destruction across the border.

—Lady Anabeth, Consort to Her Majesty Cion Livii, Queen of Aren, D'anna

IT WAS RAINING, the downpour torrential thundering against the stone alcove behind the waterfall they were huddled in. Four years ago, she had stupidly jumped off the rock outcropping just above them, and Morgen had pulled her out of the water. She was older now, much less naive about many things.

Things that included him.

The more he had told her over the years about his childhood, the more her rage had grown, and along with it, fear.

122

His father was a powerful god, one no one was willing to resist or rebel against. Morgen had grown up hidden and shamed. Few had known of his existence until the day he fled. But he had never told her what had become of his abusive father, the one whose rage was endless, who was heartless enough to bring his own son to the brink of death again and again, just to see if he would survive. Even as a child, Morgen had never succumbed, and he'd never told Nya the reason for that either.

But she was not stupid, and they both knew it. Sitting a few paces away, she thought he might be taunting her with the silence. He did not speak aloud nor down the pathway, but she could hear the word pulsing between them, nevertheless.

Ask.

Except, she did not want to know the truth about who he truly was, the one she had suspected for a long while now. She always refuted it because it *couldn't* be.

According to the short passage in a history book at home, Kronos had no children, or, at least, none who lived long enough to be born. Their mortal mothers always died before they could carry to term, their bodies succumbing to the power of the embers their child carried. And though the god-king had tried, none of the principals or their godling children had been willing to give him an heir. Nya's own mother had died and been reborn twice over rather than face that fate.

Morgen had told her once, in the hazy quiet of a very early morning, that his mother had died mere seconds after he was born, begging for her own death. His father had loved to remind him how she hadn't wanted Morgen, how every day she carried him in her womb, she wished to die 'like all the others'. His father had kept her locked up but tended to by midwives like some sick experiment to see how long she would last. Morgen had never specified who the others he spoke of were.

"I should head back soon," she said, unable to stand the silence anymore.

"It's still raining. You should at least wait out the storm."

She shrugged, biting her lip. "You know how it rains here this time of year. It could be a while."

Before she could stop herself, she stood and snatched her small, woven satchel off the stone floor. As she faced the entrance, readying to duck around the water, Morgen asked, "Will you be coming back?"

She halted but did not face him. "Why wouldn't I?"

She heard him stand, and her pulse quickened as he closed the space between them. When he spoke, his breath caressed the loos hair at her temple, and her back arched on instinct when he murmured, "You tell me, Nya."

She swallowed, giving a tiny shake of her head. "I don't know what you mean."

He laughed, the sound low and rough, vibrating across vocal chords that had never quite healed right after his father had slit his throat. His father who was—

No. It couldn't be. *He* couldn't be.

But then, Morgen turned her around, snatching her chin in his fingers and tilting her head back so she was forced to look at his eyes, glowing with silver ether and sparkling with embers of deep amber-gold.

"And now?" he challenged. "Now, will you finally admit to yourself what you've known for a while?"

Her jaw trembled. "I didn't—"

He brushed the pad of his thumb over her lips, shushing her. "Nya," he said, shaking his head. "You're not particularly good at concealing your emotions. Do you think I didn't see it, the second you started to suspect who my father really was? It's not as if I was doing much to hide it. I knew you would figure it out soon enough, given who your parents are."

"I never told you who they are," she whispered.

He looked away. "I always suspected. Like you, I ignored my suspicions, because I thought…" He exhaled an empty-sounding laugh. "I thought that Fate couldn't possibly be so cruel. To me, yes, but to you…" He trailed off again, meeting her eyes.

Her brow creased. "What do you mean by that?"

"You're right." He lowered his hand and stepped back. "You should probably go."

His eyes were still sparking with gold embers, a stark reminder of the truth of just which god's blood ran through his veins. Surely, cruelty as potent Kronos' would pass on through a bloodline, except…

Morgen was nothing like that.

He had more a right than Kronos ever had to be heartless, but even with his terror-filled, loveless childhood, he had never been anything but kind to Nya. A little broody sometimes, and hard to crack, but he never took advantage of her or hurt her on purpose. In fact, more than once, she suspected he had healed her. Bruises from clumsily tripping over a fallen branch or scrapes from the stones at the bottom of the creek sometimes mysteriously disappeared after he brushed his hand against hers.

If she left now, she was afraid she would never come back. Perhaps it was that very desperation that drove her next actions, or perhaps it was the simmering ache she had been dutifully ignoring for years, finally coming to a point she could no longer disregard.

She supposed it didn't matter. By the time she was kissing him, nothing else felt like it mattered more.

He didn't push her away or even freeze, instead meeting her with the same fervent force. His hand slid up her back, supporting her as she stood on tiptoes, her fingers fisting the rough material of his shirt. When she lowered her hands and slid them beneath the hem, feeling the hard muscles of his torso flexing beneath her fingers, he groaned against her mouth, parting her lips with his tongue. She gasped, liquid fire pooling low in her belly at the taste of him.

She nipped at his bottom lip, and he muttered, "*Fuck*," before hooking his hands beneath her thighs, lifting her to a natural ledge in the stone.

He paused, standing between her parted legs, his fingertips brushing bare skin where the material of her dress had ridden up. Their shared breaths were heavy, the roar of the waterfall fading to the background. The air was buzzing, and so was her blood, crackling with tangible energy.

"Do you want me to stop?" His voice was just loud enough for her to hear, and he looked her directly in the eye.

Her lips parted, and she forced herself to look away. She should say yes. Run. Scream in terror and tell the world what he was, because she couldn't deny the presence of Kronos' embers in his eyes any longer.

"Nya," he pushed, fingers tightening against the soft

flesh of her inner thigh. "Look me in the eye and tell me you want *me* to touch you."

He thought she was going to say no. She was sure of it. The words were supposed to be a warning, and they should have listened. Instead, she shook her head. "Don't stop."

His pupils flared, dark desire drowning out the gold of the embers. *You're not thinking straight.*

I don't care—

You're going to regret this.

She was. Of course, she was. But she didn't say that. Instead, she reached for him, threading her hand in his hair and pressing her brow to his. This way, she didn't have to see his eyes. She could pretend being with him wasn't a betrayal and ask for the one thing she wanted.

I want you. Please.

His breath caught, and he shuddered against her. "Nya—"

"Please."

She didn't want to say the word aloud, but some part of her knew it was important to him that she did. He had grown up where consent didn't matter, where women had been dragged past his door screaming and had never come back, so she understood why he needed to hear her ask clearly and without coercion.

He was nothing like that, but still, she hated herself more than she ever had for wanting him in the first place. There were too many red flags, too many people she was betraying by doing this.

She shoved the shame away to deal with later.

Slowly, he slid his fingers higher, the touch featherlight, making her shiver with every drag of his callouses against her skin. When he brushed against her undergarments, they both inhaled sharply. He paused for a second, giving her one more chance to reconsider. She only tugged him closer, kissing him hard, relishing the low sound that rumbled from his chest. He shoved aside the undergarment, swearing low and then biting her lip when he dragged his fingers through the mess already there.

He figured out quickly where exactly to touch her, paying attention to every time her breath hitched or her back arched against the stone behind her. Too soon, she felt the pleasure and ache grow to a near-blinding point, pushing her close to an edge she knew she would never recover from. This couldn't mean nothing, not with him, even if she wanted it to.

Slowly, almost carefully, he slid one finger inside her, and all the breath emptied from her lungs, her eyes widening.

"Nya," he breathed, pupils spread wide and cheeks flushed.

Then, he curled his finger, and it was over for her. Light flashed in her vision, and she saw colors she hadn't known existed as pleasure raced up her spine, so potent, she wasn't sure her body could take it. Her hands clawed blindly at Morgen's skin, seeking some semblance of an anchor as she lost all sense of what it meant to have two feet on the ground.

When she finally began to float back to reality, he was panting against her shoulder, one hand pressed to the wall next to her, the other gripping her thigh. She felt hazy, still shuddering with tiny aftershocks, but what scared her the most was that she still wanted more. She wanted *all* of him, and she knew if they did that, there would truly be no going back.

He lifted his head, something dulled now in his expression as he said, without question, "You want to leave."

She didn't say anything, wanting to agree but unable to make herself believe it enough to say it aloud. But he must have misread her expression, because he nodded and gently lifted her off the ledge before stepping back.

Her breath shook, and before she could stop herself, she asked, "Was that... Did you do that because you really wanted to, or because you thought it would scare me enough to leave?"

His brows lifted. "Are you serious?"

"It's just... Every time before, you never let things between us—"

"Yeah." He laughed hollowly, shaking his head. "I never *let* myself go there with you, Nya. That doesn't mean I didn't want to. I thought that much was made clear today."

"Why?"

"Why what?"

She bit her cheek. He was still flushed, his pupils dark as they stared at each other, as if he felt the all-consuming need for more too.

"Why did you stop yourself before?" she forced herself to ask.

He paused, his eyes fluttering shut, and when he replied, it was not aloud. *Lots of reasons, the most selfish being I knew there would be no hiding the truth once I opened myself up to you, and as soon as you finally had to accept what you've been denying, you would never come back.*

The warmth of silent tears tracked down her face, but she ignored them.

"Am I wrong?" he asked.

She took a shuddering breath, whispered, "No," and reached for him one last time.

She poured everything into the kiss, not hiding the equal amounts of shame, desire, and love. She just hoped that, even as he held her as close as possible, he couldn't read her so well that he could catch each tangled emotion.

When she pulled away, she only gave herself a few short seconds to whisper, "Goodbye, Morgen," before forcing herself to flee.

She didn't return, and two weeks later, she left for D'anna to apprentice with the Holy Sisters of the Arcane.

Life felt cold again. She hadn't even realized the warmth of the last four years until he was gone.

CHAPTER

FOURTEEN

The priestesses here suspect me. I have grown rather close to Kronos' son quickly in order to observe him and try to decipher his motives. Part of me wishes he was evil, though he does hide something I am sure is important. He often disappears for long stretches of time during the day with the dragon. Something about this feels familiar.
—Ana, Priestess to the Usurper King, Arcadia

NYA AWOKE to the familiar feeling of her mother brushing hair back from her forehead. She groaned softly, forcing herself to open her eyes, blinking rapidly to adjust to the light of the flickering torches around them.

"What—where are we?"

Her mother's ice-blue eyes were red-rimmed, but her expression was calm. "We're still in the Gods' Aisle, in a cave system within one of the mountains. The general with the blond hair and the attitude claims we are prisoners who will be kept comfortable." She snorted, shaking her head. "As if I believed him for even a moment."

Nya's brow creased, realizing she was talking about

Carus. She didn't inquire about him further, though, instead asking, "Why didn't you and the dragons try to fight them off and escape?"

Her mother's throat bobbed and her jaw tensed, telltale signs she was trying to collect herself. "I couldn't leave you or your father, Nya, love. I don't… You are my only reasons to keep any remaining faith in this world."

"Is Papa alright?" Nya asked, sitting up abruptly enough that her head spun, sweeping her gaze over the dim room. Her pulse quickened when she saw him, still unconscious on a cot a few feet away.

Her mother touched her cheek. "He's alright, Nya. It'll be a bit before he wakes up again." A small smile tugged at her mouth. "And gods save everyone here when that happens."

Nya took a slow breath. "It worked, what I did."

"Yes." Her mother's voice was very quiet as she added, "I didn't ever want you to have to feel the cold of that place. But perhaps keeping you from it was a mistake on my part."

Nya met her eyes. "I know you and Papa wanted to protect me, but I'm as much a part of this world as you are." She shrugged, adding, "All my life, you kept me away from Arcadia, but it found me anyways."

Her mother's expression clouded, and Nya knew she was about to ask about Morgen, but they both froze as her father muttered, "Where the fuck are we?"

Nya suppressed a small smile despite the circumstances, and her mother sighed and said under her breath, "Here we go."

The cot creaked as he sat up, and though he winced at

the pain, he still tried to stand, demanding, "Sora, Nya? Are you alright?"

Her mother stood, kneeling next to him and pressing a hand to his shoulder. "We're fine. Lay back down before you ruin all the work our daughter did bringing you back from the brink of death."

He blinked a few times, his eyes landing on Nya, then flicking back to her mother. His voice was steadier, more lucid as he asked, "What happened?" and Nya didn't miss the undertone of cold rage simmering beneath his mask of calm.

Her mother pressed her lips together, but before she could reply, her father's gaze shifted, and he spat, *"You."*

Nya whirled, finding Morgen leaning in the doorway, his hands in the pockets of his pants. His hair was pulled back from his face, accentuating the sharp angles of his cheeks and the shadows beneath his eyes.

"A 'you're welcome,' would be appreciated, but I'll take not getting skewered immediately by you for now," Morgen said, a single brow raised. He was breathing normally and had changed out of the bloody armor, but Nya couldn't tell if the wound had healed fully.

"You little fuck," her father seethed, trying to stand before her mother hissed something in his ear, and he settled for sitting on the edge of the cot with a glare.

"You should probably listen to your wife, given you lack the range of healing abilities I have," Morgen said. "I've no intention of inadvertently killing anyone at the moment."

"You…" Her mother trailed off, eyes narrowed. "You are Kronos' son?"

Nya looked between them, entirely unsure of what was

happening, especially as Morgen dipped his chin and said, "I'd say it's nice to see you again, Sora, but it seems, once again, we are not meeting under very pleasant circumstances."

"Sora?" Nya's father said. *What's going on?*

I had no idea he was Kronos' son, her mother said down the pathway.

Morgen cleared his throat. "Look, I know we all have the ability to speak silently to each other through various channels, but I think it might be less confusing if we clarify all of this aloud."

"Fine," her mother said shortly, her eyes still on Morgen.

He nodded once, pushing off the wall and sitting on a small woven chair closest to Nya. Their eyes met briefly, but she couldn't quite read his closed-off expression.

"Would you care to explain, or should I?" he said, glancing at her mother.

Sora cleared her throat. "What I saw, it was barely for a second, and..." She shook her head. "After I was reborn, I always thought it might have been an odd trick of my brain in those last moments, some strange image my mind tried to conjure as a distraction from the pain."

Nya did not miss the way the torches flared slightly, or that her mother casually slipped a hand into her father's.

"I saw a child," her mother explained. "Just for a flash before I was gone, near one of the pillars off the side of the throne room. A young boy with eyes..." She trailed off, looking at Morgen. "A boy with eyes both silver and gold. It was you, wasn't it?"

Morgen's jaw tensed, and Nya felt sick at the realization of her mother's words.

He dipped his head in a shallow nod, a dry, humorless laugh slipping past his lips. "I wasn't supposed to be out of my room. But, for once, my disobedience actually worked in my favor."

"They would have destroyed you if they found you," Nya's father said flatly. "So, I presume you escaped the palace before they arrived."

"Who would have?" Nya asked before she could stop herself.

Morgen lifted a brow. "The other half of the council. Your parents had just taken care of their problem. Do you think they would have let the potential of another one live?"

"How old were you?" Nya's mother asked quietly.

"Almost thirteen," Morgen replied, the ghost of a smile on his face as he added, "My birthday was the next day. Truthfully, the best present I'd ever gotten, waking up knowing he was dead and would never be coming back."

Nya couldn't help glancing at the scar on his throat. She knew Morgen noticed, but he didn't acknowledge her for more than a moment.

"Why then?" her mother asked. "Why try to take the throne if you knew what Kronos was like once the power went to his head?"

Nya resisted the urge to sit up straighter when Morgen sighed and muttered, "Right. Of course. They never told you."

Ever since she'd been brought here, Imeria, Carus, and even Morgen himself had been referencing some important factor that explained why he needed to take the throne, but no one had bothered to explain it. To her relief, Morgen didn't try to skirt around it this time, instead leaning forward on his elbows as he said, "There is a reason Sol gave the embers to Kronos in the first place."

When no one stopped him, he continued, "The embers are not only the source of Life, but the basis to this world. All the principal gods were born with a piece of them, but Sol eventually made the decision that, spread thin amongst them, the embers were not strong enough to hold the realms together. The council came to an agreement: one of them would hold the embers alone in a concentrated form and in a specific place, though Sol didn't make clear who. They all assumed it would be him, but then he gave them to Kronos, by whom they were held until he was destroyed."

Morgen paused, the gold flaring in his eyes as he glanced at her parents. "I presume you know the reason heirs exist, given you are both named as such."

"The realm would become unstable if one of the principals was permanently destroyed," her mother said hoarsely, her voice almost shocked, as if she was realizing something she hadn't before. "They aren't just gods, but manifestations of elements central to the world itself."

"Yes." Morgen sat back, stretching his legs out in front of him. "Kronos often referred to me as his 'spare.' I was always assured that once he had a true, pure-blooded godling heir, he would get rid of me so there wasn't a question as to who the title passed to." He laughed, the sound hollow. "The principals would have killed me as soon as they figured out how to take the embers, I'm sure. And then, they would have quickly realized their entire world was doomed to slowly die. Kronos was a shit king, but he was necessary, as was his place in that godsforsaken palace."

Nya's father cleared his throat. "Are you saying the palace's placement was intentional?"

Slowly, Morgen nodded. "Believe me, I'd prefer not to return there ever again. But if someone who holds the embers does not rule where the council transferred them to Kronos in the first place, Arcadia will soon suffer for it, as will the mortal realm."

"The storms we've heard about in Aren?" her mother said. "Are those a result of what you're claiming?"

Morgen's eyes flashed to Nya. "They're related, yes."

The room fell silent, and Nya bit her cheek hard enough to flood her mouth with the taste of crimson, hating how small her voice sounded when she forced herself to ask Morgen, "But why take me? Why…why marry me?"

She didn't need to look back to know her parents were probably waiting for the answer too. Morgen didn't look at them, though, his cold gaze held on her. "I meant what I said. I'm not looking for war with the council, though I will go there if necessary. Marrying you was a way to get them to listen for at least a second before they tried to murder me —and it worked."

A cold stone dropped in her belly, and she cursed the foolish, childish disappointment and the burning in her eyes. "And the blood binding?"

Now, there was a tiny crack in his indifferent, cold façade, a muscle in his jaw flickering. "A way to ensure you remained close until the negotiation was achieved and provide insurance should their cooperation ever lapse. The marriage alone wouldn't have done much if they snatched you away before proper conversations could occur. This way, you can never go far."

She lowered her chin, narrowing her eyes. "Well, this is really all so convenient for you—using me as some kind of emotional crutch until your armies were properly assembled and tossing me aside once you were done. I'm sure it was nice, though, thinking someone actually liked you for a few years there, beyond your uses with the embers. It's a shame that won't continue, especially given we're bound for life now."

His eyes dulled, almost to the point of looking human, but all he did was straighten and stand. "If that's all, I've things to attend to, but Carus will be outside if either of you would like to lose your prisoner status."

Nya's father snorted harshly, and when she glanced at him, he was glaring stonily at Morgen. "I think Nya insulted you better than I could have. We'll consider what you've told us regarding the embers."

Morgen gave a short nod and, before leaving, he said to her, "Carus won't stop you if you wish to leave this room."

"Oh, lucky me," she sneered. "I'm so glad our marriage grants me a bigger cage, at the least."

You're not a prisoner.

She set her jaw. *Keep telling yourself that.*

He inhaled sharply then turned and strode into the passageway beyond without another word, leaving her alone with her parents.

"You're not actually considering supporting his claim, are you?" she asked as soon as his footsteps faded.

Her father rubbed his temple, grimacing. "Nya, love, if he's right, it doesn't matter how much I'd like to rip his head off for what he did to you."

"Are you serious?"

He let out a slow breath, wincing. "Part of me would love to say damn the world and everyone in it, and perhaps, once, I would have actually believed that. But if what he says is true, and he does not take the throne, I'm guessing the realm doesn't have much time left for peace." His dark eyes flicked to Nya's mother, unspoken words passing between them before he added, "You've had so little time to live. If we don't side with Morgen on this, you won't have much time left at all. None of us will."

Nya stood abruptly, ignoring the lightness in her head. "I heard what Thanatos said about the blood binding. My life is over no matter what, or, at the very least, it is no longer my own."

Pain flashed across her mother's face. "Nya, we don't want this for you, but we also don't have much of a choice."

Nya let out a cold laugh. "I wonder if that's what Nyx and Thanatos told themselves when they sold you to Kronos."

It was like she had slapped them. Her mother flinched visibly, and her father paled as soon as the words left her mouth. Maybe she didn't truly mean them, but she was *so* angry. Her mind didn't feel like her own anymore, whirling emotions clouding reason and sense until nothing remained but one need: escape.

Her life.

Her body.

The *world.*

Perhaps her parents were right. Or perhaps, this world did not deserve to survive anymore.

She was out of the room and running before more angry words escaped her. Carus didn't stop her as she fled, entirely unsure of where she was going but needing to move before she brought the mountain down on them all.

CHAPTER
FIFTEEN

In his chambers within the mountain, he keeps a small satchel of river stones. When I touched one, I saw her as if through his eyes: laughing, her hair dripping water as she pulled herself onto a rocky shore. Her face, I have seen for centuries, both in my dreams and on my lost friends. It is a mockery that Fate should draw these two together. Something must be done.
—*Ana, Priestess to the Usurper King, Arcadia*

A FEW HOURS LATER, Nya retreated into the caves from the open cliffside she'd been curled on. Her entire body was shivering from the cold winds outside, her eyes dry from the tears she hadn't been able to stop, from watching the bright plumes of lava beneath her. She desperately needed a bath —preferably a warm one—and when she found herself in the same cavern where she had gotten ready with Imeria before the marriage ceremony, she thought she'd finally had some luck. At least, until she saw the figure half-submerged in the water and realized she was not alone.

"I need to bathe."

Morgen snorted softly, the water splashing as he shifted in his spot near the edge of the pool. "No one is stopping you."

She tried to keep her voice firm as she said, "You should leave," but it wobbled pathetically as she shivered.

"Believe it or not, this is *my* bathing room, and you are the one who is trespassing."

She squared her jaw. "F-f-fine, then. I'll go."

In the dim light, she saw him tilt his head. "You're trembling. Did you go outside?"

"It's n-not like anyone s-s-topped me."

He sighed, shaking his head. "It's freezing this time of the day. You need to warm up."

"Not with y-you here—"

"*Nya.*" He started to stand, and she was not sure if he was wearing even a stitch of clothing. "You're being unnecessary stubborn—"

"Fine, *f-f-fine,*" she snapped, turning away. "Jus-t-t sit down. And look a-away."

The splashing settled, and she glanced over her shoulder to see he had listened to her and was facing the wall. Quickly, she stripped down to the flimsy shift she wore under her dress and then slipped into the water on the opposite side of the pool from where Morgen sat.

"Am I allowed to look now?" he asked, a hint of amusement in his tone.

She didn't understand. How could he tease her now? Wasn't he angry? She had said awful things to him today, and she had *meant* them. Yet, he wasn't being cold with her.

In fact, he was acting almost like he had during all their meetings in the forest in Mise.

"Fine," she bit out, settling against a stone ledge as the warmth seeped back into her muscles.

He turned his head, his expression shifting into something almost soft as he looked at her. Perhaps this brought him back to swimming in the creek. She was certainly remembering those times, when Varax had splashed like a child downstream and Nya dipped underwater for river stones before handing the 'pretty ones' to him.

But she couldn't get lost in the bittersweet nostalgia of the past. She had questions.

"If you knew what my mother looked like after seeing her in Kronos' throne room, how could you claim not to know who I was the day we met? Everyone says I look just like her."

Morgen cleared his throat. "You do—except for your eyes."

"Yeah, they're my father's," she muttered, guilt eating at her as she recalled the horrified expressions on her parents' faces when she had left them in that room. She hadn't even stayed to make sure her father was alright or make sure Carus truly wasn't going to try and hurt them.

"I imagine," Morgen began, "that I ignored my immediate suspicions in the same way you ignored yours."

She said nothing, and he added, "I know you saw the embers in my eyes that first day. I can usually feel it when they're visible, and, most of the time, I'm able to keep them under control if I want. When I couldn't—"

"You'd turn away," she finished for him. He nodded, and she forced herself to look at him. "Everything you just told my parents about the embers and the palace... Were you lying?"

She wasn't sure why she was even bothering to ask. If he *was* lying or trying to trick them, it wasn't like he would reveal the truth to her now. Perhaps it was because here, this felt so similar to all those times she'd thought he was always honest with her.

"Most of what I said in that room was the truth, yes."

She flared her nostrils. "Care to share what you lied about this time, or will I have to settle for some cryptic answer now and find out later?"

"What do you think, Nya?"

He was moving closer to her, cutting across the deeper middle portion of the pool. She ignored the flutter of heat in her belly at the sight of his bare torso and kept her eyes from wandering any lower below the water.

"I don't know," she whispered as he stopped directly in front of her. "I don't know what to believe anymore."

He lifted his hand slowly, and her breath hitched loudly as he traced his fingertips lightly over the spot just above her collarbone where he'd bit her. The sensation was jarring; the spot was much more sensitive than it should have been.

"I lied about intending to do this, for one," he murmured. "That damned demi-god daughter of Juno brought it up to me in the first place before she performed the marriage ceremony."

"Ana?"

He dipped his chin, eyes fluttering shut. "I told her I wouldn't do it, even if it made some sense strategically. I doubt her reasons had anything to do with politics, though.

Children of Juno are always annoyingly cryptic and meddlesome."

"So why *did* you do it?" Nya whispered.

The scarred column of his throat worked. "I couldn't get the idea out of my head once she put it there. You hate me and have every right to. I knew it then and I know it now." He rested his hand over her neck, not tightening his grip, just feeling her rapid pulse beneath his palm. "You'll probably always hate me, and, selfishly, for just a second, I wanted to make sure you wouldn't leave me regardless. I… I'm sorry, Nya. It can't be undone, and you're the one paying the price for my moment of weakness."

Her lips parted, and his gaze dipped to her mouth. He looked away quickly, but still, she caught it, just like she caught the way his eyes darkened as his pupils spread. With a sharp inhale, he moved away, settling a few paces away against the ledge to her right. Before she could stop herself or think too much about just what she was doing, she stood, the soaked white material of her shift clinging to her skin as she approached him, heart in her throat. He went completely still as she lifted a hand to his jaw, tracing the hard edge of it and then ghosting her fingers over the curve of his neck.

"Are you alright?" she whispered.

He didn't reply right away, his eyes dipping and then bouncing back to her face, as if he was trying not to look at the places entirely visible through the water-sheer fabric but couldn't quite stop himself.

His voice was gruff when he said, "What?"

She slid her hand down, brushing her fingers over the angry-red mark on his chest. "From earlier? You were hurt."

"It healed fine."

She nodded, biting her lip. "You couldn't breathe."

He gently tugged her lip from her teeth, *tsking*. "And you're going to hurt yourself constantly doing that."

"Morgen. You were coughing up blood."

He shrugged. "My lung got punctured somehow, I think. There were lots of sharp things around, and Varax hit Heles pretty hard when we portaled. I tried not to, but it's hard to be precise when I'm distracted like that."

Her eyes widened. "You punctured your lung?"

"I presume, yes. One of the more unpleasant injuries to heal, for sure."

"Did you at least pass out while it was healing?"

He brushed a tangled strand of her hair back. "I never do. The embers always keep me conscious when my body's healing, though I'm not entirely sure why."

"So you still felt all the pain? Just without the dying part?"

His brow creased. "You don't have to pretend to be worried."

A small, disbelieving laugh escaped her. "Do you think me heartless?"

"I think you are angry with me."

Her hand was still pressed against his chest, and she pushed hard against his skin, shaking her head. "My anger doesn't cancel out everything else. I *wish* it did. It would make convincing myself to hate you so much easier."

"Do you hate me?"

She curled her hand into a fist against his skin, biting back the tears that tried to escape. For just a second, his voice sounded so unsure—almost hopeful. She knew enough about him to understand how starved for affection he was, even if he didn't ever admit to it. She didn't understand everything he had done, wasn't sure if she truly believed all he had claimed today. But even so, the split second of true vulnerability in his tone broke her heart a little.

"I should," she whispered.

He searched her expression. "Don't pity me, Nya. I made my choices, and I'm no victim."

"I don't—"

"Then why are you looking at me like I'm some wounded animal?"

"I'm not."

"You are."

"Fine!" She slapped her hands against his chest. "Fine, I am. But it's not because I pity you—it's because I don't like it when you're hurt. It's why I asked about the healing and why I didn't want to leave you when you were injured. My father was *dying*, and I…" Her breath hitched. "All I could think about was the horrible sounds you were making as you tried to breathe."

His expression shifted, morphing into something almost angry. "You went to that place to save him, didn't you?"

She blinked at the sudden shift in subject. "What place?"

"The dark place. The void."

She tilted her head. "Yes, but how do you know—"

"Observation and guesswork," he cut in, almost too quickly. "Thanatos is your grandfather."

She furrowed her brow and stepped back, confused at where this was going and growing cold as the water cooled on her skin. But when she pulled away, he caught her wrist. She stumbled, pressing a palm to his thigh to keep from falling face-first into the water. Even as she caught her balance, neither of them moved away. On a wild impulse she was sure she would regret later, she took a step closer, standing between his spread legs. He was watching her with wide eyes, both their chests heaving, when she leaned in and brushed her lips against the curve of his neck.

The action was completely instinctual, and she had little idea why she'd done it other than it felt right. A groan rumbled from Morgen's chest, and his hand shot to the curve of her hip beneath the water. When she nipped the same spot with her teeth, he tugged her even closer, his other hand sliding up her ribs. His fingertips brushed the underside of her breast, and a whimper slipped past her lips. He paused, and she dragged her teeth against his skin again, this time harder, eliciting a rough moan from him before he cupped her breast, sliding his knuckles over the pebbled skin.

"Oh gods," she gasped, fisting a hand in his hair.

His breath shuddered, and then he dipped his head, swirling his tongue across the wet fabric directly over her peaked nipple. Her back arched, and she cried out, hardly caring as the sound echoed in the cavern around them. An ache spread over every inch of her, blurring her thoughts and overtaking reason. But when she climbed onto his lap, he paused.

"Nya," he said, breath ragged as he searched her gaze.

There was very little separating them, and she could feel the heat of his hard cock brushing against her.

She swallowed hard, her voice breathless. "It's not a big deal. We're married, aren't we?"

"That does not mean—"

"Besides, it's not like it'll be anything new for you."

His brow creased. "What do you mean?"

"Imeria said you've been with lots of women."

He exhaled a short laugh, his head falling to her shoulder for a moment until he looked at her again and said, "I probably should have clarified this earlier but…she was lying."

"What do you mean?"

He traced his hand up the length of her torso, and she shivered. "I mean," he said tightly. "She was making things up. I…I've never…" He turned his head, his cheeks flushing.

She blinked a few times. He was a virgin?

"Are you lying to me?"

He shook his head and for some reason, she believed him. Maybe it was because the tops of his cheeks were still heated and pink, or the way his hands shook slightly as they traced over her body. Even so, it didn't make sense for so many reasons; he was decades older than her, and she had *seen* the way the women here looked at him. Why wouldn't he have been with one of them, and how could she possibly be more experienced in this regard than he was?

Absentmindedly, she traced her thumb over his cheek, biting her lip. When she had met him at twenty-and-two, she had been with a man only a few times, a boy she'd known since she was young from the closest village, where her parents sometimes went for various supplies. It had been brief and little more than physical, though even that part of it had been lacking, if she was honest. Other than that, she knew very little about sex or pleasure, unless she counted the way Morgen touched her behind the waterfall.

"I have," she whispered. "When I was nineteen."

He nodded, brushing his fingers over her lip again to stop her from biting it, and muttered, "At least one of us knows what the hell we're doing then."

Her gaze shot to his. Oh gods, were they really doing this?

He must have seen it on her face, because he amended, "I didn't mean—" He cut himself off, a rough, frustrated groan escaping his throat. Then, before she knew what he was doing, he turned her around and hoisted her up so she was sitting on the edge of the pool. He glanced up at her as he settled between her legs, eyes dark.

"Tell me to stop, Nya."

The words were meant to be a reminder, but they only made her more desperate. The idea of leaving now made her want to scream. She had no idea what was happening, how she had gone from cursing him less than an hour ago to touching him and watching him blush over the idea of sex, but—

Nya?

"Don't," she breathed. "Don't stop."

She thought he might have muttered, "Thank fuck," but she wasn't sure, not of anything as he went down on her with zero reservations. The way he licked and sucked like he was starving for her, all while making her writhe, made her seriously doubt his claim of being inexperienced. He figured out exactly what made her cry out and gasp quickly, and before she could make sense of it, she was already approaching the looming drop into blinding pleasure.

"Not yet. Wait," he ordered gruffly, nipping at her inner thigh.

"I c-can't—"

"Nya. Just a few more minutes."

He didn't wait for her to reply, and she thought the realization of just how much he enjoyed this might have ruined her ability to hold out any longer, because all it took were a few flicks of his tongue against her clit, and she came so hard, her ears rang, her back arching completely off the stone.

When she finally floated back to reality, she found Morgen staring at her, eyes dark and lips swollen. Just like the last time he'd made her come, she found herself wanting more—wanting everything and wishing she hadn't put a stop to it earlier when she was straddling him. Even still, she was exhausted, and he must have sensed it, because he brushed his lips to her knee then rose out of the water, heading for a pile of clothes. She didn't look away for a second, watching the muscles of his back and ass move as he walked, the afterglow perhaps making her bolder.

When he returned, he was wearing a pair of loose pants slung low on his hips, holding what looked like a robe. Silently, he knelt next to her, dragging the warm material over her shoulders and gently pulling her wet hair back. Still, he didn't move away, and it took her a moment to realize he was braiding it.

"Morgen?" she murmured, the sudden exhaustion so potent, she hardly had it in her to wonder why he was doing it.

He didn't stop, merely muttering, "It's wet. It'll get tangled if it dries like this."

She nodded but must have fallen asleep, because the next thing she knew, he was lifting her, her head lolling against his bare chest. She tried to open her eyes, her voice muffled against his bare skin when she slurred, "Where are we going?"

"Just to get you to bed," he replied.

I'm so tired.

He sighed quietly. *I know. You just need rest.*

Somewhere in the back of her mind, she knew she was supposed to be mad at him still, but she hadn't felt this warm and relaxed in a long time. There was something… something about sleep she didn't like—

Dreams?

She couldn't remember. She never could, except for those brief, gasping moments when she woke up from nightmares she never remembered and quickly forgot. But maybe with Morgen holding her, she could trust sleep would merely bring rest.

When she came to next, someone was speaking—a man's voice she recognized, hissing words that almost sounded angry.

"*Morgen.* Have you truly been covering for her this whole time?"

"Shut your mouth for once, Carus. She needs to sleep."

"Are you actually being serious right now?"

"I always pull her back before she goes too far."

A rough, disbelieving laugh, then… "But it hasn't been enough, has it? The storms are getting worse, and it's only a matter of time before more starts to happen. Look, *you* don't have a blood bond with her. It won't be pleasant, but—"

She slipped back into sleep, but it must have only been a few seconds, because the next thing she heard was: "Finish that sentence, Carus. *I fucking dare you.*"

"You know I'm right."

"Goodnight. Keep an eye on her parents."

"And the dragons?"

"Varax has it handled."

All was quiet after that, save for the steady beat of his heart. Her last thought was that she thought she recognized it in the echo of her own pulse.

CHAPTER

SIXTEEN

I did not see my mother often as a child. But the day I met Nyx and Thanatos' daughter, she came to the clearing where we played and sat down. Sora hardly looked up. She was used to seeing principals, used to feeling the overwhelming breadth of their power. After all, she was just as powerful, even as a youngling. My mother watched her quietly for a time, until she said to me: "Fate has chosen this one, Anabeth." For a long time, I thought her words a blessing and didn't realize until too late they were a warning. The hand of Fate is not a kind one.

—Lady Anabeth, Royal Scribe's Apprentice, D'anna

Her room was dark, and the only sound she could hear was the frantic heaving of her own breath. It was just like the scary place, the one filled with whispers. They called her name, and sometimes, she wanted to follow them, but she was too scared of the dark to go. There weren't even stars, just deep stretches of black. Still, she swore that sometimes, it stared back at her with blinking, deadened eyes...

She screamed, and the next thing she knew, Papa was rushing into her room, and she couldn't remember why she was scared anymore.

He sat on her bed, his eyes glowing a little in the dark. "A bad dream?"

"I think," she whispered, rubbing her eyes. She couldn't remember anymore. "Where is Mama?"

"Just resting, love."

He looked worried and sad, and she threw her arms around him. "Is she sad about my baby brother?"

Papa shivered, and she tried to hug him tighter. It was a little cold in her room tonight.

"Yes, she's sad," he said, hugging her back.

She sat back. She was shivering now too, but she wasn't sure why, because she had all her blankets. Maybe it was because she was thinking of the way both Mama and Papa had cried when her brother had been born without breathing. They had explained to her that sometimes, babies didn't get much time in the world. She didn't think that was fair. He had been so little.

"Are you sad?" she asked, biting her lip.

Papa made a funny breathing noise and tucked one of her braids behind her shoulder. "I am, Nya, love. But you know that's okay, right? And you're allowed to be sad too, or mad or confused. Sometimes, bad things happen, and there is no perfect way to feel."

"Do you think my brother went to the dark place?"

Papa furrowed his brow, and she bit her lip harder, wondering if she had said a bad thing or if she was in trouble.

"What do you mean, the dark place?"

She shrugged. "It looks like nothing, but there are sometimes eyes. Maybe they're his?"

Papa cleared his throat then hugged her tight again. "Maybe," he said, but she didn't think he meant it. He didn't sound happy like she thought he might.

He sounded scared.

〜

Nya opened her eyes to find Morgen staring at her. She blinked a few times, trying to clear her head of the dream. It was odd that she remembered it at all.

Morgen was still looking at her, brow furrowed, when he said, "You had a brother?"

"How…?" she rasped, clearing her throat. "Why are you asking me right now?"

"Did you, Nya?"

She glanced around the room, not entirely sure how she had ended up in his bed. She remembered the pool…what they had done…but after, her memories were hazy. Carus had been there, or his voice, but she wasn't entirely sure what had been said.

"I… Yes, I did. But he was stillborn."

Morgen rubbed her jaw, muttering, "Of *course*. This is about to get a lot more complicated." She opened her mouth to ask what he meant, but he cut her off, asking, "Are you aware that when a god dies, their soul is eventually reborn? Mostly, it's just gods and godlings, but if a demi-god is particularly powerful, they may get caught up in the cycle of rebirth too."

She furrowed her brow. "Yes, it's why my parents came back after they died along with Kronos."

He nodded. "Usually, resurfaced memories from a past life become clearer with time." He hesitated before he continued. "I've always suspected this isn't Carus' first life, but he's never remembered anything clearly. He's always said he can recall feelings that don't feel attached to anything in this life, so I figured perhaps his last life was a very long time ago. But maybe he has no memories because he didn't make any."

Nya's eyes widened, sudden heat rushing to her face. "Are you saying you think Carus is my *brother?*"

"I'm saying I don't know, but he holds a striking resemblance to your father, and his magic is fire-based."

"He doesn't look like…" But she trailed off, realizing Morgen was right. Carus had her father's nose and high cheekbones, and his eyes were the same as hers. She hadn't seen it before because why would she? It didn't make any sense. "But I thought Carus was a demi-god?"

Morgen shook his head. "Both his birth parents were mortal. They died when he was young, and he ended up on the streets in D'anna. He crossed the border into Arcadia when he was thirteen."

"How old is he?"

"Twenty."

"I thought he was older," she whispered, shaking her head.

"Most do," Morgen said with a sigh. "But he's incredibly powerful and has lived through more than most do in a lifetime. Those things tend to age someone past their years."

Her throat worked. This was…too much of a coincidence. Wasn't it? Morgen couldn't possibly be right, and even if he was, what did it mean? Everything was complicated enough already.

"Did you see my dream?" she asked. "Is that how you figured it out?"

Morgen paused. He was already dressed, and she had no idea what time it was. She needed to go back to her parents, make sure her father was okay, and apparently figure out if she had a brother. But this felt important. She couldn't remember her own dreams most of the time, but if Morgen could see them, maybe she could finally figure out the source of her nightmares.

"Yes," he finally answered, not explaining further.

"Is that new?" she pushed. "You being able to see my dreams?"

"Not entirely," he said. The air shimmered with the pulsing energy of his magic, and she wondered if it was on purpose, or if some of his control was slipping.

"Okay," she whispered, holding his gaze. "I have more questions about that, but for now, where is Carus?"

Morgen cleared his throat. "Still keeping guard."

Nya winced. "Keeping guard outside the room holding my parents, who might also be his parents?"

"We should probably head that way," Morgen said carefully, rising from the bed. "Imeria brought clothes for you. I'll be waiting in the hall."

She almost brought up what had happened last night but let him leave instead. If he didn't want to talk about it, perhaps that was for the best.

She dressed quickly in the thick pants and too-big shirt Imeria had left, tugging on boots she assumed were for her too before joining Morgen. His eyes landed momentarily on her face, though he looked away quickly. She wondered if he felt the same urge to stare, paired with bitterness when he *did* look at her.

He sucked in a short breath, and she wondered if he'd heard the thought. All he said was, "If you can find it in you to be gentle about this, I'd ask you to try. I know you don't like him, but this might be a bit…sensitive, for Carus. He's been looking for his true parents for a long time."

"So he's always known his mortal parents weren't really his family?"

They started to walk. "I think so, yes. Obviously, I've never been reborn, but I hear there is usually a strong feeling of dissonance with the circumstances you're born into. Your parents are quite familiar with that feeling, I'm sure."

"Are gods usually reborn so quickly?" she asked as they rounded a corner, passing a few soldiers who nodded respectfully at Morgen but did not really look at her. "My brother was only born a year before Carus was supposedly reborn."

Morgen didn't answer right away, his expression contemplative. "I'm not sure the amount of time is important. The Fates just pull souls back into the world when it's their time again."

After that, neither of them spoke until they reached Carus, lingering in front of the room where Nya's parents were and looking bored.

"Anything to report?" Morgen asked casually, but Nya could hear the tension in his voice at the end of the words.

Carus shrugged. "Not really. They're pretty boring prisoners for being heirs. Just a lot of hushed talking."

Morgen nodded, and Nya's stomach whooshed as she really allowed herself to look at Carus. Morgen was right. He could absolutely be her brother.

"Why are you both looking at me like that?" Carus ventured, eyes narrowing.

Morgen shifted, his boots scuffing on the stone floor. "Nya had a dream, which I saw."

"Really?" Carus mused, though his voice hardened, his tone almost cold, and for a moment, Nya felt like she was the one missing something here.

"Yes. It was a *memory*," Morgen said firmly. "One I was unaware of."

Carus raised a brow. "Okay?"

Morgen glanced at her, and she took a deep breath, realizing he wanted her to continue. "I had a brother," she forced herself to tell him. "But he didn't live. He was stillborn."

Carus stiffened. "My condolences, but I'm not sure why you're telling me this."

"He was born when I was five, about twenty-one years ago. Morgen told me you don't think your mortal parents were your original birth parents."

"Why would you tell her that?" Carus snapped, silver flashing in his eyes. Though she didn't know him well, Nya had a feeling he didn't often get angry like this, at least not visibly.

Morgen didn't balk though, replying calmly, "I started to have suspicions when I saw her father. Nya's memory just confirmed them."

"What does her father have to do with—"

"You look just like him, Carus."

"I look like a lot of people." He paused, jaw clenching, and when he continued, his voice was quiet. "I've been searching faces my whole life. It doesn't usually mean much."

"And how ironic that the one time you're not looking close enough, it's exactly who you've been looking for."

Carus shook his head, backing away like he was going to run. But for him, for herself, for her parents who had lost a child all those years ago, Nya called, "Carus. Wait."

He turned but said nothing, his eyes wide, shining with unshed tears. But he stopped, waiting for her to speak.

"Morgen said you have memories of emotions." She took a deep breath, trying to soften her voice. "Can you tell me what they were?"

He shook his head, shutting his eyes and muttering, "This is a waste of time."

"Maybe, but wouldn't you rather make sure than wonder if you were wrong for the rest of your life?"

He opened his eyes, identical to hers except in their shape, slightly closer to her mother's. "I remember sadness mostly, but it was almost bittersweet, like…like the sadness felt unfair because it was so entangled with joy."

He paused, hesitating for so long, she thought he wouldn't continue. Eventually, he let out a slow breath, unfurling his fisted hands.

"There were words too. Just one phrase. I never told anyone, because I was sure that after looking for so long, I'd probably just made them up because I *wanted* to remember something."

"Maybe you did," she said quietly, tilting her head. "Still, what were they?"

Carus didn't look at her, his voice barely a hoarse whisper. "He looks just like you."

The tunnel fell silent, aside from the quiet murmuring of her parents in the room beyond. Nya took a short breath. "I wasn't there, Carus, not until later, when they let me say goodbye, so I can't confirm anything. But they can."

"I shouldn't." He was backing up again. "I can't."

"Carus." She reached out to him. "Just come with me. I'll do all the talking. But this way, you can at least have an answer."

"Do I want it?" he asked, not her, but Morgen, who stood just behind her. "This would mean… I don't even know what this would mean."

"You want to know," Morgen said. "Believe me, Carus."

Unspoken words lingered in the air: *They would love you if they knew. Don't waste that.*

They would, Nya was sure of it. They had never *stopped* loving her baby brother. It didn't matter that he was gone. Morgen had never had that love from the people who brought him into the world, and he never would. It made sense why he was pushing Carus to find out the truth.

"Alright." Carus paced back and forth a few times before stopping in front of her. "*Fuck…* Fuck. Okay, you can ask."

She nodded silently, and he followed her as she ducked into the room. Her parents were sitting on one of the cots together, and they immediately looked up when they saw her, their eyes wide and full of relief. Neither of them looked upset, despite the awful things she had said to them yesterday. Guilt clawed at her, but their lack of anger didn't surprise her. They had never let anything get in the way of loving her unconditionally.

"I'm sorry about what I said," Nya said first, crossing over and sitting in the chair across from them. "I didn't mean it."

Her mother nodded, tucking a loose curl behind her ear.

"We know, Nya. But I understand why you're angry. Nothing about this is fair, and I wish more than anything I could take that away."

Nya bit her lip, tucking away her own emotions for now. This wasn't about her. "I know." She glanced back at Carus, who watched them with wide eyes. She blinked once at him, a silent warning, then faced her parents again. "I need to ask you both something."

"What is it?" her father asked, brow creased.

She cleared her throat, folding her trembling hands tightly in her lap. "When my brother was born, did either of you say anything in particular?"

She knew they were going to be taken aback by the question, and, sure enough, her mother's lips parted in surprise, and her father paled slightly, his shoulders stiffening. It took a moment for either of them to speak, but finally, her mother said in a tight voice, "We talked to him for a while." Her voice broke as she added, "He was loved, Nya, just like you, and we needed to make sure he knew that before—" She cut herself off, quickly brushing at her eyes.

Even after all these years, she could tell their pain was still just as potent. That alone made the next words even harder to force out, but she did, for all their sakes.

"But was there anything in particular you remember?"

"Nya, what's going on?" her father asked, his usually steady voice wavering.

There were very few times she had seen her father cry. The night her brother was born had been one of them, and she hated bringing the memories to light again.

In her periphery, Carus took a step back, and she thought he might have been about to leave, so she said firmly, "I'll explain, I promise. But first, please, was there anything you remember saying of note?"

Her father took a deep breath, exchanging a look with her mother, undoubtedly speaking to her down the pathway, currently closed to Nya.

"When you were born, Nya, until the moment you opened your eyes, you were like a tiny replica of your mother," he said, his smile bittersweet. "Your brother never got the chance to open his, but he… He looked—"

He cut himself off, looking down abruptly, but her mother finished for him. "He looked just like your father, Nya." She smiled too, even as tears tracked down her cheek. "I remember that most."

Nya did not smile, her eyes widening. Their words matched Carus' memory far too closely to be a mere coincidence. She glanced back at Carus, who wasn't looking at her now, instead staring at her parents with a disbelieving expression. Morgen, who lingered in the doorway, nodded once at her. *I think we were right.*

"Nya, what's going on?" her mother asked, obviously aware of the sudden tension.

Nya saw the exact moment her father noticed Carus standing with a hand pressed to the wall. Her parents did not know what their son would have looked like grown. She wasn't even sure they thought he would be reborn, so she didn't blame them for not realizing it right away. It was the same reason neither she nor Carus had noticed their own resemblance. The mind did funny things to rationalize things it thought impossible.

"Carus was born to mortal parents in D'anna," Morgen

said quietly. "Obviously, he's not mortal, but he never knew who his true parents were."

"Stop talking about me as if I can't hear you, asshole," Carus muttered in a thick voice, though his eyes were still on Nya's father.

Morgen lifted his hands in the air. "I was just filling them in on the basics, since I presume you weren't going to."

"How old are you?" Nya's father asked hoarsely. Her mother's eyes were huge, ether illuminating the tears rolling steadily down her cheeks.

"Twenty," Carus said, clearing his throat, adding, "Everyone says I look older."

Her father nodded slowly. "I got that a lot too as a teenager."

"Carus," Nya said, and he finally looked away from her father. "Tell them what you told me, about what you remember."

Carus took an audibly shaky breath, glancing at Morgen before looking at her with a pained half-smile. "You have turned out to be a hell of a lot more trouble than I bargained for, sweetheart."

She shrugged but offered a small smile back at him. "I'd say I'm sorry, but I'm not big on apologizing to people who helped kidnap me."

He didn't laugh, instead looking at her parents, his eyes a little wide. Nya had meant it when she'd said she thought Carus appeared older than twenty, but right now, he looked…young, unsure and boyish, with a vulnerability she was certain he usually hid under sarcasm and humor.

"I doubted for a long time what I was feeling—that sureness I didn't belong where I was when I was young—because I didn't have memories," he started. "Once I came to Arcadia, I met a few demi-gods who had been reborn, and they all said eventually, everything about their past lives came back to them. All I had was the memory of brief emotions and a single phrase: that I looked like him." He paused, glancing upwards and clearing his throat again. "I guess it makes sense now, and I'm sorry for making all this more complicated than it already is. I won't take it personally if you're not interested in knowing me. We *did* take you as prisoners."

Silence fell over the room, broken only when her mother stood slowly, her entire body trembling. "Did you hear a word of what we said to Nya a few minutes ago?"

Carus' brows rose in surprise. "Yes, but surely, you can't actually apply those words to me. I almost killed you yesterday," he said, glancing at Nya's father. "I helped kidnap Nya and am leading a campaign to put Kronos' heir back on the throne."

"Fortunately, I'm still alive," her father said. "And Morgen's explanation made sense."

Carus shook his head. "Still—"

"But it wouldn't have mattered," her father cut him off, ether flaring in his eyes. "Nya could stab me in the heart and twist the knife, I'd still be trying to make sure she was okay."

Carus shut his mouth, still stiff at the wall. Her mother took a tentative step towards him. "You don't know me, and I don't want to smother you with the assumption you want a relationship with either of us. I know how terrifying it is to have someone tell you how much you mean to them with little understanding of those emotions, even if you feel them yourself. Being reborn is complicated; each life is your own, and you are not expected to uphold anything from your past ones. But…if you want to know me, I would very much like to know you."

Carus stared at her for a long time, long enough that Nya saw a little of the hope die in her mother's eyes, at least until he tentatively said, "So you're Nyx and Thanatos' daughter?"

Her lips twitched. "In my first life, yes."

"I can see the resemblance."

She took another slow step, nearly in front of him now, tilting her chin back to meet his eyes. "Of course you're tall," she said with a soft laugh. "I swear, I have a permanent crook in my neck."

"My birth mother said the same thing," he said, his lips twitching strangely, as if he wasn't sure if smiling was a proper reaction. "She hated it. Neither of my parents were tall, and I think she was worried her husband suspected an affair on her part. I… Sorry. If that's strange to bring up."

"Not at all," her mother said. "I know it's odd, being born into a family and being completely out of place, but no one expects you to talk about it as if it didn't happen."

Nya glanced back at Morgen, who was watching Carus talk to her mother with a blank expression. He looked entirely emotionless, but Nya knew better. Though she was sure he was happy for Carus, it couldn't be easy watching this. She imagined a part of the reason he and Carus had bonded in the first place was because of their childhoods— or lack thereof. Now, Carus was getting what Morgen would never have.

"Papa," she said quietly. "I'll give you three some time to talk, okay?"

He glanced at her, having been watching Carus talk to her mother. He nodded then stood and pulled her into a tight hug.

"You're still my favorite," he said in her ear, and she laughed, pulling back and flicking his nose.

"That's mean, and you hardly know him yet," she said. "But I will take your favoritism gladly."

He smiled, but it fell slightly. She could tell he was worried. "Are you alright?"

She looked at the doorway, finding Morgen had left. "I'm alright," she said. "I'll be back. Be nice."

He followed her eyes, a flicker of sadness on his features before it cleared and he patted her cheek. "No promises."

As she walked to the door, Carus gave her a smile that looked more like a grimace. But still, he was sitting with her mother and talking, and when her father joined them, he remained.

The tunnel was empty when she stepped out, and, on a hunch, she said down the pathway, *Varax?*

He's out here.

Care to share where 'here' is?

Nya waited, leaning her hip against the wall. A few minutes had passed by the time she heard Morgen say, *It's a bit of a climb. You don't need to bother.*

Nya sighed loudly. *Varax, would you be so kind as to give me directions?*

Just down the hall from his chambers, there is a set of stairs set into the stone that leads out to the side of the mountain. After that, you'll just have to hike.

Nya didn't bother replying, instead hurrying towards the

direction of his room. She was surprised to realize she had already started learning her way around the tunnel systems.

When she reached Morgen's room, she found the stairway with little trouble, though by the time she climbed it to the top, she was panting. She swore softly when she emerged and saw the worn footpath that wrapped around the side of the mountain. It was less steep than most of the peaks surrounding them, but still, she had no idea how far up Morgen was. He had probably portaled there, but she was too stubborn to ask for him to come get her.

The sun was setting by the time she reached the outcropping where he sat against a large boulder, Varax curled behind him. The clouds had cleared enough to let some of the orange-red light seep through at the horizon, casting an eerie glow over the valley.

Nya wondered if, sometimes, he came up here, watching the clouds and deadened valley below, and considered sending one enormous strike of that lightning she'd seen him wield across the mountains, turning all of it to ash.

Perhaps there was something wrong with her, for even after seeing Carus and her parents meet today, she still thought turning all the terrible, wonderful pain of the world into nothing wouldn't be so bad.

CHAPTER

SEVENTEEN

I pray they will forgive me for what I have done, but he must see the truth of their connection. It may be the only way to save us all.
—Ana, Priestess to the Usurper King, Arcadia

"I TOLD YOU—YOU didn't need to bother," Morgen said when she sat down next to him. "You should probably be with Carus and your parents."

She shook her head. "They need some time alone to figure things out."

Morgen blew out a breath, hanging his head between his bent knees. "Carus has been searching for so long, I don't think he ever stopped to imagine what would happen if he found what he was looking for."

She didn't know what to say to that. The wind howled through the mountains, and she remained silent next to Morgen for a while. Eventually, she asked, "How did you meet Carus?"

He glanced sidelong at her. "I suppose he won't mind me telling you now, given you're technically his sister."

She shrugged, though her stomach whooshed. Hearing the words spoken aloud felt odd.

"Varax was hunting in a small forest just west of here, and when she dove for a sheep, it turned out to be a boy wearing a sheepskin who, according to her, screamed very loudly and then set himself on fire trying to fend her off."

Nya's brows rose. "Are you serious?"

Morgen nodded, the ghost of a smirk on his face. "Completely, unless Varax is lying. Besides, Carus has yet to come up with a believable story."

I am not lying. He shrieked like a very young female child.

Nya glanced over at Varax, who was already closing the single amber eye she had opened and evidently going back to her nap.

"Varax called for me, and by the time I got there, Veeron—Carus' dragon—had shown up too and claimed Carus. I portaled all four of us back here, and then you can imagine what happened after that."

A surprised laugh bubbled up before she could stop it. "So, you 'rescued' him, and then he took care of you while you were magic-drunk." She shook her head. "No wonder he was so grumpy when it happened the other day."

"It was a memorable start to our friendship," Morgen said dryly.

"And Imeria? How did you meet her?"

His hand twitched where it was resting against the cold ground, and she resisted the urge to take it. Despite their marriage, neither of them wore bands, and she wondered briefly if it was a way for him to keep it from feeling real. She knew she should be relieved, but it only made her feel a hollow pang of disappointment.

"Do you remember I told you some of my friends had known me for a long time?"

She looked up to meet his eyes. They were dull, barely even illuminated by ether, much less the embers. "Yes. I presume Imeria was in his palace?"

"She was one of Kronos' personal servants. She was very young, younger than was traditional, which made the others dislike her. But she was lucky, because he never touched her, and sometimes, sent her to deliver messages to me. The day he died, she was just supposed to tell me to stay in my room, but she also told me there was a demi-god killing guards outside the throne room."

Nya's eyes widened slightly. "My father?"

Morgen nodded. "It was impressive, really. All the palace guards had been trained practically from birth, and all of them were dead before Vane reached Kronos. They had to be; they were ordered to die than let anyone touch their king. Imeria saw, and I think she hoped someone was finally going to get close enough to kill him."

It was odd to hear, to connect her gentle, albeit sometimes grumpy, father with a demi-god who had slaughtered highly trained guards with ease. But when she thought about why he'd done it, she could make sense of it. He would do anything for her mother.

"I was young and stupid, so I ran to the throne room." His lips turned up, almost as if recounting a happy memory. "I wanted to watch it happen, to see him finally die. Imeria followed me, begging me to come with her, to run. She understood what I didn't yet: if and when Kronos was defeated, I needed to be gone before more of the council arrived."

"And she's been with you since?"

He shrugged. "She's loyal."

Nya bit her cheek, thinking of the day Imeria had helped get her ready for the wedding ceremony. Something she had said sat strangely with her, and she wasn't sure why.

"Why did she tell me you weren't a virgin?"

Morgen huffed out a silent laugh. "Bringing that up again, are you?"

"It's just an odd thing to do. I mean, she made me think you'd had countless lovers and that they were all going to be spiteful. When we went to breakfast in the mess hall and everyone was glaring at me, I assumed she was right."

He shook his head. "They just don't know you. I'd never tolerate them being hostile or threatening you, but I understand why they're wary."

She bit her cheek, turning her attention to the sun fading in the sky. It was nearly nightfall, and a deeper chill was beginning to spread through the air.

It was probably just jealousy her own mind had disguised as something else, but she didn't like that he couldn't see an issue with what Imeria had done. It was just strange, and most people would be bothered by it. Then again, Morgen wasn't most people, and his idea of trustful relationships was assuredly skewed in many ways.

"We should go back," he said, touching her arm. "You're cold."

She did shiver at the brush of his fingers against her skin, but it had little to do with the temperature. Turning to face him, she asked, "What happens now?"

He touched her face, tracing her cheek almost absent-mindedly. "The principals rejected our terms. Even if your parents stay for you and Carus, that remains true. We're running short on time, Nya. More cracks will form, and the stability of this world will start to waver. If the council won't bend, I'll have to force their hands."

"So there will still be war," she whispered.

"We'll see, but knowing Sol…probably."

She searched his gaze for a moment, wholly focused on her, before inhaling sharply and wrapping her arms around him, hugging him tightly.

It just felt like the right thing to do, with what had happened today and all that had already passed. They had so much history between them but so few, shaky ways to bridge the gaps that were naturally always going to live between them. Holding him like this felt like finally forcing herself to connect all they had been with all they were now.

He stiffened at first, arms at his sides, before slowly relaxing, sliding his hands up her back. She waited all the time it took for him to return the embrace. Though he was surrounded by people who believed in his claim, she had learned quickly he trusted very few, and even then, he did not really open up emotionally to anyone, even Carus and Imeria. But she had the luxury of knowing him in a time and place that was entirely separate. Perhaps without that, he would have never been able to be vulnerable with anyone, and, as angry as she still was that he had lied and forced her into all this, she could understand to some degree. It was not right, but as Carus had said to her the other night, Morgen had no idea how to treat the people he cared about, and she could no longer say he did not care.

Neither could she.

Lightning lit up the sky in the distance, and he

murmured in her ear, "We need to go inside before the storm hits."

She nodded against his shoulder but asked, "The lightning; what is it like?"

It must have taken him a moment to realize she was referring to his magic, because he didn't answer right away. "A little terrifying," he eventually admitted. "It always has been. It's a difficult element to control properly. You could just as easily destroy your enemies as your friends if you're not careful."

She pulled back slightly to look at him. "I understand that," she whispered before really thinking.

He paused, a few faint veins of gold sparking in his irises. "Do you?"

"I…" She trailed off and for a few moments, her mind went blank, and then she shook her head. "Probably not, actually. I hardly ever use my magic, so I can't even say for sure how it manifests."

He didn't look convinced for some reason, but still he murmured, "All right."

A sudden wave of anxiety churned her stomach as she realized how dark it was. The wind was picking up, and the mountaintops were only visible when the lightning flashed.

"C'mon," he said, pulling her up. "Just hold onto me for a moment, alright?"

"We're portaling?"

"Mhm. Not sure I trust you not to trip over a rock and break your ankle, especially in the dark."

She smiled, despite the cold fear she suddenly couldn't shake as the sun dipped below the horizon. "That was *one* time. I did not break it, and even you said you didn't see the root."

His laugh was soft in her ear. She wondered if anyone else had ever heard that laugh before as he tugged her close, one arm wrapped around her waist, the other outstretched as he summoned the portal. She watched closely as the ether in the air shimmered, visible even in the dark, and just before they stepped through the opaque silver, she told him, "I portaled during the battle. That's how I got down to you so fast."

The next thing she knew, they were standing in the mess hall and Morgen was a few paces away, staring at her with wide eyes.

"What?" she asked, a little breathless.

He shook his head slightly. "That's just…highly improbable."

"What, me portaling?"

"Yes."

"Well, it happened, so—"

"Morgen!"

They both turned at the sound of Carus' voice.

"Where are Sora and Vane?" Morgen asked immediately.

"Where I left them," Carus said casually, though Nya heard the slight catch to his voice. "Don't look so worried. I didn't kill them. In fact, we had a proper heart to heart. I cried, it was beautiful, and I've taken Nya's place as their heir, firstborn son and all."

Nya scowled. "That's not a thing."

He shrugged. "Fine, you got me. Yes, we spoke, but there were no tears on my end, and Nya, you are still their first choice of heir in the very unlikely circumstance it ever comes to that. But Morgen, we need to talk." He glanced at Nya and added, "Alone."

Morgen gave a curt nod. "You should go find your parents," he said to her.

Nya narrowed her eyes at Carus. She was sure, being one of his generals, there were plenty of things he needed to talk to Morgen about, but they were supposed to be on the same side now. She didn't like that they still kept secrets from her.

"Right, of course," she muttered, slipping away before either of them could say more.

She didn't go to her parents, though, instead lingering in one of the tunnels off the mess hall before quietly walking to the war room, keeping her head down and eyes downcast. Sure enough, her hunch about where Morgen and Carus had been going was right. She could hear their low voices when she paused outside the room.

"—you ask if they know?"

Carus huffed out a breath. "Not directly, no. There were lots of other things to talk about."

"Do I need to remind you that *you* were the one who brought it up to me and suggested we murder my *wife*."

Nya's breath caught, but she didn't think they heard it, because Carus didn't even pause before answering.

"Not my finest moment, I admit, but you can see why I thought of it as a possible solution. Besides, it's not like you can actually claim to care that much about her. I know you two had some odd friendship before, but look me in the eye and tell me that wasn't a part of the ploy. At least I can say she's my sister."

Morgen made a noise somewhere between a laugh and a snarl. "You didn't know that until this morning."

"Morgen." She heard Carus' footsteps against the stone floor of the cavern, presumably moving closer to Morgen. "Seriously. Your marriage is a farce, and we both know it. Forcing her under threat isn't exactly the start of something long and happy."

"It was *your* idea, you *eejit!*"

Carus blew out a loud breath. "Yeah, and I still don't think it was a bad one. But don't act like I'm some monster and you're not just because you suddenly claim to care about her!"

There was a long pause, and then Morgen said, almost so quietly, she couldn't hear, "And if I do?"

Something scraped against the floor, a chair perhaps, and Carus said, "Look, as much as it pains me to say this, because, apparently, she's my sister, but someone needs to ask: are you sure it's not just because she's the first person you've ever taken to bed? You do know that sometimes, people *think* they're in love, and then the afterglow wears off, and you realize you were just really fucking horny."

Morgen didn't say anything. Hearing what she thought was footsteps, Nya glanced behind her. No one was there, so she remained, despite the dizzying racing of her pulse. She should go, but something held her frozen. This felt important.

"Wait." The chair scraped again. "Morgen. Please tell me you're not that stupid."

"You're going to need to elaborate."

Carus let out a rough laugh, loud enough that it echoed into the hall. "You *did* legitimize the marriage, right?"

"It's an archaic practice."

"Of course it is, but this is *Arcadia*, and you are trying to take the fucking throne! You do realize that until you do that, the marriage does nothing to stabilize your claim in the eyes of the council. Not to mention, if anyone were to find out, this makes her incredibly vulnerable. There are plenty of women who I'm sure would love to be queen, and if they knew the marriage ceremony was never technically completed, they might feel there's an opportunity here."

"They wouldn't dare."

Carus barked out a harsh laugh. "They don't *know* Nya! To them, she's just some outsider you brought in and forced to marry you. Perhaps they would even think they're doing her a favor by slitting her throat."

Nya took a step backward, her hand shaking as she brought it to her throat. Everyone here had assumed she and Morgen had sex that night…that they were *supposed* to. Worse, they probably thought he had forced her, given the circumstances of the marriage in the first place.

"Nya?"

The unfamiliar whisper came from close behind her. Too close. She whirled, and a hand covered her mouth before she could scream. She smelled something sickly sweet, and her vision tilted. She tried to call for Morgen or Carus, but her lips felt stiff.

She was falling…

Someone caught her, but their hands were rough.

Morgen. I think he was right.

She couldn't tell if she'd actually accessed the pathway, or if she had just thought the phrase. Before she could try again, her vision blurred, and the world went dark.

CHAPTER

EIGHTEEN

My big brother says I should write from time to time. Words are whispers of Fate, according to him. I suppose he would know. He has our mother's name, so he must be important. Sora did not come back from the palace right away. It has been happening often. Today, I will ask her where she goes.
—Anabeth, demi-god daughter of Juno, Goddess of Fate (and sister to June)

"Just fucking do it!"

A loud sigh. "Maybe this was a bad idea. He did say he would kill anyone who tried."

"Yeah, and he also said he'd automatically assume it was Harren and Laen if anything happened. C'mon, she'll wake up soon, and I don't have anything else to knock her out with."

Nya stayed very still as heavy footsteps drew closer. When they stopped right next to her, she forced herself to open her eyes and move, panic and adrenaline cutting through the haze of whatever they had drugged her with.

She'd never even heard of something that could knock out gods, but then again, she didn't know much at all about Arcadia.

"Shit!"

She tried to bolt for the exit, but someone caught her roughly around the waist before she could reach the doorway. They were in a small, cloistered chamber lit by a single torch, the light flickering wildly and casting long, frantic shadows over the walls. She didn't recognize the man in front of her, but his gray eyes were wide as they met hers.

"Feron, you *eejit.* Do it now!" the other voice boomed in her ear, and she thrashed as she screamed. The man covered her mouth, but he roared, *"Fuck!"* when she bit his palm hard.

The man, Feron, approached, trembling and ghostly pale.

"Don't!" Nya rasped. "You don't understand what you're doing, either of you."

"What?" her captor sneered. "Because you're some distant relation of Nyx? Believe me, girl, most of us can claim connection to one principal or another. You're not unique in that respect."

"He'll kill you if they don't first," she wheezed around the hand holding her throat.

"Feron, give me the damn knife."

She tried to grab the hilt of the dagger as it was handed over but only managed to wrap her hands around the blade. Still, she didn't let go, blood streaming down her wrists from her palms. Her captor grunted, twisting and letting go for a moment, giving her one more chance to scream before he gripped her throat tightly with one hand and forced the blade down with the other.

For just a flash, she saw his face hovering above hers, faint silver ebbing in the muddy hazel of his irises. Then, his eyes widened, and he choked, blood coating his lips. She gasped, coughing, when his grip loosened and she could finally breathe again. A moment later, his body was flung against the far wall, smacking limply as it slid to the floor. She only saw his blank, empty gaze for a moment before the screaming started, and someone lifted her off the floor.

She thrashed blindly, tears mixing with the blood on her face as she screamed, "No, no, *no*—"

"Nya, hey, hey, it's okay. It's just me."

Vaguely, she knew she was sobbing openly, still trying to escape because she did not want to die, not yet, not like this—

"Nya, shh, it's alright. It's me. It's Carus." She opened her eyes to find him gently cupping her face, his brown eyes wide and familiar. "I'm getting you out of here, okay?"

In the corner, someone—Feron, she thought—was screaming and pleading. Energy crackled through the room, so potent, she could taste it. Her eyes darted to the sound, but Carus shook his head, pulling her face away.

"Don't look. It'll be over soon, but we need to go now, alright?"

Hazily, she nodded. This time, when picked her up, she did not fight, clinging to him as he carried her out of the room.

"Please, please tell him!" Feron screamed. "He told me to, but I didn't do it! Please...*Nya*—"

The last thing she heard before Carus rounded the

corner was a low laugh, another shrill scream, and then Morgen speaking in a voice so cold, she hardly recognized it.

"What makes you think you can fucking say her name?"

She shut her eyes, tucking her face against Carus' chest. Her body was shaking so hard, it hurt, her tensing muscles unable to relax. Neither of them spoke, not until they reached what she vaguely recognized as Morgen's room and he had tucked her into several blankets on the bed.

"What will happen to Feron?"

Carus gave a low laugh, his eyes darkening with fury. "If he's lucky, he's dead by now."

"And if he's not?"

He raised a brow. "My guess is that Morgen is taking his time, and Feron is wishing he slit his own throat with that dagger rather than following along with his piece-of-shit friend's plan."

She shifted, wincing as the adrenaline and terror began to fade and the pain set in. Her throat felt bruised from the inside out, her aching hands covered in drying blood. She healed faster and easier than mortals, but, unlike Morgen's healing abilities, it still took time.

Carus frowned, looking at her hands. "I can't heal you, but he'll do it as soon as he returns."

"Do they know?"

"Who?"

She swallowed, tightening her jaw at the sensation but forcing herself to continue. "Our parents."

A flicker of emotion crossed Carus' face, but he didn't address the way she'd spoken of her family as his too. Instead, he shrugged and said, "I figured it would be best not to mention it until you were safe. I kind of got the impression they're 'the tear down the mountain to keep you safe', 'ask questions later' kind of people, and while I appreciate the sentiment, it would have been a mess."

Her lips twitched with a barely-there smile, even though she really felt like crying. "You're definitely right," she croaked. "Thank you for realizing it."

"They love you." His voice softened as he said it. "A lot. I didn't think… I thought that kind of love was something people made up."

She shivered, and he added another blanket around her shoulders.

"I'll warn you, it can be kind of overwhelming sometimes," she said. "Having someone care that much with zero expectations of anything in return."

"I don't know if they'll ever feel that way about me."

She paused, wondering if it was her place to convince him of anything. But Carus had been alone and searching for so long, and her parents had been mourning all that time too. Letting him waste time wondering if he was allowed into her family suddenly seemed foolish, especially with the approaching conflict.

"They're no stranger to second lives," she told him. "But they fell in love with each other every time they came back, and you…" She lowered her gaze. "I've never heard my mother scream the way she did when she realized her baby wasn't breathing, and I hope I never do again. And when it was time, the midwife had to practically shout in their faces and push me into their arms because they wouldn't let you go. Believe me, Carus, they'll love you just the same as me if you let them."

He looked away, eyes glassy and jaw tight. After a moment, he gave a short nod, and then neither of them spoke for a while. She shut her eyes, willing her body to calm and telling herself Morgen would take away the pain soon.

Nya?

She opened her eyes. *I'm fine. Carus is with me.*

You're injured. I should have healed the wounds first.

Even down the pathway, his voice was breathless, as if he was moving very fast. She was sure he would appear at the doorway any moment, so she didn't reply. Sure enough, within less than a minute, she heard him say through ragged breaths, "I would have portaled, but I just used a decent amount of magic, and I didn't want to——"

"Relax, Morgen," Carus said, standing. "She's fine. Just heal her so she stops bleeding all over the blankets."

The words did not help calm him. The air thickened and shifted, the torches flickering, and his fingertips sparked as he clenched his hands into tight fists.

"Hey." Carus stepped directly in front of him, momentarily blocking her view. "Take a fucking breath, or you'll accidentally kill her trying to heal a few cuts."

Morgen stiffened, and she couldn't see his expression, but the air stopped buzzing and the torches calmed.

"I'm good," he said gruffly. "Go."

Carus didn't hesitate this time, leaving the room without another word. Slowly, she lifted her head from where she had been resting it on her curled knees and met Morgen's eyes. She expected him to get angry again, but instead, the glow of the embers softened, and his terse expression fell.

Tentatively, he moved closer, one hand slightly outstretched, as if not to startle her.

"Can I sit?"

She nodded, trying and failing to stop from shaking. The mattress bowed, and she whispered, "I'm fine."

"You can try to feed that bullshit to Carus, but it won't work with me. I know you're not, Nya. I can feel—" She heard him take a deep breath. "Let me heal you at least. Please?"

Now that he was closer, she could see the specks of blood on his cheeks she was sure weren't his. Maybe it should have frightened or made her feel worse, but the knowledge the men who had done this to her had died painful deaths was comforting. More than. She was *glad* Morgen had killed them the way he had. If that was wrong, she couldn't find it in herself to care at the moment.

"Go ahead," she said, her breath hitching.

He nodded, moving closer. She didn't fail to notice the way his hand shook as he placed it lightly against her sternum.

"This might hurt, just for a second, but it won't be as bad as the last time I healed you."

She didn't reply, instead watching his eyes as the embers flared bright gold, nearly blotting out the ether and light brown of his irises. A burning sensation spread up her throat and across her hands, uncomfortable but not any more than the injuries themselves. The feeling only lasted for a few seconds before fading completely, taking the pain with it.

"There," Morgen murmured, starting to pull away. She

caught his hand before he could, holding it to the same spot it had been on her chest.

Before he could protest or say anything at all, she blurted out, "I heard what Carus said to you, about legitimizing the marriage."

Morgen stiffened. "You were listening to that?"

"Yes, right before I was snatched and drugged by *your* soldiers, so you don't get to be angry with me about it."

He started to pull his hand away again, shaking his head. "Nya—"

"And I think he had a point. If not doing that is going to cause issues or make it more likely that people will try to stab me in the back, I think it would be stupid not to."

Now, she let him pull away. He sat back, long arms draped over his bent knees on the bed. She didn't mistake his posture for anything relaxed, though. His jaw was tight, his voice tense when he said, "There is no way for anyone to know we haven't."

She raised a brow. "Except they obviously figured it out. Carus made it seem like people would be more apt to swoop in and get rid of me if they thought we weren't *really* married. I don't know much about marriage traditions in Arcadia, but I'm getting the impression it's all taken a lot more seriously than in the mortal realm."

He sighed. "Not necessarily. Pretty sure the mortal royals are also sticklers about consummation."

"Okay, yes, fine," she said, rubbing at the slight ache in her neck. "All I'm saying is that it sounds pretty likely someone got Feron and his friend to do their dirty work for them. Meaning at least a handful of people here are aware, and there are probably others eyeing my spot. The easiest way to get that to stop would be to get it over with and be obvious about it."

"Or I could just track them down and kill them, like I did Feron and Sillas."

A humorless laugh escaped her. "Really? You'd rather kill your own soldiers than touch me?"

"I'm fairly certain you know that not to be true, Nya. *You* were the one who just framed sex between us as something to get over with."

"Then why?" The words came out quieter than she wanted, almost hushed.

He leaned his head forward, his hair falling in his face. "Lots of reasons. Because I never want you to think that's expected of you. Because you were forced into this marriage. Because I've seen enough men use 'duty' as an excuse for consent—and worse."

She took a deep breath. "You're not your father, Morgen."

"Perhaps not yet. I imagine it took time for him to become a ruthless tyrant who took pleasure in taking advantage of women and watching them die as a result."

"It was always in him, I'm sure," she whispered. "But you are not like that, and you never have been. The fact that we're even having this conversation is proof. I know you saw far too much when you were young, but that doesn't mean you're going to flip a switch someday and change completely."

He sighed deeply then surprised her by tugging her closer, his head resting against her torso. His voice was muffled when he said, "I'm sorry for what happened today."

After a moment of stunned shock, she let herself relax into his embrace. "It wasn't your fault."

His arms tightened around her. "Maybe. Or maybe it was selfish not to tell you the risks."

"I was well aware there was risk." She laughed dryly and added, "I married you under threat, after all."

He groaned, pressing his face to her stomach. "I'm not a good person, Nya. It's obvious."

"You are not," she agreed softly, a little amazed he'd said it without pushing her away entirely. It wasn't like him; none of this was. "But I don't believe anyone is *truly* good. They're lying if they say they are, and you're only hurting yourself trying to convince anyone you're the only one in the entire world who has moral flaws."

He let out a soft puff of air against her but didn't respond. His lips brushed the strip of skin where her shirt had ridden up, and she inhaled sharply, threading her fingers through his hair. Her skin felt oversensitive and fragile, every light touch of his mouth and hands making her shiver.

He had come for her. And not only that—he'd made sure that those who had hurt her suffered for it.

She was still reeling and shaky, and not for the first time in her life, she wanted him to ground her. Except that, unlike all the other times before, when he'd kept a safe distance between them, he was right here, touching her, and she needed *more*.

"You should rest," he murmured, even as he nipped lightly against the thin skin at the top of her ribcage.

A soft, unbidden moan slipped past her parted lips. His hands tightened, though his touch was still achingly gentle as he slid his fingers up further to press against the undersides of her breasts. When he didn't go further than that, she whimpered softly, moving her hips instinctively against him, seeking any friction, because she was starting to *burn*—

He groaned again; this time, it was a mix of frustration and something darker that sounded exactly like what she was feeling.

He glanced up at her, eyes dark with desire and crackling with a deep shade of amber-gold.

"Please," she whispered.

"You need—"

"*This* is what I need."

He searched her gaze, as if he could pull the truth from within her eyes. She was about to protest, to *beg*, but she didn't ever have to go that far, because his mouth had closed around one of her nipples, and she cried out in surprise as he flicked his tongue over the pebbled surface. Her back arched, and he pulled back, forehead against her sternum. They were both breathing fast, and through half-lidded eyes, she saw his hand was fisted in the sheets next to her.

"Morgen?"

He lifted his head, his cheeks flushed and eyes glassy. "I want…" His voice was hoarse. "Can I see you?"

She didn't hesitate a second, tugging her shirt off and letting it fall to the floor. The blankets pooled around her waist, and Morgen stared at her with wide eyes, his gaze sliding slowly over every inch of her. His lips were parted. his chest rising and falling in quick succession. She thought she might have shocked him by moving so quickly.

Finally, he touched her again, splaying his hand over her

sternum. She wondered if he could feel just how hard her heart was beating.

"You are so singularly beautiful," he breathed, and she shivered. "It's a little overwhelming."

Heat rose to her cheeks. "You did see me nearly naked in the pool the other night."

He shook his head and muttered, "That damned shift was in the way. I swear, I'm going to burn every last one of those."

She opened her mouth to tell him he was being ridiculous, but then he sucked on the scar at the base of her neck, where he'd bit her after their wedding. She cried out in surprise as a shocking bolt of pleasure raced down her spine. When he swirled his tongue over the same spot, the sensation intensified again, and she gasped, "Wha—What... Why does that feel like *that*?"

He did it again, ignoring her question, instead asking, "Do you think you can come just from this?"

"I don't know—*Oh gods*."

She fisted her hands in the material of his shirt as another wave of that confusing, blinding ecstasy spread low in her belly and all the way to her center, the ache nearly painful. Maybe she *could* come from this. Maybe she was nearly there.

He lifted his head slightly, and when he spoke, it was barely a whisper against her ear. "I want you to do this to me next."

He bit down softly on the scar.

Her head emptied.

She was reduced to nothing but sensation and a wave of overwhelming pleasure she hadn't even known was possible.

The feeling was violent. Demanding. Destructive.

She almost thought for a moment she was dying. But if this was death, she wanted to die a thousand times more, and she wanted Morgen to be the one to do it.

When she came back to awareness, she was panting against his shoulder, shivering with tiny aftershocks. For a split second, she had the urge to do exactly as he'd said, to bite him and taste his blood.

To *claim*.

"Do it," he rasped, his hand fisted in her curls, tugging just enough to make her feel it without hurting her.

"I shouldn't—"

I don't give a fuck about what we should or shouldn't be doing.

Even down the pathway, his voice was breathless. She straddled him and let herself graze her teeth along his heated skin, but still, she fought the growing need to mark him as he'd marked her.

You're not thinking straight.

He looked her straight in the eye, letting her see every raw emotion laid bare on his face when he replied in a place that was for them alone. *I never am around you.*

Maybe his words should have given her pause. They *were* a reminder that, though their marriage was a farce, the feelings between them were very real, even if neither of them liked to acknowledge it. What they were doing now wasn't just about her safety or even his political maneuvering, not anymore. Perhaps it never really was.

Before she even really knew she was moving, her teeth sank into his skin. Color and light exploded across her vision when she tasted his blood, fleeting images flashing before her eyes.

Two daggers. A familiar voice whispering, "Together?"

Drops of blood in a pool; a ceremony. "Great and terrible things lie ahead…" An orchard of trees and an angry roar.

A blaze.

Endless darkness.

Eyes of amber-gold and a child's echoing laugh—

Nya gasped, her eyes flying open. A knot tightened painfully in her chest, and she knew without explanation what had happened, could feel the beat of her heart forever syncing to his.

Her eyes widened, and she lifted her head to look at him, almost expecting horror on his face. "Morgen, what did I—"

He kissed her hard before she could ask what exactly she had just done, his lips moving feverishly against hers. When his tongue slipped into her mouth, she whimpered in the back of her throat, grinding against him without even realizing it. Everything about the moment felt feral and terrifying, uncontrolled in a way that should have been enough warning to both of them but only urged the frenzy on.

He bit her lip hard enough to draw blood the same moment he jerked his hips up. She gasped, and he muttered, "From now on, I'm the only one who gets to do that to you."

It took her a moment to make sense of his words, to realize he was referring to her habit of biting her lips when she was worried.

"I can't—help my bad habits." She pulled back, shaking her head, her breath shuddering. His lips were stained with both his blood and hers. "What just happened?"

His throat worked. He seemed to be having as hard a

time concentrating as she was. "Ana, the priestess who performed the ceremony, told me the blood binding would only work until the sun rose the next morning."

She nodded, her breath shallow as he traced his hands lightly up her sides, leaving goosebumps in the wake of the touch. She was fairly certain he didn't even realize he was doing it. "I remember."

"It seems that rule only applied if the ceremony was complete."

Her eyes dropped to the spot where she had just bitten him, the broken skin healed by the embers. But a scar remained, just like hers. The logical part of her wanted to be horrified; if she died, he would too now. But some other part, the same part that could still taste his blood on her tongue, only wanted to finish things. Complete the ceremony, then do it again, and again, and…

"Nya." Morgen touched her face, his voice still rough but quieter now. "I'm not upset. I didn't know that would happen, but it doesn't change anything."

She knew it didn't, that *none* of what had happened had really managed to change anything. It was eternally confusing. How could she both love him and hate him, all while wanting him more than anything? How could he threaten her, force her into a marriage, and then stare at her now like she was something sacred? Their entire relationship was a tangled mess of threads she could not separate, and she was drowning in feelings she couldn't make sense of. Sometimes, it felt useless to even try.

"Let's make sure it doesn't happen," she whispered. "You dying because someone goes after me, I mean."

It took him a moment to understand her weak attempt

at asking for more, for *everything*. But she saw it the second he realized what she meant; his pupils darkened again, spreading like storm clouds across the bright golden glow of his irises. He looked beautifully inhuman, and she thought she could finally see it now, the side of him that commanded so much respect and fear from others.

But she didn't fear him. She was fully aware that even as he looked like *this*, even as the energy of his magic crackled through the room, disturbing the torches, he would do anything she asked.

She almost started to speak—to say what, she did not know—but he cut her off gently with a shake of his head and leaned forward, eyes shutting as he brushed his nose against hers. The act felt intimate and soft, and she wanted to deny that those feelings belonged here, but she just couldn't anymore. They had far too much history between them for this to be nothing more than a necessity or even a way to find pleasure. Perhaps he was just quitting while he was ahead and accepting this for what it was. Maybe she should too.

"Lay back for me," he murmured, kissing down the curve of her jaw.

She leaned back onto the pillows, watching raptly as he tugged off his shirt and tossed it somewhere off the side of the bed. His torso and back were a mess of scars that had never fully faded, even with the embers. They were a map of the terror and abuse of his childhood, but beyond wanting to resurrect Kronos and kill him herself, none of it mattered to her. He was extraordinary and beautiful, every hard ridge of his muscles a testament to years spent training and years spent *surviving*.

He looped his fingers under the waistband of her bands and ordered softly, "Hips up."

She did as he said, biting her lip without thinking, and as soon as he had dragged everything away, leaving her completely bare, he *tsked* and nipped hard at her mouth, muttering, "What did I say?"

"I don't know," she said, voice breathy, her pulse fluttering in her neck.

He was distracted, cheeks flushed and eyes wild and dark. Still, he teased in a rough voice, "No?"

"No, I don't recall—"

He dipped his fingers into the mess already between her legs, and her hips bucked, a surprised moan echoing through the room. He swore under his breath, chest heaving.

"Are you always this wet for me, Nya?" he asked, and she couldn't tell if he was teasing or serious. His eyes shamelessly slid through the very center of her as he circled her clit. "Because every time I touch you, you're ready to be fucked."

He slid a finger inside her, and she fought to get the words out around the dizzying pleasure blurring her mind. "You—haven't touched me many times… *Oh.*"

"I'll have to make a habit of it then." He added another finger, still watching everything her body did. He curled his fingers inside her, groaning as she fluttered around him. "You're going to come again, aren't you?"

She didn't have it in her to reply, not as she did exactly that. He kept touching her the entire time, until she brushed away his hand and kissed him hard, whispering down the pathway, *I want you. All of you.*

He inhaled sharply against her mouth. *Bear with me here. We'll have to go slow.*

She couldn't help the smile that tugged at her lips. "I know," she whispered. "Don't worry. You can't possibly do worse than the first boy I was with. He lasted all of thirty seconds."

A low, almost animalistic sound rumbled from his chest, and he snarled, "Don't talk about that," then sucked at the mark on her throat, punctuating the sentiment.

She understood the possessive drive, as barbaric as it sounded. Perhaps it was made stronger by the bond, but the thought of anyone else touching him made her want to draw more blood.

"Show me then," she whispered, finding his wild eyes. "Show me you are mine and that I am no one's but yours."

He didn't waste a second after that, dragging his pants down and kicking them off before pushing into her with one, hard thrust. She was ready for him, but still, the feel of him, huge and pulsing inside her, had her gasping. His eyes widened, his hand grasping hers, pushing it into the mattress next to them. Slowly, tentatively, he started to move, both their breaths hitching as he hit an even deeper spot, her muscles spasming around him and sending delicious sparks of pleasure up her spine.

His head fell against her shoulder, and he shuddered, mumbling against her bare skin, "I want to fuck you forever."

She laughed, the sound broken as a moan clawed up her throat. When she managed to speak, she said, "You're just saying that because you've never been inside a woman before."

He dipped his head, kissing across her breasts then glancing up at her. "No. It's because it's you."

She stared at him and, for a moment, she was completely terrified. Not because of who he was, or his magic, but because she wasn't sure she could go back to the way things were even a few minutes ago, not after this. The problem was, she wasn't sure he even knew what he was doing. When he had come for her at the temple, she had immediately assumed all his words and actions had been intentional and calculated, but now…

Almost everyone who held power like his had motives for everything they did. Perhaps when it came to his campaign to reclaim the throne, he did, but for the first time since coming here, she really considered that the things he said to her in moments like this were just what he felt.

She wanted to believe that.

She *wished* she could, fully and without fear.

Instead, she kissed him hard, letting herself be lost in the feel of him moving inside her. He went slow but deep, whispering nonsense against her skin and paying attention to the angles that made her gasp and arch. But when she felt his muscles tense for the third time, she touched his cheek and whispered, "You don't need to stay in control anymore. You can trust me. Let go."

He took a ragged breath, nodding against her forehead and sliding one hand up her leg, lifting it and deepening the angle before fucking her so hard, the bed shook. It only lasted about a minute before he swore loudly and thrust his hips as he came, but that was all it took for her to come again too. She thought she might have screamed but couldn't tell if it was out loud or down the bond. As he pulsed inside her, he muttered a rough litany of curses and praises, half-aloud and half down the bond in broken intervals.

Eventually, they both stilled, and he pulled out of her, though he didn't let her go far, dragging her against his chest, breathing slowly, his lips pressed to the crown of her head. She closed her eyes, and the blurred edges of sleep began to drift in.

Just before she drifted off, Varax muttered grumpily down the bond, *So glad you two idiots finally stopped being so stubborn. But next time, do* try *to leave me out of it.*

Morgen laughed against Nya's temple, and she smiled hazily when he replied, *Apologies, Varax. But cut me some slack— it was my first time.*

She practically felt the dragon sigh. *And the world rejoiced.*

CHAPTER 19
TWO YEAR AND THREE MONTHS PRIOR

I tried to speak to Morgen's dragon today. She snapped at me, and the other rider's dragon, Veeron, told me Varax does not want my warnings. When I left, the boy with the hauntingly familiar eyes asked if I was alright. I tried not to stare too long at his face. If I seek interest in him, it could raise questions I should not yet attempt to answer.
—Ana, Priestess to the Usurper King, Arcadia

"WHAT KIND of dreams do you have?" Nya asked Morgen, her eyes on the clear blue sky above.

She could feel his eyes on her from where he was sitting against a large boulder. Her feet were in his lap despite his grumbling about getting dirt on his pants. She wasn't sure if he actually cared about that, or if he just didn't like her being this close. Sometimes, when their hands accidentally brushed, or they looked at each other a little too long, he would get standoffish and quiet. She'd started to teach herself not to take it personally. She knew he liked her, but he had made clear he was never going to let their friendship go *there*.

"I don't dream often."

She sighed. "Of course you do. You just don't remember them."

"Do you remember yours?"

"Not usually," she said quietly. "But I got nightmares quite often as a child."

"About?"

"No idea. Sometimes, I think I still get them, but all I ever remember when I wake up is Varax's eyes, and that's only occasionally. I assume she's just being nosy, but I don't know. I've never asked."

"Hm."

She sat up, smirking. "What? Does she not make special appearances in your dreams too?"

"Maybe she does. But like I said, I never remember."

She tilted her head, trying to make sense of his sudden shift in mood. He didn't seem angry or even really upset. There was just something off about the way he kept avoiding looking into her eyes.

"Are you okay?"

"Of course," he replied. Then, he surprised her by asking, "What do you know about your magic?"

She lifted a brow, taken aback. "Oh. Ah, not much. I can feel it, but I never use it, and I'm not even entirely sure how it manifests." She shrugged, chewing on her lip, a surge of odd anxiety twisting her stomach. "Probably like my mother's. Why?"

He nodded, though his brow was creased in what she thought might be concern, or even worry. "I was just curious."

"You're being weird."

"I am not."

She rolled her eyes, attempting to dissipate the tension. "Yes, you are. Do you think I can't tell?"

"You don't know me, Nya," he said, his voice uncharacteristically sharp. He wasn't looking at her, and she flinched when he added, "You may think you do, but you exist in a bubble. You don't even know yourself here."

She scooted away and scrambled to her feet. "If that's what you think…I should probably just go."

He shut his eyes, muttering something she didn't catch under his breath before he stood and faced her, finally looking her in the eye. "I crossed a line," he said, taking a deep breath. "I'm sorry."

"Did you mean it?"

"I shouldn't have said it like that."

Her jaw tightened, and she swallowed to banish the sudden tightness in her throat. "Fine."

She turned, stalking away, but he caught her wrist, and she whirled, hating that he saw the angry tears in her eyes.

"Nya, I didn't mean—"

"That I'm some sheltered child who you just indulge with visits when you escape what I'm sure you think is the 'real' world?" she snapped, hot tears cascading down her cheeks.

His fingers slid down her wrist, his touch light. But he didn't let go when he spoke, and she was so stupid and needy, she was willing to take anything from him, even upset like this.

"No. All I meant was that I think there are things about yourself you don't acknowledge, your magic being one of them."

"Perhaps," she whispered.

His fingers tightened slightly. "And I don't come here just to humor you. I probably shouldn't keep returning at all, but—"

"Varax insists, I know."

"No, Nya," he said quietly. He hesitated, and she swore she saw his jaw tremble before he steadied it. "Because *I* do. Varax is old and cranky and doesn't always want to make the journey. I never want to miss seeing you, though."

"Oh," she whispered, the tears threatening to return.

He let go of her, and she had to make a conscious effort not to grab his hand, to hoard his touch and beg for more.

He nodded stiffly. "You can go if you want. I just wanted to make sure you didn't spend the next few weeks assuming I thought so low of you."

"You won't be back for a while?"

He cleared his throat. "I'm not entirely sure how long. Before the end of the moon cycle, probably, but Varax will let you know."

"Alright."

She wanted to touch him, to hug him goodbye, to press her face to his chest and listen to his heart. But he didn't want those things, would never allow that closeness between them. So, she merely said, "Goodbye, Morgen," and began the trek home.

CHAPTER

TWENTY

*I once heard that when Nyx and Thanatos were married, the priestess
could actually see the threads of Fate tangled between them as she
mixed their blood. A fable, I had always thought, until today.*
—Ana, Priestess to the Usurper King, Arcadia

"Shh, Nya. Look, it's gone, it's gone…"

She was vaguely aware she was thrashing and crying
when she woke up, that Morgen was murmuring in her ear,
but his words didn't make any sense. What was gone? And
why was her skin so ice-cold when his was blazing warm?

She forced her eyes open, trying to make sense of it. The
room was dim, the torches burning low, and she had no idea
what time it was. It was nearly impossible to tell in the cave
system. When she touched her cheeks, she flinched. Her
tears had turned to shards of ice against her skin.

"Morgen?"

He was smoothing down her hair, tugging the blankets
tight around her, as if to ward off the strange, frigid chill.
"You're alright."

"What happened?"

He paused for too long. "You were dreaming."

"About what? You saw my dream the other night, the one about Carus. Did you see this one?"

"I don't...I don't think so."

She lifted her head. "What do you mean, you don't think so?"

He took a deep breath. "I mean—"

But he cut himself off as someone banged what sounded like metal against the stone just outside the room. She jolted, but Morgen shook his head and muttered, "It's only Carus," before slipping out of the bed and shrugging on a loose pair of pants.

Thankfully, she remembered she was completely naked before she accidentally flashed her newly realized brother, who was speaking in low tones to Morgen at the entryway. She heard Carus give a loud, exasperated sigh and mutter, "Of course I'm right. Just stay here."

Once he was gone and Morgen turned back to face her, she asked, "What was that about?"

Morgen grimaced, shifting back and forth on his feet. "He's going to have Imeria spread a rumor."

"Oh. I assume about what we..."

"Yes."

She cleared her throat. "Well, ah, that's good, since I'd really like to avoid any more attempts on my life."

He crossed back to the bed, his fingers brushing his neck over the exact spot where she'd drawn blood. "That's not going to be an issue again."

It took her a moment to realize exactly what he meant; that now, if someone tried to kill her, they would also be threatening his life. His soldiers might not trust her, but she was fairly certain most were loyal enough not to turn on him too.

"I suppose that's good."

He nodded, and she sat up, not realizing she had lost hold of the sheets until his eyes dipped down and darkened. She made to grab the sheets, but he stopped her, shaking his head.

"I should get dressed," she whispered.

He traced his fingertips down her collarbone, ghosting a light touch over her breasts. "Or not. Ever."

She was fairly sure he was trying to make a joke, but it didn't land. His pupil-spread eyes were too wide, rapt as they slid over her body, and when he took a breath, it was audible. She tried to push down the overwhelming ache already spreading like liquid heat across her body. It had been probably only a few hours, yet she wanted him inside her again.

Someone just outside the room spoke in a harsh whisper and then giggled. Nya stiffened, and Morgen shut his eyes and muttered, "Busybodies," before adding, louder this time, "I know you are well aware I can hear you!"

Nya pulled the sheet over herself as the voices faded along with quick footsteps. He shook his head before dropping his forehead to her shoulder.

"It appears Imeria took Carus' order to spread gossip to another level," he mumbled.

"Well, it'll probably work more efficiently. Pretty hard to dispute a rumor we had sex when multiple people obviously just saw me naked in your bed."

"Mmph," he grumbled.

She bit her lip then quickly stopped, remembering last night. If he saw, if he reminded her only *he* was supposed to do that. They would never leave this bed, and she needed to create some distance until she figured out how to make sense of what had happened between them—what she was *feeling*. Far too much, probably, given his recent betrayals and lies. Even if he'd had his reasons, she couldn't forgive him so quickly. Could she?

She wondered if he sensed the sudden tension in her body, because he lifted his head and sat back, eyeing her. "There's a few pieces of clean clothing that will fit you on top of the dresser."

She didn't ask why he had clothing for her even though she wanted to. She needed some distance to think. When he was this close, she went back to her old habit of forgetting and forgiving far too quickly.

She left the warm tangle of sheets and quickly dressed in the loose shirt and thick leather pants she found laid out. When she reached back to redo her braids, he was already behind her, brushing her hands away.

"Let me," he murmured.

She swallowed, her throat tight. "Alright."

Neither of them spoke, but each brush of his fingers against the back of her neck made her shiver, and she swore she felt his hands shake a few times. Last night had changed things; she supposed now, it was just a matter of acknowledging it. Neither of them were good at doing that, though, so perhaps they would exist in this new state of tension for another four years.

He stepped back before she had even realized he'd finished, and she turned, opening her mouth then shutting it before she could speak. Thankfully, he didn't notice, busy knotting half of his hair back and searching for a shirt. He had just located one when Carus burst into the room unannounced.

She jumped, and Morgen started to say, "Carus, we talked about barging in. You seemed to have it down earlier this morning, so I don't see—"

"Principals," Carus panted between heavy breaths. "Outside."

Morgen's expression immediately hardened, the mix of humor and irritation replaced by harsh resolve. "Who?" His voice was curt and demanding.

"Bella and Janis."

"Sol?"

Carus shook his head. "Not yet, but I'd bet the bastard is hanging around close by to fortify if need be."

"Understood," Morgen said shortly. "Two minutes."

Carus nodded once and promptly left the room, though Nya was certain he wasn't far. When Morgen turned back to her, she immediately said, "I'm not staying back."

"Nya—"

"No." Her voice brooked no argument. "This is about me too now, and I will not let you shove me somewhere for safe keeping every time there's danger."

To his credit, he only hesitated a few seconds before relenting. "Fine. But do not engage with them, Nya. I'm serious. The principals may appear human, but they've been alive for several millennia and are *very* good at manipulating people."

"I would never mistake them for human," she said, thinking back to Thanatos and Nyx.

Though both gods had exhibited genuine emotions and obviously cared for her mother, there was still an unmistakable ancient coldness to them. If that was what the principals were like when they loved someone, she didn't want to know how they appeared when angry. She supposed she was about to find out.

Morgen inhaled sharply. "Good."

It took him barely a minute to dress and attach more weapons than she could keep track of to his body with belts and harnesses—a variation of daggers, throwing knives, and even a dart she assumed contained some kind of poison, which he placed carefully in his breast pocket. When he was done, he approached her, brow creased in concentration as he knelt.

"Step up."

"What—" But then, she saw a weapons harness in his hands and shut her mouth.

He slid the leather belt up her body, then tugged the clasps tight. His mouth was set in a thin line as he stood then placed three small daggers in various pockets around her waist. He hardly looked at her as he stepped back and picked up a heavy sword leaning by the doorway.

"Are you ready?"

"Let's go," she said, her voice tight.

She followed him into the hallway, finding Carus bouncing on his heels. As soon as he saw her, he glanced sharply at Morgen. "She's coming with?"

"*She* is even more wrapped up in this mess than she was before because of you two, so yes," Nya snapped. "Where are our parents?"

Carus' nostrils flared. "You don't understand what we're walking into here, sweetheart."

"I asked you a question."

He narrowed his eyes. "They're meeting us in the mess hall."

She didn't bother to speak after that, and neither did he or Morgen. There wasn't time to argue about whether she followed them or not, and she knew it as well as they did.

When they arrived in the mess hall, it was eerily silent, despite being filled to the brink with armed soldiers, obviously on standby. Her parents lingered near the front of the crowd, her mother standing with her arms crossed against the cavern wall and her father mirroring her. She could tell they were speaking; the odd, silent twitches of their faces and the prolonged eye contact were easy tells, though she couldn't hear down their pathway at the moment.

"What are they doing?" Carus asked just before they reached them.

Her lips twitched, despite the situation. "Talking. They do this a lot, sometimes without realizing it. You'll get used to it eventually."

"Strange," Carus muttered.

She glanced sidelong at him. "Did you tell them what happened yesterday?"

He shook his head. "I figured I'd let you have that honor. Later, when we're not about to have this fun little confrontation."

"Right," she said, but her voice was barely more than a rasp.

Morgen approached her parents and asked curtly, "The dragons—are they ready?"

Her father nodded. "They're waiting with Varax."

"I don't know if it was worth them hiding," her mother said, brow raised. "Bella and Janis will likely sense them no matter what, and even if they didn't, Sol surely will."

"We don't know for certain he's nearby," Morgen replied, though he didn't sound so sure.

Her mother's expression darkened, and Nya's stomach dipped when she said, "He is. So is Nyx. I imagine she and Thanatos figured out what was happening rather quickly."

"Can we trust them?" Carus asked, gaze flicking between her parents. "Nyx and Thanatos, I mean?"

The ether in her mother's eyes was brightening. Seeing her like this, with a short sword at her hip and the ominous cloud of her magic pressing against Nya's senses, she remembered what her mother really was.

Not a prisoner nor a captive. Not even a woman. A *goddess*, and an heir at that. She usually hid her true nature well, letting the influence of the mortal body she had been reborn into trick the eyes of others, but she had never been mortal, just as Nya herself had never been.

"To back us against Sol, yes," her mother said. "As for the rest of it..." She glanced at Morgen. "I don't know where they stand, not yet. They withheld information. We'll have to see if their reasoning was made in an attempt to protect us, or if it was a betrayal."

"That will be a problem for later," Morgen said, voice low. "We need to go before they grow impatient and come knocking in a less pleasant way."

He strode ahead without a moment's more hesitation. Nya glanced at her parents. "Are you alright? Wasn't the last time you saw Sol...?"

Her mother's blue eyes were still silver-bright, but she did not look afraid. "The last time I saw Sol, he treated me like a disobedient child up until the moment I destroyed the throne room, blasted him on his ass, and killed his king. I imagine he is more nervous than I am right now."

Carus' brows rose, and Nya cleared her throat. "Right," she said.

They hurried after Morgen, and though her father looked a mix between on-edge and enraged, he still teased quietly, "Don't underestimate your mother, Nya. She's quite scary when she wants to be."

Nya gave a weak laugh, but it died in her throat when they stepped out onto the cliff, and she saw two figures standing at the edge.

The goddess, Bella, was tall and muscular, with an angular face and short, jet-black hair. A long sword was strapped to her back, and, unlike Morgen, she wore all her weapons in full sight. Fitting, Nya supposed, for a goddess of war. Janis, on the other hand, was dressed in loose blue robes, his dark hair a messy mop of waves atop his head. Where Bella looked agitated, he appeared almost bored, shifting on his feet and occasionally staring up at the sky. His nonchalance made Nya more nervous than anything.

"Are you two just going to stand there loitering, or did you come here to say something?" Carus called.

Bella snarled, the noise so feral, it was more animalistic than human. Janis put a hand on her arm, which she promptly slapped away, causing him to roll his eyes.

"Despite what you might believe, we're not here for a fight," Janis said dryly.

Nya felt a prickling sensation at the back of her neck, and she whirled as Janis' voice whispered directly in her ear, "We just want the girl."

Suddenly, he was everywhere, surrounding them with the same apathetic expression mirrored across each face. Morgen stepped in front of her, and Carus casually moved behind her, a hand resting on the pommel of his sword.

"Come now, you don't need to make such a fuss," all the Janises said with an innocent tilt of their heads. "Sol just wants to speak with her."

"Then he should stop being such a fucking coward and come talk," her father snapped, flames burning hot in one of his hands, a sword held in the other.

The Janises groaned in unison, hands rubbing at their temples. "My, my, you have *not* developed a sense of humor with time, have you, Vane? You know, I always found it odd you had absolutely none of your father's temperament. It's a shame. Vulcan can be so funny."

"I'm not sure what's funny about any of this," her mother said. Shadows crept from her, crawling towards each and every Janis, and Nya swore she saw the sword and half-moon mark flicker on her father's forehead.

The Janises watched the shadows warily and sobered a bit. "Ah, and Sora, I see you have not forgotten or forgiven."

"And I never will," her mother said in a deathly quiet voice.

"All of this talking," the Janises mused, his voice echoing around them. "But I haven't heard a peep from you, Nya Evva. You must know what an anomaly you are."

A bolt of crimson lightning narrowly missed one of

Janis' duplicates. "She doesn't need to talk to you, coward," Morgen growled.

The closest Janis looked directly into Nya's eyes. "No?" He smiled, and the cold, bemused expression he wore sent a shiver down her spine. "Have you even told her?"

"Told me what?" Nya asked, breath shallow with a sudden nervous anticipation.

Janis laughed softly. "That you, my dear, are the reason our world is slowly falling apart at its seams."

Nya shook her head, an immediate jerk reaction, even as she felt her face go cold. "No… That's because Kronos died and no one with embers took the throne."

Janis glanced at Morgen. "Ah, so that's what you told her. A small tip from someone who's been in love more times than the number of years you've lived—if your lover is about to unintentionally destroy the world, you should probably let them know." He paused, his gaze sweeping around and landing on Carus. "You knew, I think, based on your lack of confusion. But…" He snorted. "Sora and Vane, you had no idea. Did you truly think neither of your children would find themselves tangled in the threads? Are you so unaware of the hand you were dealt by Fate? It would not let you go so *easily*!"

Her mother was shaking her head, mouthing soundless words as she took a step back. Nya didn't even look at her father, didn't want to see the same horror play out on his face over something everyone but her seemed to understand.

But then, she heard him whisper hoarsely, "No… Her nightmares?"

Janis raised a brow, snorting softly. "It took you this long to understand?"

"Understand what?" Nya asked, her voice shaking. "What does this have to do with my dreams?"

Janis forms shimmered and morphed all into one more quickly than her eyes could track. He stepped directly in front of Morgen, completely ignoring the blade pointed at his throat.

"Before this world was born, there was a void. Nyx took form in the darkness, bringing with her Sol, who shed light upon the world she had created. We all followed, but Thanatos was the last to linger, because he understood what the void was. It was everything and nothing; death in its purest form, the very beginning and eventual end of this world's cycle. It would never go away, though as time passed, Thanatos alone could still see that place. Some of us even forgot it existed. I imagine he had to be very careful, for it held a particular temptation to him especially. But you, my dear, have never been careful."

Her eyes widened, and Janis nodded. "Yes, you have been there—many times, it seems—although we did not realize it was you until quite recently, thanks to your parents keeping you away from Arcadia. I imagine Sora could touch that darkness too, but she was always more of Nyx's daughter than Thanatos'. Besides, she will never see in the darkness like you can, not without your fire. Had Kronos' bastard not found you the night you reached just a little too far into the void, I daresay our world would be long gone by now. Instead, he sacrifices embers that will forever be lost to that darkness in order to keep you alive."

He glanced at Morgen and uttered words that would haunt Nya for the rest of her existence. "They are not yours to give, nor are they hers to destroy."

Nya took a step back, bumping into Carus, who was looking at her with a mix of wariness and pity. She shook her head, her field of vision closing in at the edges, fading and warping as her heart raced too fast.

Nya.

She couldn't breathe.

Oh gods…

The storms, the earthquakes, even the deadened valley around them—it was because of *her.* Morgen knew, had known all this time, and hadn't told her.

"No," she whispered. *No, no, no.*

She didn't ever use her magic, hardly even knew what it looked like. Except that wasn't true; she just never remembered. All the destruction she had once accused Morgen or even the principals themselves of was, in truth, a result of her reaching again and again for the void, threatening this world each time, all because she couldn't resist its call.

Nya.

That voice wasn't Morgen's…was it?

She was vaguely aware of voices shouting around her, some of them saying her name. There was a blast of heat and light, but all she felt was an empty, bitter cold. It would probably be best if she left now… Yes. Save them, at least for a few moments, before she failed to hold out again, and the darkness consumed them all.

"Morgen! The air—"

Someone grabbed her wrist as the air parted. An outstretched hand was trying to tear apart the threads of shimmering ether before the portal could complete, but it was too late. She dragged them along with her through it, and everything went dark.

Nya.

There was that voice again, calling for her in the empti-ness. She was supposed to resist it, but she couldn't remember why. It understood her loneliness when no one else could.

No one will see the truth of your soul without shying away, Nya. No one but me.

Cold tears froze on her cheeks. She smiled wide, a silent scream echoing around her as she welcomed its embrace.

When the void rose from the ashy earth in the center of the deadened valley and opened its eyes, it saw those wretched golden orbs staring back.

"Hello," said the god with hair like the deepest shade of blood.

It smiled, sighing softly. "You do know you can't win. Not anymore."

The god shrugged, and the void was reminded of the king before him, the one who had been born nameless all those millennia ago. It had dreamed of a balance when it imagined him, without realizing that dreams, once real, would take on a life of their own. That king had not deserved the name he had been gifted, nor the power, and now, he was gone, collected once more. His soul had hardly satiated it.

This one, however, would be exquisite to collect. Things had lined up nicely; the girl who had become the void was a perfect mix of bloodlines for this task, and the god she

would take Life from was powerful enough that his destruction would mean that of this world.

"What can I say?" the god said with a smirk that made
the void remember that old dream. "I like a challenge."

CHAPTER 21

MORGEN

Death calls to all of us, even gods. The strength of that call is just greater for some.
—Lady Anabeth, Royal Scribe's Apprentice, Royal Rider's Training Camp

MORGEN KNEW he was probably going to die today. The power of the nameless being who had taken Nya's mind wasn't comprehensible, and the chance of reaching her now was small. Not even the principals themselves understood it, not anymore. He doubted many of them, other than Thanatos, even remembered the true nature of the void they had been born from.

Nya's familiar brown eyes were gone, and not even the silver glow of ether permeated the depths of the onyx pools that now stared at him with such apathy.

They are coming, Morgen. You need to try and reach her, Varax urged.

He didn't take his eyes off Nya, not even as he heard

screams in the distance. There was no telling how far away they were; sound tended to echo in these mountains. *Is it Sol?*

Yes. Carus and his father are keeping the principals at bay with fire, along with the other dragons, but we will not be able to hold Sol back forever, especially not with Janis and Bella at his side.

What of Sora? And Thanatos and Nyx?

There was a pause, and Nya cocked her head in a jerking motion, as if she could hear Varax too, curious for the answer.

They are gone. I presume to find Nya.

The pathway went silent again, and Morgen didn't move as Nya laughed, an empty, cold sound that sent a shiver up his spine. When she spoke, her voice was nothing of the kind, stubborn woman he had come to care for. "Hello, Thanatos. And Nyx, it's been a while."

"What—" He heard Sora begin, but she stopped speaking abruptly. Morgen glanced back to see Thanatos' hand on her arm. He was pale as a corpse.

"Hm, *you* were always too careful," the void murmured, eyes on Sora. Its voice jerked and rose on random syllables, as if it had not quite mastered the art of human speech. "You know, I wanted you to do this, though I am glad I waited. The demi-god's fire made her much more well-suited for the task... Even you wouldn't have been able to see my stars without it."

"You want the embers, I presume?" Thanatos said, letting go of Sora and moving closer, though he didn't venture further than where Morgen stood.

Pure shadow crept towards them, flowing freely from Nya's hands. The magic didn't manifest translucent like

220

smoke, but rather like wisps of solid obsidian. She uncurled each finger slowly, and they became engulfed in the same fire Morgen had seen her hold close to her heart many times in dreams.

Nytfire, the lifeless light of dying stars.

"You've had your fun with this world," the void spat. "But I'm bored and hungry. Taking that one's embers over the years has whet my appetite, and I want the rest."

"You'll have to kill me first," Morgen said, fighting to keep his voice calm. He had to keep his head here. If he lost focus, he would lose her too. "And when that happens, her soul will follow. You won't have much time."

"Shame," the void breathed.

Morgen felt the earth begin to slip beneath his feet. The void didn't have the capacity for pause and would not hesitate to destroy what it desired to.

"Get back *now!*" he roared, ducking as a wave of nytfire burst from Nya's hands, exploding in a plume and then racing their way.

He yanked hard on the embers, taking all he could from the whisper of Sol's magic within them. When the nytfire reached them, he threw up a wall of light to dissipate it. Still, shards of the icy heat found their way through his barrier, slicing tiny cuts all over his skin. He ignored the sting, pushing back against the blaze with fire, now from Vulcan's magic.

Nya! he roared down the pathway. *Wake up.*

The void only pushed harder against the failing shield of fire and light, laughing. Morgen's breath was ragged, and he felt the wet warmth of blood dripping from his nose and ears as the pressure of his own magic built to a blinding agony. His body was still half-mortal, and it had limits the void, and even Nya, did not.

Please. Nya.

"Give up," the void whispered, its voice all around him, echoing in his head and pressing violently against his very thoughts.

Something integral inside him was beginning to tear. Perhaps it was the embers, perhaps it was his soul, but he had a feeling once it was ripped free, there was no going back. It probably should have frightened him more, but he had never feared death. Once, not so long ago, he had even longed for it.

That changed four years ago, when he had pulled a young woman, soaking wet and sputtering, from the undertow of a waterfall. If he died now, so would she, and he would let the world crumble before he stood by and let that happen. There was a reason he had never said anything all this time, why he had let the void take embers in her place. If the principals had known, she would have hunted and put down like a dog. They would have claimed they had no choice.

But Morgen had a choice, and he made it years ago.

Her.

He'd thought they were tied by Varax and the blood binding, but as his vision began to swim and pain lanced up his muscles as they gave out, he realized what he had failed to see.

One dragon did not bond to two riders. Heles and Thessilnn bonded with Vane and Sora with a circular thread of Fate, but Varax…

Varax never claimed Nya. The dragon had accepted her long before she saw her, long before Nya was even *born*. It had occurred the day the dragon found Morgen lying half-frozen in a creek bed in Arcadia. Binding his blood to Nya's had only brought to light what had always been true.

His breath caught, the pain so potent, he did not know how he was not screaming. He could feel the exact place where they were tied as it threatened to rip apart entirely.

Their soul.

Maybe Fate itself had done this, or perhaps this was an unintentional after-effect of his father binding Sora's soul to his own. It didn't matter now, not as Morgen fell to his knees, red filling his vision as he grabbed at every last piece of magic in the embers. Lightning flashed behind his closed eyelids as he tried one last time.

Nya.

The force of the nytfire increased, and he tried to speak aloud, only to cough violently. The thick, iron tang of blood filled his mouth, and he fell to his knees.

Morgen?

He inhaled raggedly and dug his fingers into the ashy soil. *Nya, I need you to come back. I can't hold on much longer.*

It's dark.

I know. Just follow my voice. It's going to be alright.

The blaze dimmed behind his eyelids, just slightly.

Morgen? Her voice was small and pained as she said his name again, and his gut clenched with fear, not for himself but for her.

He choked on more blood. *Right here. Just a little further, I promise.*

I'm afraid. It knows I'm trying to—

Agony lanced up his back, and a scream echoed across the valley, but the voice was not his.

All at once, the nytfire blaze disappeared into smoke, and he opened his eyes just in time to see Nya collapse, her scream still echoing down the pathway. He crawled across the ash-stained earth, ignoring the pain. When he reached her, she was curled up and trembling, tiny whimpers escaping her with each labored breath.

He was shaking just as hard, but he pulled her into his lap, pressing his lips to her brow. Her skin was so cold, and he willed the embers to heal him faster. He was too weak to do anything for her until his body repaired itself, and he hated it.

"Morgen," she rasped. "I almost... I—"

"I know," he murmured. "But you're alright. I came for you, just like I always do."

He could hear footsteps behind them. Nyx, Thanatos, and Sora stood a few paces away when he glanced back, holding up a trembling hand in a pitiful attempt to stop them. Nya was fading, and he could feel his own conscious-ness slipping too.

"I'm about to—pass out," he forced himself to say through gritted teeth. "Get... You need to make sure—"

His vision tilted, and when he came to again, he found Sora kneeling next to him and Nya, her wide blue eyes glassy.

He jerked, and she shook her head. "It's alright," she said softly. "You can trust me with her, Morgen. I'm one of the few people you can."

In a haze, he tried to nod, but instead, his head hit the

ashy earth. Just before he lost consciousness completely, he slurred, "You looked like a newborn star when you died. I could never get…the image out of my head."

The last thing he saw was a tear slip down Sora's cheek, imbued with sparkling silver.

TWENTY-TWO

Sora told me of him today, the man she meets with in secret. I have never seen her so happy, and I have never been more afraid. Perhaps I should try to stop her from going to him. Or, perhaps, it is already too late.

—Anabeth, demi-god daughter of Juno, goddess of Fate

NYA LAY wide awake in an unfamiliar room. She'd only realized she was in Nyx's house because she recognized the night blooming rose garden just outside the window behind her. She didn't bother trying to leave and had a creeping feeling the door was locked anyways. In the hall beyond, angry, hushed voices raised every few minutes until someone scolded them to be quiet.

Mostly, it was her father arguing with Thanatos and another male voice she was fairly certain was Vulcan's. Occasionally, Carus would interject, along with a feminine voice she recognized but could not place.

No one came into the room, but she tried to reach out to Morgen several times down the pathway.

He did not reply.

It had been several hours since she had woken here alone, and she was so terrified of facing the truth, she'd hardly moved. She had hazy memories of him pulling her close, his face covered in blood, his body shaking so hard, he'd barely been able to hold her. She couldn't quite remember exactly what had happened, beyond piecing together the basics from the argument outside.

The void had called to her, and again, as she had nearly every night of her life, she had answered. But this time, she had been awake and fully able to wield her magic. Morgen had been the only one able to stop her from letting the world fall into the hands of that endless darkness.

"It might be for the best," she could hear Vulcan saying for the third time in the hour. "We should at least try—"

"I am not letting you drug my daughter!" her father snapped, this time not managing to keep his voice quiet or level.

"Vane, it's for her own good. Just until—"

"Until when? Until you and the others figure out a way to take away her magic? Unfortunately for you, I'm not stupid enough to believe that's even possible, not without killing her."

"We've been over this. We won't hurt her, especially not with her tie to Morgen."

A silence fell. Then, her father spoke in a voice so low, she could barely hear it through the door. "Yes, of course. But tell me, both of you: if not for him, would you say the same? You need Morgen. I understand that. Just stop lying that you care about your granddaughter—tell me the truth:

you wouldn't hesitate to kill her yourself if doing so didn't kill Morgen and, in turn, destroy the embers."

Neither of the gods replied. Nya shut her eyes and buried her face in the stiff couch cushions, forbidding herself to cry.

Her father laughed coldly. "I thought so. You all pretend you understand what love is, that you're even capable of feeling it, but you only love others when it's convenient, even your own children."

Someone sighed loudly, and Thanatos said, "She's awake, by the way. Has been for a while, probably eavesdropping." His voice faded along with his footsteps as he added, "The walls of that room are thin. Sora often took 'naps' in there when we had council meetings at the house —at least, until we figured it out…"

There were more footsteps, a few low murmurs, and then the door opened, flooding the room with light. Nya hadn't realized there was a hearth in the corner, but flames roared to life within it as her father entered the room, shutting the door behind him quietly. She didn't sit up from the couch, hardly even looking at him as he sat on the edge of the armchair facing her.

"So, they want to sedate me." Her voice was hoarse and grating, and the back of her throat tasted like iron.

He scrubbed a hand over his face, blowing out a breath. "I'm not going to let that happen."

"Maybe you should."

"Nya…" He shook his head, looking at her with a crease to his brow.

"Maybe it's the best solution. Since they can't just kill me."

Silver flared bright in his eyes, and even as it dimmed, his voice was unyielding. "Don't even go there, alright? You are not some problem that needs to be fixed."

"The principals out there sure made it sound like it," she said. She felt emotionless, even as a cold tear slid down her cheek.

"Yes, well, fuck them," he said, but his voice caught. He rubbed his eyes, the gold band on his finger catching in the firelight. "I should have realized what was going on. I'm so sorry, Nya."

She looked away, curling her hands into fists. "I never told you or Mama. How could you have known?"

"Except you did. I knew you were having nightmares, and I just brushed it off. I should have known it was more." He sounded angry, but she knew even now, it wasn't directed at her. "I'm supposed to protect you. It's my one job, and I failed at it."

She pushed herself up and took a deep breath, trying and failing to keep her jaw from trembling. "Yes, well, I think if every father was able to keep their children out of trouble their entire lives, the world wouldn't be the way it is."

His smile was very sad. "I suppose you're right, but I still wish I could. If you have children someday, you'll understand."

She dropped her gaze, worrying her lip between her teeth. "Where is Morgen?" The question had been burning in her for hours now, simmering slowly into a festering fear the longer the pathway between them remained silent.

"Unconscious still."

Her stomach dropped. "Here?"

"Yes." He cleared his throat. "The others—the principals—were talking about taking him somewhere else, but Varax made quite the fuss about separating you two. Watching her argue with Heles and Thessilnn was like looking at three enormous cats get into a spat."

Despite everything, her mouth twitched. That *did* sound like Varax.

"Nya," he began. His expression was just shy of a grimace, and he looked uncomfortable enough that she knew exactly where this was going. "I know there's a lot happening right now, but—"

"I don't know," she blurted out. "You were going to ask about what's going on between me and Morgen, right?"

He cleared his throat again, leaning back. "Your mother vouches for him now."

Nya bit her lip, gaze dropping to her wringing hands. "I'm just…I'm confused. I knew him as one person all those years at home, and when I realized that was a lie, I hated him. But now, I'm realizing I might have been wrong. He was never two different people, not really. I'm just angry he withheld information."

"Do you think he had a reason for not telling you everything right away?"

She raised a brow. "Are you taking his side on this?"

"Not… No." He knotted back his hair, something he did sometimes when he was nervous. "But I do think that sometimes, telling someone the truth right away, just for the sake of being truthful, can often do more harm than good. Some truths need to be handled carefully, or instead of providing clarity, they have the potential to only cause more pain."

She met his eyes, his expression always gentle and kind for her. She wondered for a moment if her fervent tenacity towards caring for the few people she really loved came from her father too. Sometimes, she wished she could feel less ferociously; loving someone regardless of risk wasn't always the smartest or safest choice. But she thought of her conversion with him mere days ago, when she'd asked if he ever wished he hadn't met her mother, and how he had said he didn't, without a second of hesitation. To love as they did, in a world like this one, was a tragedy.

He would understand her next request, even if no one else did.

"I need to see him," she said firmly. When he hesitated, she felt a flash of power rise like fire in the back of her throat, and she added, "Say it, whatever it is."

To his credit, he didn't sugar coat it. "The principals kept you separate on purpose. They're worried for Morgen if you slip again."

"Oh, *now* they care?" She laughed coldly. "They always knew he was the only one with embers, so I don't see…" But she trailed off. "Or did they?"

Her father shook his head slowly. "It seems Sol kept some, just a small amount that he was somehow hoping to increase. I presume he fed the council lies that he was the reason the stability of the world had yet to digress."

"But they realized that's not true, didn't they?"

"I meant what I said in the hall, Nya." She opened her mouth to say she hadn't been listening, but he only gave her a pointed look and continued, "They tend to care about things only when it is convenient for them."

She cleared her throat to ease the tightness there. It felt like the circumstances of her life were constricting around her, and she was powerless to stop it. If the situation were reversed, she knew Morgen wouldn't let a few doors stand in his way, but maybe this was for the best. This way, she might actually be able to force herself to leave.

"I'm tired," she said, avoiding her father's eyes.

He paused, and she was sure he was going to push more about Morgen, but instead, he sighed. "Alright. Get some more rest; we're right outside the door."

He patted her cheek and stood, letting the fire die as he left. She waited a long while after that, for the voices in the hallway to quiet and for the darkness of night to deepen. Then, she quietly unlatched the window and slipped outside.

"You are a stupid, *stupid* bastard, and they are going to kill me for this."

Nya jerked, nearly tumbling off the cliff she was dangling her legs from. She had walked aimlessly for over an hour before finding the waterfall. It was much larger than the one in the forest at home in Mise, and she was sure the chances of surviving a fall would be slim.

"They won't kill you, and they won't kill me, so calm down."

Nya's breath caught, a mix of relief and apprehension turning her stomach. That was Morgen's voice.

"*Apparently*, they need you now, but they don't need me!

I'm just the reincarnation of some dead baby, and now, I'm going to be a dead—"

"Carus, calm the fuck down. You're giving me a headache."

"Sorry to break it to you, but I think your headache is just a result of all the bleeding you did out of your face. You can't blame me for that."

"Try me."

Their footsteps shuffled closer then stopped abruptly. She bit her lip when it started to wobble, tears threatening to spill over her cheeks.

"Nya." Morgen's voice was even, but she could detect the hint of alarm in it, in the brush of his magic stirring the air. "What are you doing?"

She didn't turn right away, forcing what she hoped was a composed expression before she twisted and found Morgen leaning slightly against Carus, who had an arm slung around his shoulders to support him.

"I really hope you didn't portal here," she said. Her voice was as flat as she suddenly felt, as if all the emotion had drained out. She was an open wound, but even the worst wounds stopped bleeding eventually. "Otherwise, I'm going to have to agree with Carus and call you stupid."

Carus let out an exasperated sigh. "I told you, Morgen." He shook his head, catching her eye. "I told him, but he would not listen."

"You shouldn't have let him."

Carus barked out a harsh laugh. "It was that, or let him attempt to kill everyone in that house when they tried to stop him."

She narrowed her eyes. "Does anyone else know I left?"

"Not yet," Carus muttered. "But they will soon, and they will not be happy!"

She ignored his outburst, glancing at Morgen. "You knew, though."

"Of course," Morgen said, voice impatient. His eyes kept darting to where her legs dangled, and she wondered if he knew just how dark her thoughts had turned. "For several reasons, which I will explain once you get off the cliff."

"As if I'm going to jump," she said bitterly.

His eyes grew hard. "Why? Because you don't want to, or because you know it will kill me too?" When she didn't bother replying, he paled, eyes so dull, they looked nearly black. "I thought so."

"It would be for the best, and I would do it if I could," she said in a hollow voice.

Carus' eyes widened, and he opened his mouth, but Morgen cut him off with a snarl. "Don't *ever* fucking say that again."

She didn't reply, staring at the churning water below, imagining how *easy* it would be. Easier for her to not have to feel this pain, easier for this world and especially for the council of principals. She did not actively want to die, but she was so tired of the burden of living.

"Nya," Morgen said, his voice much softer now, almost a plea. "Come away from the cliff."

She shut her eyes, digging her fingertips into the dirt below.

Breathe, he said down the pathway. *Just breathe. You're not alone in this, I promise.*

She opened her eyes, finding a pale white moth flitting through the air in front of her. It flapped its delicate wings and then disappeared behind her, toward Morgen and Carus, away from the cliff. A small thing of simple beauty, one of many tiny facets that made this world what it was. If she died, so would Morgen, and everything would be reduced to ash. She did not want that.

She wiped the tears from her eyes and scooted back, away from the edge. When she settled on the ground, picking at the small blades of grass beneath her, Carus eyed her warily.

Morgen ducked out of Carus' grip, his eyes on Nya as he said, "Be somewhere else for a while."

To his credit, Carus didn't hesitate, meandering towards the nearby patch of trees. Once he was out of sight, Morgen sat down next to her. She didn't look at him, not even as she whispered, "This is my fault. All of it."

He was silent for a long minute. Then, he said, "Maybe it is."

She turned her head in surprise. "So why are you here?"

He lifted a hand and brushed his fingers under her chin, tilting it so she had no choice but to look directly at him. "Lots of reasons."

"Care to explain this time?"

He didn't balk at the bite in her tone. He just stroked his thumb up her cheek and said, "Because if it's your fault, it's mine too."

"That's not—"

"Because Carus wasn't lying—I would have done anything to reach you now. Having a bunch of dead principals on my hands would definitely not help my cause."

"Which you need to return to. There are lots of people counting on you—"

"*And* because if you're going to throw in the towel and decide you're done with it, I'd prefer to be there with you than die alone in some stuffy room."

Her breath caught, and she shook her head. "I wouldn't have actually done it. The world might be better without me, but it needs you."

"Screw the world."

"You don't mean that."

He looked towards the cliff, slowly slipping his hand from her face. "I do. I've always known what the embers meant, and once Kronos was gone, I understood what would happen if I wasn't here to carry them. That doesn't mean there weren't a few times I considered…not caring."

Her eyes widened. "Morgen," she whispered when she realized what he was insinuating.

"So, if you're feeling selfish right now, imagine how I felt when Imeria or Carus, or even Varax, had to pull *me* away from some cliff edge, or even from the bottom of some creek bed. Highly unpleasant, not to mention demoralizing, especially when your body pretty much refuses to die no matter what you do." His lips twitched in a sad smile. "But alas, the world needs me, even if it has never loved me."

She almost said the words, but whereas before, when she'd hated and feared what she felt for him, now, her love just felt selfish, a chain he would never be able to detach himself from. Perhaps never saying it aloud would at least make the shackles of their connection less heavy.

"Thanatos and Vulcan suggested drugging me." She laughed, the sound a little hysterical. "I have no idea with what, or if it would even make a difference. Maybe I should take them up on it. I'm sure whatever they have growing in Arcadia is stronger than gardroot."

Morgen frowned, his nostrils flaring. "Did they happen to mention how long they planned to keep you drugged?"

She had the distinct feeling the question was more rhetorical, because he already knew the answer as well as she did. Even still, she muttered, "Probably forever."

She laughed again, tipping her head back to stare at the dawn-hued sky. She was vaguely aware she was unraveling a bit, especially when she rambled on, "Do you think they'd wake me up so I could pop out a few heirs for you? Or do you think they would enlist someone else? I bet Imeria is interested, which is probably for the best, given my magic. I'm sure they don't want a repeat problem."

When he didn't respond, she lowered her gaze from above and found Morgen staring at her with something akin to horror on his face.

"What?" she whispered. "All the principals need heirs. It's not that far-fetched to think they'd go to horrible lengths to get one."

His throat worked, the scar pulling taut against his worryingly pale skin. "They can kill me and find a new king if they want that. I am *never* fathering children."

She blinked a few times, taken aback. Someone else might automatically assume he meant children with her specifically, but she knew enough about him that it took all of a few seconds for her to understand why he felt the way he did.

His mother. All the women before and after her who had died because Kronos had impregnated them and their bodies could not withstand the embers the unborn child

within them held. He thought that would happen if he…
To *her.*

"Does it work like that?" she asked quietly. "Since you're only a demi-god?"

"I'm not finding out." He took a ragged breath. "All those women he brought into the palace wasted away within weeks, and they died writhing in pain and begging. And he *enjoyed* it, just like he loved telling me how he had to chain my mother up to keep her from trying to cut me out of her belly because she knew what would happen to her if I was born."

His eyes were so dull, he looked nearly mortal for a moment, until a tear slid down his cheek, clearly imbued with silver ether. Clearing his throat, he swiped it away quickly.

"I would never risk that. Not with anyone, and especially not with you."

They both fell quiet, the roaring of the waterfall below a constant in the background as dawn bled into morning. Now that it wasn't dark, she could see the wide expanse of the lush field she had trudged through, dotted with wild-flowers and long grasses. Birds called to each other in the forest Carus had walked into, a mix of pine and spindly trees with trunks of peeling white bark.

Life.

Morgen was right. Having children would be a mistake, especially knowing what kind of magic she could pass on. Still, some long-buried part of her quietly mourned the death of the idea. It would be a lie to say she had never glanced over at him during those hazy afternoons in Mise and wondered if their children would have his eyes or hers,

238

or if they would be tall or short. Not that it mattered anymore.

Nothing mattered, except finding a way to break their connection and save him and everyone else.

"I know what you're thinking," he said.

She was sure he did, and not even because her thoughts had been ferried down the pathway. He knew her too well.

"Even if we managed to find a way to break the blood binding—which, by the way, is impossible—it wouldn't change anything."

"I could ask the principals," she pushed. "There might be a way. Maybe Thanatos knows—"

"*Nya.*" His eyes were wide and intent. "It wouldn't change anything."

She had the distinct feeling he wanted her to know what he meant without him saying it.

Think about it.

She bit her lip, and his eyes briefly dropped to her mouth. *I don't understand.*

Varax chose me as her rider, but she never actively chose you. She just accepted you, remember? I pulled you from the waterfall, and she didn't even need to look at you.

Nya furrowed her brow. *Are you saying I'm* not *her rider?*

No, not at all—

"Fates, there are two sets of you now," Carus said, and they both jumped. "It's unnerving enough to watch Sora and Vane do the silent talking thing, but Morgen, the embers flare every time I assume it's your turn. It's creepy."

Morgen shut his eyes, sighing sharply. "What do you need, Carus?"

He snorted. "Perhaps to get back before they think we

kidnapped Nya and Vulcan sends a fleet of Vemon dragons our way. But mostly, it's just cold, and I'm bored."

Morgen glared at him, but Nya wondered silently how Carus managed to be so flippant and droll, even with everything that had happened to him. He was younger than her and had endured more, and yet he still seemed to have a less pessimistic outlook on the world. Then again, Carus had not been targeted by a nameless creature of darkness.

She discarded the thoughts for now and glanced at Morgen. "Are you even well enough to create a portal right now?"

He hesitated. "Ah…most likely."

"Good enough," Carus grumbled, striding closer to where they still sat on the ground.

"Are you sure?" she pushed, standing and offering him a hand.

Morgen took it but let go quickly. He didn't reply, evidently confident he was ready to or convinced enough by Carus' whining that he didn't want to argue, because the air began to shimmer in front of his outstretched hand. It shook as the portal turned silver, and his tan complexion turned pale.

"Morgen—"

He cut her off, speaking through gritted teeth. "Just go through."

She wasn't exactly keen on returning yet, but she was also sure if she didn't listen, Morgen probably wouldn't have the energy to draw up another portal. Carus was likely also right about the reaction of the principals and her parents to the three of them suddenly missing.

She stepped through, followed by Carus, and the folded

pocket of space choked the air from her lungs for a brief handful of seconds. When she emerged on the other side, she was standing in the middle of a flower bed in Nyx's garden. Morgen flickered into existence next to her half a second later and fell to his knees before either she or Carus could catch him. Her chest constricted painfully, and her vision blacked out. Then, just like last time this had happened, the agony disappeared as if it had never been there at all.

"None of these flowers are blooming," he muttered, his words already beginning to slur. "What is the fucking point of the garden?"

"Shit," Carus said under his breath. "He's magic drunk."

"Yes, thanks to you," Nya snapped just as the back door opened. "We should have waited longer."

A figure appeared in the doorway, and at first glance, she thought it was her father. Quickly, she realized he was a few inches too tall, and his eyes were a slightly different shape.

Vulcan.

"They're back!" the god of fire called into the house.

She allowed the shock of seeing her grandfather for the first time register for only a few short moments before kneeling next to Morgen.

"Nya," he groaned, shaking his head. "I was trying to tell you, and it was important, but now…" His head fell to her shoulder. "My head is so fuzzy."

"Hush," she murmured, threading her fingers through his hair. Thanatos and Nyx hurried out, followed by her parents, and then Juno and another woman who she realized had to be Anabeth. She pulled him close, a hum just beneath her skin as her magic rose instinctively to protect him. "You just need to sleep this off."

"I can't sleep," he said, voice muffled against her shirt. "What if it comes back and I didn't tell you?"

She had no idea what he was talking about and couldn't tell if it was nonsense or something genuinely important. If it was the latter, now probably wasn't the time anyways.

"It's all right," she told him, and he made a low noise, the vibration of it buzzing against her chest.

Vulcan stepped forward. "What's wrong with him?"

"Magic drunk," Carus replied. His expression was tight, but still, he laughed dryly, dragging a hand over his face. "Very magic drunk, by the looks of it." Apparently, this was a phenomenon unique to Morgen, because they all stared at him blankly. "When he uses too much magic, usually when he portals too far or twice without pause, the mortal part of him begins to die with the strain. The embers react and flood his system with way too much magic, making him all loopy."

A long moment of silence followed, broken only when Morgen lifted his head and whispered loudly, "Nya, why are they all looking at us?"

Vulcan snorted. "Fates, he really is drunk."

"Wasted," Nya's father said, rubbing at his temple as Morgen started to monologue about how useless the garden was.

Her mother glanced at Anabeth, her expression wary and a little cold. "Do you know anything about this? You spent time with him after you abandoned Cion."

Anabeth pressed her lips together. She no longer wore the robes of a priestess, instead donning a blue wrap dress.

She looked younger, standing next to all the others, and Nya almost felt bad for her when she replied in a quiet voice, "I told you, I did not abandon her. She practically begged me to investigate when rumors of Morgen started to float over the border. You know I never wanted to come back here, same as you."

"That's not what she asked you," Nya's father said, his tone flat. "Have you ever seen this happen before?"

Anabeth frowned at him, some unspoken hurt in her eyes as he glared at her. Anabeth had hinted during the marriage ceremony that she had been friends with her parents, who weren't necessarily being hostile now, but who weren't acting as her friends. Nya assumed it had to do with Anabeth assisting Morgen, though her mother *had* referenced that she'd 'left Cion.' Could she really mean Aren's elderly queen? Had she and Anabeth been friends, or even lovers?

The questions promptly left her mind when Anabeth said, "It might be best if you keep your distance right now, Nya. You're both weakened, and he has no way to defend himself if you—"

"No, no, no." Morgen cut the demi-god off, laughing. "No... *You* are not giving me advice anymore, cryptic lady. You told me to do this." He slid his fingers over the scar at Nya's throat, and she had to bite back an entirely inappropriate noise for the current situation. "Bad, bad advice, even if I liked it. Now all our colors are even brighter, and when she's gone for too long, it hurts my head."

Anabeth sighed, evidently understanding exactly what his ranting referred to. "I did not explicitly tell you to do anything. It was merely a suggestion, and I warned you it would likely make your preexisting connection to Nya even more elevated."

"What do you mean by that?" Carus asked, brow furrowed. "What preexisting connection?"

"Their soul," Anabeth said, as casually as if she were talking about the weather. "They share it. It's why Varax claimed them both as riders."

Nya froze, and it took her only a few short moments to realize everyone besides her and Carus were already aware of what Anabeth had just revealed. She found her mother's gaze, hardly able to speak, half-mouthing, half-speaking to her down the pathway, "*How do you all know?*"

"Anabeth told us when you were sleeping," her mother said gently. "None of us knew before that, Nya. I swear it."

With his head still buried in her shoulder, Morgen snorted softly and mumbled, "Bad Morgen, I know. Probably should have mentioned it before, but please don't be mad."

Suddenly, everything Morgen had been saying mere minutes ago by the waterfall made complete sense.

Many things made sense now.

Their immediate connection when they had first met, his ability to reach her in her dreams, Varax, even the discomfort she used to feel in her chest when they went too long between meetings… It was because a part of them had been and always would be the same.

"I can explain it, if you wish," Anabeth said, as if she were merely offering to tell Nya why the seasons changed or what made the trees green.

"No," she said, her arms tightening around Morgen. "Not now. He needs to sleep this off."

Carus glanced at her when Juno nodded but said firmly, "Away from you."

"Good luck with that one," Carus muttered at the same moment her father chuckled and said, "I'd like to see you try to make that happen."

Nya saw them look at each other for a brief handful of seconds, Carus offering him a wry smirk. She let herself feel the fleeting burst of joy, watching her father's eyes light up at the interaction, before she said, "They're right. I'm not leaving him when he's like this."

"Nya, you don't understand—" Nyx began, but then Thanatos cut in, surprising Nya, and apparently everyone else too.

"She understands the risk more than any of us can. Just get the poor boy to a bed before he crushes more of the roses."

Juno looked like she was about to argue, but then Morgen slurred, "Any of you *assholes* try to put your hands on my wife..." He shook his head, grinning at Carus. "No more spines."

Carus nodded, offering him a hand. "That's right, no more spines. Wouldn't be the first time."

"Nope," Morgen sighed, letting Carus help her drag him to his feet. "Carus, there is *so* much magic in my head. More than the last time, right?"

"Does this happen often?" her mother asked, obviously fighting a smile.

Carus shook his head and muttered to Nya, "Try to get him to lean most of his weight on me, sweetheart. It'll make this easier. You're far too short to carry the big bastard."

She didn't argue. Her head was beginning to spin with

the overwhelm of the last three days. Still, just before she and Carus dragged Morgen into the house, she glanced back and made herself ask, "Do we need to worry about Sol?"

Thanatos shook his head. "Not yet. This house is heavily warded against him and has been for a long, long time. We have at least a few days."

Nya had little idea of what a ward even was, beyond being a protective barrier, but she took him for his word for now.

It's a biiiiig portal, but it's only open one way.

She glanced at Morgen to find his eyes half-lidded but focused squarely on her. Carus grunted and all but carried him down the hall, muttering, "Make doe-eyes at your wife later, preferably not when I'm around."

Morgen muttered something incoherent and then grunted as she and Carus managed to drop him on a large couch in one of the endless sitting rooms.

Carus swept a scanning gaze around the room. A general combing the space for danger, she supposed. "I can stay if you want?" he said.

She shook her head. "I've got it. And if I... Well, if anything is wrong, I'll make sure Varax knows to alert Thessilnn and Heles. She'll be aware if there's a change."

"Alright," Carus said, his expression tightening slightly. Still, he trusted her enough to head for the door, only stopping when she called his name.

"Back at the waterfall," she began when he turned. "He mentioned there were times he tried to..." She trailed off, not sure if she could make herself say it aloud.

Carus understood, though, nodding curtly. "He can't kill

himself, Nya. Not with the embers. I'm glad for it, because if he could, he'd already be dead."

The blood drained from her face, hearing Carus confirm it. "Right," she managed to say.

He left without another word, and she curled up next to Morgen, counting, recalling facts about dragons, reciting poetry, making lists of herbal plants used for healing…

Anything to keep her awake and out of that place.

CHAPTER

TWENTY-THREE

This morning, Kronos' guards dragged us to the border, our hands bound and our mouths gagged. Kronos didn't even let Vane wash off Sora's blood. He kept looking at it, dried on his clothes and hands, as if he couldn't quite believe it was there. He would be dead from his wounds if he were mortal, and I couldn't stop thinking how that would be a mercy. The mortal king of Aren owns us now. My brother, June, found me before Kronos sealed the border to Arcadia, vowing to stay by my side. It's a small comfort.
—Anabeth, D'anna

WELL AFTER SUNSET, Morgen finally stirred, restlessly murmuring Nya's name. She was propped up on the couch behind him, his head in her lap. She touched his face carefully and asked, "How are you feeling?"

He groaned softly, tugging her down. "Why were you sitting up?" he asked in a sleep-roughened voice. He sounded mostly lucid again.

"Should I not be?"

He blinked a few times, obviously trying to get a sense of

his surroundings. She had surmised the small room they were in was off the back of the house, lit only by dim gas lamps that had begun to glow of their own accord just as dusk set in.

"It's nighttime, isn't it?"

She nodded against the pillow he had practically shoved her against. "You needed to sleep. You used too much magic portaling us back."

"Mm, 'figured it would happen. You need to sleep too. I can tell you're tired."

She said nothing, fairly certain he drifted off again until he sighed against the hollow of her throat. "You're staying awake on purpose, aren't you?"

"It was safer that way. You were…very much not yourself."

He made a discontented noise then he slid his tongue over the scar at her throat, nearly causing her to cry out. She stopped herself at the last minute, but he did it again, and a soft moan escaped her lips before she managed to ask, "Are you still magic drunk?"

"No," he replied. "Just a bit tired."

"Then why are you—*Oh.*"

He sucked against the scar, and at the same moment, he cupped her breast under the loose tunic she wore. Her back arched, and, on instinct, she reached for him, clutching at his shirt.

"I'm trying to help you sleep," said in her ear, circling her nipple with his finger. A maddening ache began to pool at her center, slowly, and then all at once as he pinched the puckered flesh lightly between his fingers.

"I can't sleep," she gasped. "It's not…not safe."

He nipped at her lower lip. "Hush."

She whimpered, the sound dragging itself up at the back of her throat when he slid his hand between them, pressing firmly against her throbbing core.

"Is that what you want?" he breathed against her mouth.

She shook her head slightly, and he paused and started to move away, misunderstanding her. She caught his hand and whispered, "No, I mean I need *you*."

In the dark, his eyes met hers, the embers ebbing faintly in his irises. "We're not alone here," he said, and she opened her mouth to say she didn't care, but then he added, "I'm going to need you to be quiet. If you think you can't, bite my shoulder. Understood?"

She nodded, and he parted her lips with his fingers, his gaze dropping to her mouth. "Good."

"I want to do something first, though, okay?" she whispered, guiding him up so he sat with his back against the couch cushions. "Something you're going to need to stay quiet for too."

His nostrils flared as she moved onto her knees. "Nya, you don't need to—"

"Believe it or not, I want to," she said, brushing her nose against the indent where his hips met his pelvis. "Unless you don't?"

He shivered, lifting her chin so she met his eyes, shining in the dim light "Not too fast, alright?"

Her lips curved as she palmed his erection through his pants. "I'll try to go easy on you," she said in a low voice.

His head fell back, throat working. "*Fuck*, I'm serious, Nya. I don't want to—"

But the rest of the words were lost as she undid the clasp of his pants and loosed his cock, wrapping her fingers around the thick base and pumping a few times. She had only ever done this once and was sure it hadn't been good. But with him, everything felt right, every motion driven by some innate, primal instinct within her.

She darted her tongue over the tip where it dripped salty precum, and his cock twitched in her hand. When she wrapped her lips around him and started to suck, he fisted a hand in her hair, a low moan escaping him.

She glanced up, releasing his cock with a soft pop. "I thought we agreed on being quiet."

He stared at her, wide-eyed and chest heaving. Then, without another word, he tugged her into his lap, kissing her fiercely. She slid her hands beneath his untucked shirt, moaning as she felt every time his muscles flexed and twitched beneath her touch. He hooked his fingers under the waistband of her pants, tugging.

"Off," he moaned, hardly breaking the kiss.

She slid her nails over his abdomen with just enough pressure to make him hiss. She pulled back momentarily and tugged the pants down. The fabric got caught around her ankles, and as she struggled with untangling herself, he slid his fingers between her legs. She gasped softly and dropped her head against the pillow when she couldn't hold back her moan. He tugged her pants, managing what she apparently couldn't when he freed them from her ankles, all while still keeping a slow, steady rhythm against her clit with his other hand.

"Nya, look at me," he said gruffly.

She shook her head, face still pressed against the pillow. "I can't…can't stay quiet."

"I know. But I'd rather you bite me than the pillow."

A shiver raced up her spine. She was already *so* close. It was dizzying, the notion he could wring an orgasm out of her in less than a minute. She dragged herself off the pillow, pushing away his hand even as the unresolved ache at the loss of his touch made her want to scream. His brow creased in confusion, though only for a moment. He gasped as she positioned herself over his cock and slowly joined their bodies.

"Now you can touch me again," she managed to say between heaving pants.

He did, and she drew blood at his shoulder by the time she came. His eyes were closed, muscles completely tense, when she found her surroundings again.

Gently, she touched his cheek and whispered, "Morgen?"

He exhaled slow. "One moment."

"You know you don't have to do this, right? I'm honestly impressed you haven't come yet, and I don't need you to keep holding out. I *want* you to come."

His jaw tightened beneath her fingertips. "I know, but I really didn't trust my ability to pull out when you were coming around me." He opened his eyes. "Which I should. I should have the first time too, I just… I was being stupid."

For some reason she didn't fully understand, her stomach sank a little. Which made no sense. She didn't want a child any more than he did, and even if she *did*, now was most definitely not the time.

He smiled sadly at her expression and brushed the tip of

his nose to hers. "I know…I know. It's okay. That feeling you have right now, it's just the embers. Life trying to make life."

"How did you know?" she whispered, shutting her eyes.

He kissed her again, slower this time, and the world grew hazy. "Because I feel it too, *oíche rionn*. Fates know I'll always wonder what that would be like with you, Nya, and not just because of the embers."

Her breath hitched. He had not called her that in so long.

She ignored the tears when they started to run down her cheeks at the unfairness of it all. Neither of them had asked to be what they were; choice didn't exist when you inherited power like theirs, not in Arcadia.

But, for once in her life, she *chose*. She let herself fall fully into Morgen and finally gave herself permission to love him without stipulations or shame.

"Nya, I—"

"Shh." She kissed him softly, moving her hips in a slow, steady rhythm. "I know."

He lifted her abruptly, panting against her mouth as he came.

She didn't say it, and she didn't let him either, even though she knew they both felt it clearly within every touch, saw it reflected in each other's eyes. Telling him felt too final, and she had a terrible feeling stirring somewhere in the back of her mind that it *would* be.

So, they pretended it wasn't important. They didn't talk about their shared soul, or the impending doom of the void, or the fact that Sol was assuredly breathing down their necks. She just held him until he was asleep and began to silently recite her histories and poems and lists.

CHAPTER
TWENTY-FOUR

Sometimes, I feel like a chess piece. My friends and I have suffered so much because of the fickle nature of gods greater than us. It pains me to watch the child from my dreams take on such a burden. And to my surprise, I feel sorrow for Kronos' son too. He cares for her, more than he will likely ever have the luxury of telling her. They have inherited the inevitable doom of their bloodlines.
—Ana, Priestess to the Usurper King, Arcadia

JUNO WAS STARING AT HER, had been the entire morning. Nya tried to ignore her, but her ability to put on a brave face and pretend she was fine had been worn down from her lack of any sleep the last two nights.

Yesterday, nothing had happened, not unless she could count watching Nyx walking on tiptoes around her parents or Heles landing in the garden with an entire goat hanging from her mouth.

Morgen and Carus were growing more and more on edge as the hours passed. They had left behind an entire army in the Gods' Aisle, but each time they brought it up to any of the principals, the gods insisted it was unsafe to leave the house. The one saving grace was that Nya was pretty sure Carus and her father were cooking up a plan to allow for some kind of escape. She didn't ask them or Morgen about it, though. She was simply too tired, and as the day dragged on, it began to feel like she hadn't slept in two *weeks.*

It was why, as Juno stared at her with narrowed eyes for the third time that hour, she snapped harshly, "What?" at the Goddess of Fate.

Juno's brow rose, but to her credit, all she said was, "Something is wearing thin in you, Nya. I am simply trying to figure out what it is."

From the corner table where he stood behind Carus and her father, Morgen turned his head, and Nya was grateful he was the one who asked in a sharp voice, "Care to explain what you mean, Juno?" because she didn't have the energy.

Juno tilted her head. "I'm surprised you don't know what I'm referring to."

He took a single step closer to her, eyes narrowed. "I'm surprised it took *you* this long to notice."

Juno fell silent but went back to staring, this time at him. Thanatos and Nyx spoke in low tones by the hearth, Anabeth making stilted conversation with her mother, and Nya just...couldn't. The air was so tense, she felt like she hadn't been able to breathe in days. No one was speaking their minds, and everyone was whispering.

She stood abruptly. "I need some air." Her parents exchanged a look, and she added, "Alone. It's fine; I'll just be in the garden."

She could feel the weight of Morgen's gaze as she

headed for the hallway and the back door, but he didn't follow her.

Nya.

She took a sharp breath, hurrying into the garden. *I'll be back. I just need a second—*

Her steps faltered when she rounded the corner of the house and saw a man standing there, observing the flowerbed she, Carus, and Morgen had crashed into a few days ago. He had dark skin and light hair just shy of golden. Though he was tall, he was more willowy than broad, and his eyes…

He had the same eyes as her mother.

"Hello, Nya," the god said in a deep, well-mannered voice. "I don't believe we've ever had the pleasure of meeting."

They hadn't, but she knew exactly who he was.

"Sol," she whispered, echoing the name in her thoughts and sending it down the pathway.

His eyes flickered, ether mixing with a brief hint of gleaming gold light, perhaps the handful of embers he had kept for himself.

"You look quite like Sora," he said, tilting his head to the side. "Not your eyes, though. Those are most definitely from Vulcan's bloodline. Not that there's much to be seen for it. Shame he devoted himself so fully to a mortal, he never produced any other offspring."

"Shame indeed," she said quietly, "that a few of the principals actually figured out how to be loyal to the people they care for. I might even call it love."

Sol chuckled dryly, taking a step closer to her. "They may think so, yes, but here is the truth none of them want to admit: we are not capable of such a thing, nor should we be. We are the results of power and obsession, and we seek those things above all else. Why do you think the void calls to you so?"

She retreated, and he glanced briefly behind her. "Because you, my dear, will never be the carefree mortal girl your parents so wished you to be. You are just like the rest of us, the principals you blame for the misfortune of your bloodline. But unlike us, you do not have the luxury of understanding what calls to you." He leaned in, and she stiffened. "That is a problem, Nya," he whispered in her ear.

The back door slammed open, and Sol grabbed her arm roughly, a hand outstretched in front of him.

"Sol, no!" Nyx shouted.

Sol smirked, and Nya tried to twist out of his hold as he mused, "Sorry, little sister, but you knew it had to be done. I simply possessed the backbone none of you did to do it."

The portal formed, but even as he dragged her through it, Morgen bellowed down the pathway, his voice echoed by Varax's shrill roar. The garden disappeared, and a searing pain blinded Nya, tearing the air from her lungs and pressing a suffocating pressure against her chest.

Seconds later, the portal closed behind them, and Nya found herself surrounded by the familiar craggy peaks of the Gods' Aisle. Sol shoved her down onto the ashy earth, and she coughed violently, spitting out bright red blood. The pain was only getting worse. She could hardly breathe, gritting her teeth against the scream building in her throat.

"Interesting," Sol said, crouching and looking at her with something like mild irritation. "It's been a long time since I've been around someone stupid enough to bind their blood to their betrothed. I forgot about the matter of distance, though I don't recall the discomfort usually being this severe."

Her vision tilted, and she shut her eyes as her stomach roiled, as she tried to breathe through the pain and focus. There was a faint noise coming from... Where was it coming from?

"Up!" Sol barked, tapping her with his foot.

The noise... It was a voice. She was sure of it now.

Nya... Nya, please.... Where, where, where—

A foreign pain lanced up her back, but she forced herself to focus enough to say two words.

Gods' Aisle.

The voice faded after that, and Sol dragged her by her hair up a steep slope into a shallow cave, dimly lit with torches. As soon as they were inside, Sol restrained her with heavy chains hammered into the stone itself. There were four figures she could see in the cave, two of whom she recognized.

Bella and *Imeria.* But...why? Why would she betray Morgen like this?

"Took you long enough," Bella grumbled, picking at her nails.

"Patience is an attractive quality, you know," Sol said lightly. "Though, regretfully, one you have never mastered."

Bella rolled her eyes. "Oh, now you've really insulted me." Her gaze landed on Nya, and she snorted. "So that's what happens when you mix Nyx and Vulcan's bloodlines. Always wondered, but they're both such prudes when it comes to reproducing."

"You're forgetting Thanatos. He *is* her grandfather," Sol

mused. "Fates, Bella, it never fails to puzzle me how hung up you still are on him."

Bella's nostrils flared. "Oh, fuck you, Sol."

The two gods bickered, and Nya tried and failed to get Imeria to look at her. The demi-god who had *claimed* to be Morgen's friend stood silently in the corner with two others Nya did not recognize, her eyes downcast and her hands folded tightly in front of her.

Fine. She just had to hold on a little longer. It was only a matter of time before Morgen and Varax portaled here.

Nya Evva.

She almost answered aloud before realizing no one in the cave had spoken her name aloud. Tentatively, she reached out down the unfamiliar mental pathway. *Who are you?*

My name is Veeron. Your brother is my rider, which is why I am making this concession to speak to you.

Sol turned to face her, and she kept her expression flat even as Veeron added, *You need to leave the cave the god Sol took you to. It is heavily warded. Varax is in the mountains, but neither she nor her other rider will be able to find you if you remain there. You cannot remain there, Nya Evva. They intend to do terrible things to you.*

The pathway went dark, and the pain in her chest and head had eased considerably, replaced with a dizzying surge of fear and adrenaline.

Bella and Sol were still bickering when Imeria approached, eyes shining and wide. Nya lifted her head, her jaw set. "Why are you here?" she rasped.

Imeria's gaze settled on a point somewhere above Nya's head. The coward couldn't even manage to look at her as she betrayed them.

"He told no one about you, Nya. Not even me or Carus," she began, and Nya knew she was talking about Morgen. "For so long, I thought if I just waited long enough, he would come around. I have immortal blood, and I knew once he was king, he would need someone to provide an heir, even if he refused to marry. But then, he brought you here, married you within hours..." She trailed off, shaking her head. "I couldn't bring myself to defy him, but that didn't mean I couldn't try to protect him from his own poor choices."

"How noble of you." Nya laughed hollowly. "So you went to Sol, of all gods?"

"I will do my duty," Imeria whispered, even as silent tears tracked down her cheeks. "I wish it did not mean harming you. It would have been better if this had ended when I sent the assassins."

"So that was you?"

Imeria glanced over to where Sol now watched, his conversation with Bella over. "I will do my duty," she repeated. "Sol promises to ensure it is I who gives Morgen an heir. You are too corrupted."

Nya blinked a few times, a dull headache forming at her temple, making it hard to think. "Either Sol is tricking you, or he is unaware," she told Imeria, not even sure why she bothered explaining it to her. "For your sake, I hope he wasn't lying to you, though I doubt it."

"What do you—"

"Morgen will never have an heir. He's too afraid of hurting anyone. Even if you somehow managed to convince him to touch you, he won't risk the embers killing anyone like they killed his mother."

Nya knew he was more likely to rip Imeria's head off than bed her after today, even if Sol did not harm her in this cave. But perhaps she felt some small seed of pity for Imeria, pining all these years for someone who would never be hers.

It didn't matter if Imeria believed her or not, though; Nya doubted she would live long enough to know what happened to her. Heavy boots stopped directly in front of her, and Sol lifted her chin with his fingers, his touch unnerving delicate. Imeria scrambled away, retaking her place with the other three women in the corner, her head bowed in submission.

Sol smiled, eyes on Nya. "Bella. Let us see if we can get our old friend to say hello, shall we?"

Bella knelt, examining Nya as if she were some sort of specimen, not a person. "You're sure about this?"

Sol sighed, tipping his head back. "Now, now, don't tell me you've gone soft?"

She shrugged. "The last time we fucked with Sora, it did *not* go well."

"We bounced back, and we always will, because I have something they do not."

Nya laughed, spitting blood on the stone floor. She was vaguely aware she might be unraveling, but she didn't pay that fact any mind. She was too angry to care.

"You think because you stole a few of the embers, you have some kind of upper hand?" she said, smiling and tasting the iron tang of blood on her teeth.

Sol raised a brow. "Perhaps I would not, had Morgen not made the idiotic decision to bind his life to yours. I always had a hunch he would fail in this role, and so did

Kronos. They do say no one knows a son better than his father."

"You knew about Morgen," she breathed. "You *knew*, and you did nothing to stop what Kronos was doing to him."

"Of course, I knew." He laughed, and the sound was as cold as her skin suddenly felt. "And when your mother destroyed Kronos, I left him for dead, which is exactly what Kronos would have wanted. It's a shame he escaped before the rest of the council arrived."

"He was *twelve*," she snarled. "What kind of monster decides an abused twelve-year-old boy deserves to die because he hasn't checked off all your preferred qualities for a king?"

Bella opened her mouth, but Sol knelt next to her, putting a casual hand on the goddess' wrist. "A practical monster. Morgen was weak and soft, even as a child."

"*Even* as a child? Do you hear yourself right now?"

"Sometimes, if Kronos hit him hard enough, he would cry for his mother." Sol snorted softly. "It always seemed so ironic when Morgen wanted her, some useless mortal woman who would have killed him the second she had the chance if she was alive to do it."

Rage overcame her in a wave so potent, it burned her throat. It was only with the cold of the rising fire was that she realized her mistake in letting Sol goad her. Perhaps he had intended Bella to torture her to the point that the void would emerge but had realized all he had to do was talk about hurting Morgen.

She tried to stop it.

Her hands clawed at the darkness closing around her.

It whispered her name, promising an end to pain, to loneliness, to responsibility and burden…

She tried to stop.

But all she had the strength to do in the end was reach for the pathway one last time.

I'm sorry.

The darkness was drowning her, stealing the air from her lungs and icing her heart until it was nothing but a dead weight in her chest. Soon, it would take her mind, and then Sol would carry out whatever he had planned. She was probably going to die today, Morgen with her.

Nya, stay with me!

A tear tracked down her cheek. She couldn't breathe. Nytfire blazed in her hands, and a suppressed scream built in her throat. *I wish we had more time, but this is how it was always going to be.*

NYA—

The chains around her wrists shattered.

A distant roar cut through the mountains, and the void smiled, laughing softly as it looked at Light. "You were always too arrogant for your own good."

The god's eyes were wide with delicious fear. "The world would not exist if not for me. I would just call that truth."

"You still think that?" The void cocked its head to the side. "No, no, no… It was there when your sister awoke. You just couldn't see it."

The cavern plunged into darkness.

CHAPTER 25
MORGEN

The dragon, Varax, finally spoke to me. I could sense it, when she opened the pathway between us, but as soon as I began to tell her of the coming danger, she told me she has heard the same warnings from her kind for many years. She chose them anyway. I left her after that, wondering if her choice was made out of love or foolishness. Perhaps they are one in the same.
—Ana, Priestess to the Usurper King, Arcadia

THE LIGHT WAS UNNATURALLY LOW, even for the Gods' Aisle. Varax landed with a deafening thud atop the ashy floor of the valley, shaking her head in aggravation. Morgen knew she could feel the unnatural tether on the other end of the bond just as well as he could. He reached for Nya again, only to be met with the same suffocating press on his lungs, like he was drowning in ice.

Don't, Varax warned when he pushed.

He pulled back, coughing as he opened his eyes. When he pressed his hand to his lips, it came back coated in crimson.

Nyx, Thanatos, Juno, Sora, Vane, and Carus all waited below. Heles, Thessilnn, and Veeron were perched on a nearby cliff, huffing and restlessly slapping their tails against the rocks. Vulcan was still circling above with his dragon. Carus had gone earlier to warn their forces to lay low for now. None of them had protested, despite their absence over the last several days. They were used to obeying orders. He just hoped Sol would be too occupied to target them.

Nya, Morgen tried again, his heart beating frantically. The agonizing pain he'd felt earlier had subsided when he portaled into the mountains, but the relief had been short-lived.

"I'm sorry," she had said, like it was already over, like it was another way to say goodbye. He would not accept it.

He wiped the blood from his hand against his pants and dismounted, choking down the iron tang when his chest spasmed again.

Sora rushed towards him, Vane close behind her. "Anything?" she urged, her blue eyes huge and pulsing with silver.

He coughed wetly, and Carus looked at him sharply. Morgen ignored him.

"I heard her, but neither Varax nor I could track where she was. Sol must have put up wards, strong ones at that."

Sora's hands curled into fists at her sides, but she did not cry or delve into hysterics at the bad news. Instead, she squared her jaw and took a slow breath before she asked, "What did she say?"

He hesitated and found his gaze drifting behind her, landing on Vane. Morgen still remembered Imeria's frenzied words from decades ago now, when she had told him there was a warrior cutting down Kronos' guards like they were nothing but nuisances. As a child, he almost hadn't believed her. Such a thing wasn't possible; his father's guards had been trained practically since birth. But when he had raced to the throne room, determined to see Kronos' demise himself, he'd realized how the warrior had done it.

It wasn't merely skill that had secured the impossible victory of reaching the throne room. Incomprehensible love and reckless devotion were what had felled his father's guards in the end. They were also what had led to Sora and Vane's deaths and reincarnations.

Morgen wondered if those same things would save any of them now.

"It has her, doesn't it?" Vane asked, his expression hard and determined.

Morgen swallowed hard, nausea rising at the metallic taste still coating his mouth. "Yes," he replied with a short nod. "It does."

"Morgen!"

The familiar voice had him whirling, but he stiffened when he found Imeria standing a few feet away, covered in blood. Varax growled, the sound low and rumbling across the rocks. Heles and Thessilnn mirrored the sound, all three dragons crawling closer.

Something was wrong.

"Imeria." From behind him, Carus said her name slowly, an edge to his tone. "What's happened?"

She was trembling and breathing hard, as if she had just run a great distance. Morgen almost asked her if she was alright, but then she said, "Sol *made* me. I swear, Morgen, I didn't want to hurt anyone—"

"Made you what?" He somehow managed to keep his voice level, but he was about two seconds from losing it. Magic hummed beneath his fingertips, surges of deadly electricity begging to be released.

"There were others," she whispered, her eyes huge and shining with tears. "We were supposed to help keep her contained while Sol talked, but she killed them. You need to flee *now*. I can get you somewhere safe——"

"Who?" he cut in sharply. "Who killed the others you were with?"

"Nya." She said her name like it was a curse, and his anger flared into something dangerously close to uncontrolled. "I knew there was something wrong with her, but no one would listen! They all said we just had to follow your orders."

He took a single step closer, suddenly hyperaware of every sound and sensation around him. Tiny rocks crunched beneath his boots. The air smelled acrid and hummed wildly with the energy of all the powerful gods behind him. Imeria was breathing fast, and the scent of blood that wasn't hers clung to her clothing and skin.

The blood smelled familiar, he realized, like fire and metal and something else that was unnamable and ancient.

Nya.

"Did you send Feron and Sillas to kill her?" he asked in an emotionless voice.

Imeria took a step back, a shaking hand held in front of her. "Please, I was just trying to keep you safe."

Varax snapped her jaws behind him, and this time, Morgen did not suppress the magic slamming against his skin. A bolt of crimson lightning exploded, close enough that Imeria yelped and fell back.

"I am fully aware of my own wife's magic." He dragged in a breath through his teeth, the temptation to strike her down where she stood growing stronger by the second. "And if you were truly loyal, you wouldn't have questioned that or tried to turn my own soldiers against me."

"Morgen, please. You don't understand!" Imeria cried out, holding her hands in front of her. "It's not just magic. There is a terrible place, a dark void no one should be able to touch, and she willingly reaches for it!"

He smiled, dipping his chin. "Oh, I know. I've been there more times than I can count."

Beneath the droplets of blood, Imeria's face abruptly lost all color, her lips parting in horror. The sky darkened abruptly, and Sora called, "Dragons!"

"Sol's fleet," Vulcan said, adding, "Be careful. They have riders."

Imeria turned and ran, but this time, Morgen didn't bother with her. He would deal with her later—if there was a later.

"Morgen."

He turned and stiffened when he found Sora in front of him. She reached up and touched his cheek, her blue eyes nearly blotted out with ether.

"Find her," she said. "We'll hold off the fleet."

He stared at her for a long moment. Shadows danced behind the silver in her eyes, subtle and fleeting. Even still, he could feel the force of her magic under her fingertips; dark and velveteen death. Sora coaxed living things to death softly, in the same way he coaxed them to life.

"I will," he vowed quietly. "Stay alive."

She raised a brow, the ghost of a smile on her lips. "That's never been a guarantee. Not for me."

She pulled her hand away, hurrying towards Thessilnn. Vane glanced his way and gave a curt nod, before turning to Sora. Morgen looked away when they bowed their foreheads together, speaking words no one else could hear.

"I'm coming with you to look for her," Carus said. "Don't argue. We don't have time, and you need me. Veeron says we should be looking for a cave."

Veeron, who had landed next to Varax without Morgen noticing, ruffled his wings and screeched at the approaching fleet.

"Fine," he bit out. "Does Veeron have any idea where?"

"No," Carus said. His eyes followed Thessilnn and Heles as they took off. Vulcan soared above, riding an azure dragon and motioning to Sora and Vane.

Defense, Morgen thought distractedly. He was signaling for a defensive strategy.

Nyx, Thanatos, Juno, and Anabeth had all disappeared by the time he took his eyes off the sky, but he didn't care enough to question it, not when he hadn't been able to reach Nya down the pathway since he landed.

He was just about to tell Carus to mount Veeron when Varax roared abruptly. Carus shouted his name, and Morgen whirled, his blood running cold when he saw what had caused them such alarm.

Nya strode slowly towards them, her steps almost casual. Her eyes were completely flooded with inky black, and she gave them an empty smile when she paused at the edge of the empty clearing. But it wasn't the knowledge the void had a complete hold of her that made his lungs empty out, his heart beating so fast, he could hardly breathe.

There was a deep gash just above her collarbone, the wound gushing freely. If he didn't heal it soon, she would lose too much blood.

She would die.

"Oh," the void said, brushing Nya's small fingers across the wound and coating them in crimson. "Sol thought it might be fun to try and cut out the blood binding. He's always been a little too confident in his ability to control anything and everything. Don't worry; I made sure to numb the feeling of his silly efforts on your end. It would have been beyond agonizing for you otherwise."

Morgen took a step forward, ignoring Carus when he said his name in warning.

"She's going to die if she keeps bleeding like that," he said hoarsely.

The void chuckled. "Oh, yes, she's close. While I'm here, I can hold that off, but as soon as I let her go..." It shrugged. "She will join me in the dark within a few moments, I'm sure."

The void seemed pleased at the thought.

Above them, dragon fire lit up the sky, and someone shouted. Sol's riders had met Sora, Vane, and Vulcan. Morgen didn't dare take his eyes off Nya, though, not as the void closed its eyes and murmured, "It's been so long since someone like her has walked between the worlds. You have no idea how long I have been waiting alone."

The air quivered, and for a flash, he swore he saw each individual strange of ether pull taut. A fissure cracked the stone beneath his feet, and Carus swore.

Prepare yourself, Morgen. The dragon sounded almost resigned, as if she knew as well as he did how little chance they had.

Nya opened her eyes, fixed on him. The raspy, feminine drawl of the void whispered a slew of words that sounded almost like the Old Language. One of the phrases—a name —was just close enough to familiar that he understood it.

Eater of Worlds.

"Get behind me, Carus," Morgen shouted, shoving him back when he began to protest.

The clouds above swirled in a circular vortex, and the wind picked up. The fissure at their feet widened, revealing red-hot lava beneath, and a deafening *crack* split through the air. Thunder boomed, and the ground shook violently enough that he almost lost his footing. Carus was trembling when he gripped his arm, still trying to pull him away.

Nya, I need you to fight.

The dragons were beginning to lose control in the high winds, several of them landing to avoid crashing into each other. But as a moon-pale Vemon dragon dove for the safety of the ground, a streak of strange black lightning exploded, causing her to swerve. The rider flew from her back, falling too far and too hard against the side of a cliffside.

"Sora." Carus rasped, his voice barely audible.

Thessilnn and Heles shrieked, and, even over the wind, Morgen heard Vane bellow her name as Heles raced to the spot where she had fallen. The void slowly turned its head, eyes glittering with empty stars as it cocked its head. A strong wind slammed abruptly against Heles, knocking Vane to the ground too. Morgen did not see him get up.

Carus, who had fought and trained soldiers triple his

age, who hadn't done more than grimace when he'd been nearly disemboweled at sixteen, who was more likely to make a joke than admit he was afraid… He was shaking so hard, Morgen was surprised he still stood as he gripped his arm.

"You were right," the void crooned, looking at Carus. "Sister or not, you probably should have killed her. A shame for your world that you had to be so human."

"Nya!" Morgen shouted over the wind, this time aloud. "I know you're there."

The void shook its head. "She is gone, and soon, you will be too. Close your eyes, god of life. It will be easier that way."

He did as it said, letting it assume his defeat. But just as a wall of nytfire erupted that could destroy him and Carus, he forced up the same shield he had used against it days ago, yanking on each and every ember he had been painstakingly awakening over the last few minutes. The void cackled, and his weak barrier faltered, almost to failure, until pure light flared behind him, bolstering the defensive wall.

Sol, he realized, after a moment's confusion.

Next to him, Nyx, Thanatos, and Anabeth stood, all with hands on Sol's back. Morgen didn't trust any of them, but right now, he had no choice but to accept their help. With the added force, the wall of nytfire began to ebb and then faded completely. Even the storm calmed slightly. Out of the corner of his eye, Morgen saw Vane limping towards Nya, Sora at his side.

"Nya could stab me in the heart and twist the knife, I'd still be trying to make sure she was okay," Vane had said to Carus.

He hadn't been lying.

Morgen took a casual step towards Nya, not trusting the moment of victory. She was oddly still, but her eyes remained flooded with midnight. He motioned subtly to Carus, and his most trusted general gave him the smallest of nods, understanding his silent order: *Retreat.*

"Step aside, all of you," Sol said. His hand was still outstretched, blood running down his forehead. "It's time to finish this."

Nyx shook her head, reaching for him. "Sol, you promised you wouldn't—"

"I said I would help you end this, Nya," he snarled. "I am."

The Goddess of Night dipped her chin, and shadows swirled at her feet. "You do this, and I am never trusting you again."

"If I don't destroy the girl now, it won't matter! Nothing will!" he bellowed, a burst of pure light flaring at the crown of his head, so bright, it singed the air.

"Nya, he's right," Juno urged.

Nyx shook her head. "Not you too, Jun." A silver tear tracked down her cheek, and she whispered, "They named her for me."

Juno glanced at Thanatos, who was uncharacteristically still and silent behind Nyx. An odd look passed between them.

"Enough!" Sol snapped. He turned his attention back to Morgen, Carus, Vane, and Sora where they stood around Nya. "*Move.*"

"He's right. You should step aside."

Morgen's head snapped back at the sound of Nya's voice. Her face was completely expressionless and her voice was flat, but her eyes were flashing rapidly between silver and black. Hope clawed at his chest, crawling from the wounds despair had wrought there all his life. Maybe just *once*, the fates would pity him.

"Nya?"

Her eyes settled. The hope crumpled and faded to ash, and he did not know if he could take another blow. He felt like he was dying, and it had little to do with the blood in his mouth.

The void spoke again, its voice harsher now. "I told you. *She is gone.*"

Nyx screamed, the only warning as Light exploded from Sol so pure, it was just as blinding as the deepness of the void itself. None of them had time to move fast enough, to protect Nya or themselves from the inevitable end.

The end, something he had always thought would come at the hands of a vengeful god. As a child, he had even prayed silently for it, that one day, Kronos would push just a little too far, and finally, he would stop existing.

Morgen?

He opened his eyes, and the world seemed to be moving in slow motion. The light hovered all around them, and in front of him, he saw a small form with unbound silver hair haloed by the glow. Her eyes were still gone to the void, but within that never-ending midnight, stars flickered. In her palms, she held something close to her chest—a dying star, cold and untouchable. But she saw its beauty. Perhaps that was why he had fallen in love with her in the first place. She had an ability to look at things everyone else presumed dead and see wonder all the same.

This is goodbye. Her voice was in his head, echoing

between their shared soul down the pathway. *But I need you to know I love you. I've loved you for years, and I'm sorry I never said it.*

He tried to speak, tried to scream at her that this wasn't over, that she couldn't do this. He was supposed to martyr himself for the world, not her. Their lives were tied, but he did not know how he would survive her death, even in the few moments before it took him too.

Shh, don't try to talk. She reached out but didn't quite touch him. *This moment isn't truly real, and I'm probably close to gone now. I suspended things for us, just for a second. You won't have much time either once you open your eyes, but please, if you get the chance, tell my parents how much I love them, that this was not their fault. They won't believe you, but say it anyway. And make sure Carus knows to keep trying, because they love him too.*

His lips formed her name, and she smiled sadly. Her fingertips brushed his face, and though the sensation of her touch didn't register, he could still feel the energy of her magic.

Don't reach for me this time, okay?

He gave a slight nod, wondering if she could see through the lie or if she ever expected him to listen in the first place. If she doubted him, she didn't say.

Nya turned away from him, and, in a sickening rush, time resumed, the Light pouring from Sol hitting her body and inverting. A great chasm opened in her chest as the magic was sucked into the void itself. Light and Darkness mixed, the sight blinding. The mountains shook, and thunder roared, so deafening, his ears rang.

The maelstrom was over within seconds. Every last bit of power Sol possessed faded, absorbed into Nya's small body as she crumpled to the ground.

Flecks of white ash fell around her, haloing her head. Morgen fell to his knees, and tiny shards of glasslike silver and sparkling onyx sliced into his palms and knees. He hardly registered the stinging sensation. He just crawled to her, holding tight to the tiny, fraying strand of Life gripped by her soul—*their* soul.

His hands were shaking so hard, he could hardly pull her into his lap. It only got worse when he saw her face. Her lips were pale, her eyes and mouth coated in blood. The gash at her neck was still a jagged open wound, and her tunic was blackened and charred where the void had opened up at her chest. He didn't know…he didn't know if he could fix this. But he had to. *He had to fix her.*

"Morgen, don't," she rasped weakly. He froze at the sound, the proof of life within her. Her eyes fluttered beneath her lids but would not open. He could do this. He had to. He could feel her chest rising and falling in tiny, stuttering gasps. As long as she was still breathing, there was a chance.

But then, her breath stalled. The blood wasn't gushing from her wounds anymore, and even in his delirious state, he knew what that meant.

"No," he said firmly, even as his failing body shook with broken sobs. "No, you are not going to die today."

He thought Sol might be shouting, thought that maybe, someone else was crying. He didn't care, hardly even noticed the rest of the world existed as he pressed his palm to her sternum and forced the tired, burnt-out embers from his body into hers.

"Live," he whispered over and over again, until the word

lost its meaning. The embers failed to take each time he gave them to her. He kept trying anyway.

He didn't know if she was breathing. He didn't know if he was.

"Nya, please." *Please.* "I love you," he said, cupping her face and leaning his forehead against hers as a broken, agonized sound he didn't recognize escaped him. He pushed the embers into her body again. Just one more; one more, and she might live…

His vision blurred and his chest caved open with a pain so potent, his back bowed. Still, he did not let go.

"It's over, Morgen."

He stiffened, and when he lifted his head, he found Sol standing over him. An old memory flashed across his failing mind; Sol watching with the same stony expression as Kronos' whip tore at Morgen's bare back. He had been seven or eight and had tried his luck at asking the God of Light about his mother. He informed Kronos, who then resolved another attempt to beat the 'weakness of love' out of Morgen.

They had been so utterly wrong. Love wasn't weakness, but the strongest force in existence. It was why he was still breathing, still trying to bring her to life when he should have been dead. Love carried out the impossible, against all odds. It did not care what the chances were and was far more ruthless than the strongest magic in Arcadia.

"She's too far gone to save, and you are dying." Sol sounded impatient. "I need the embers."

Morgen made a sound somewhere between an empty laugh and a dangerously wet cough, tasting iron in his throat. "Fuck you."

"The world will die if you do not hand them over to me."

"*Then let it die.*"

Fury glazed over Sol's stony features, twisting them into something ugly no physical beauty could mask. He lunged, his hand digging into Morgen's hair and dragging him away from Nya before he slammed to the ground.

Pain blinded him so completely, he lost consciousness for a few seconds. When he came to, he wondered why no one was coming to help him. It was a fleeting thought, the dying hope of an unloved child.

Sol gripped his throat directly over the place Kronos had once tried to slit it, pressing his thumb against the scar like a reminder. Morgen was completely alone in the world. No one had ever cared, not until *her*. He had failed to save the one person who made him want to live. She had shown him there was beauty in the world, however broken.

"Here." She handed him a smooth, dark stone, still damp and sandy. Her hair dripped with creek water, and her eyes were bright. When their fingertips touched, she blushed.

"Why?" he asked, glancing pointedly at the stone.

She shrugged, her lips tugging upwards. "I thought it was pretty. Add it to your pouch."

Beams of sunlight shone through the trees as he stared at her. She found the simplest, oddest things to be worth her attention. He found he had involuntarily begun to see things he hadn't before. Sometimes, he heard her voice in his head when he was alone, commenting on a bird song or a tree. It took him a while to realize he found her disarmingly beautiful too, more than anything she ever pointed out to him. He had viewed his life through black and white for years. She was a vivid burst of color.

Sol kicked his side, and the memory faded like smoke, bringing Morgen back to cruel awareness. The god's eyes were aglow with rage and desperation.

"You are pathetic," Sol spat, baring his teeth. "You are not worthy of the embers or the power you inherited."

Morgen smiled, a delirious, empty expression. He could feel the blood coating his teeth and dripping down his chin. There was nothing left to lose.

"Go ahead, Sol," he choked out. "Take my life. I never wanted it anyways. You've proclaimed it many times before yourself: you never needed me because you kept a couple of the embers. Good luck with that."

Sol roared in fury. His features morphed, and Morgen caught a glimpse of the immortal beast beneath his human face, formless light curled around a heart long blackened by an excess of power. The vision was gone in flash.

"Give them to me!" Sol screamed, his hand squeezing, suffocating until drawing air was nearly impossible.

Morgen knew it was over. He was teetering on the edge of a chasm he could never return from. The embers still attempted to revive him, their efforts agonizing as they tried and failed to heal too many wounds. The magic flooded his broken body in one last riotous attempt to revive it. A drunken stupor hazed over his mind, but he forced himself to stay awake, to look at Sol and offer up one last taunt before he left this world to collapse in on itself.

"*Beg.*"

Sol's fingers spasmed, burning where they touched Morgen's skin. "You worthless fucking—"

"You should probably listen to him if you'd like to live, Sol."

For a moment, Morgen thought he was already dead, because that voice…

It was Nya's.

Through his clouded vision, he saw her standing behind Sol. Her eyes were no longer filled with midnight, instead glowing with strands of silver and the most beautiful shade of blazing amber-gold.

CHAPTER
TWENTY-SIX

The child runs for the small house, a simple cottage nestled amongst the trees. Her laughter echoes strangely, and I am aware I am dreaming, though I do not wake. When she reaches the threshold, she is scooped up and held tight. A familiar voice pierces the dreamscape, making it feel too real. But when I turn, all I see is darkness.
—Account of a dream, Lady Anabeth, Consort to Her Majesty Cion Livii, Queen of Aren, D'anna

NYA HAD BEEN FULLY aware she was dying.

The ancient creature that called itself World Eater hadn't been so kind as to numb to pain as it locked her away in her own mind, screaming and thrashing, watching helplessly as it hurt the people she loved.

When it looked at Morgen, though, she sensed the strangest emotion.

Jealousy.

The void was utterly alone. It had been listening to itself breathe in utter darkness for millennia. It wanted companionship and could not fathom Morgen's willingness to die for

Nya. It *hated* them. Hated her parents, too, for it had watched her father wait decades for Sora's return. When the void was forced to relinquish her, it wept.

It wanted to love but did not understand the concept. It no longer knew how to do anything but take and destroy.

Once it had created. Nyx had been its favorite, crafted from its understanding of itself. Thanatos was torn from a piece of its cloak's fabric. Juno was threaded from the silver essence of the dying stars, and all the others came from dreams the creature had when it managed to sleep. Most of them forgot it quickly. Only Thanatos remembered, though he could not recall its true name, merely referring to it as 'the void.'

Nya was the first living being who had blinked back at it without fear since this world had come to be. Once she understood that, all she had to promise was the gift of a bit of fire to stay warm and a vow she would remember its true name.

It was nothing more than a terrified, ancient child.

Sol had unknowingly given her exactly what she needed to calm it when he unleashed the full brunt of his magic. In return, it had given her a hollow space of time, a pause to say goodbye to Morgen before they were both swept away, an assurance it wouldn't let Fate return them here. This was to be her last and only life.

She thought she had closed her eyes for the last time until she found herself staring at a slate-hued sky and heard Morgen's voice from afar.

Nya, love.

She blinked hazily, finding her mother staring down at her with wide eyes and a spray of blood on her cheek.

Mama?

Her mother touched her cheek gently. *Can you stand?*

Nya's lips quivered, and she bit back a whimper when she realized just how much pain she was in. *It hurts.*

I know, my brave girl. I know. It will just be a moment, and then I promise, you can rest.

"Give them to me!" Sol screamed.

Nya forced herself to sit up. He was hurting Morgen. Morgen, who had not stopped fighting for her until the end, even when no hope remained.

There was a blisteringly hot, heavy weight in her chest, and she pressed a hand to it, thinking there must be a wound there. But when she pulled it back, no new blood coated her fingers. On a hunch, she slid her hand up and touched her own throat, finding the deep wound Sol had carved into her skin completely healed. This pain wasn't from a wound. It was the same sensation she experienced when Morgen healed her, but *everywhere,* crawling underneath her skin and knitting her back together against her body's will.

The embers.

It had worked.

She reached for her mother. *Help me stand.*

Sora glanced behind them, and Nya followed her gaze. Carus knelt next to her father, who was hunched over, a hand pressed against his torso. She met his eyes, and he nodded, a small smile tugging at his lips despite the pain.

Go on, Nya.

It was Carus who stood and walked to her on a silent gait, offering her a hand. He searched her face, an unspoken question in his eyes. *Can you do this?*

He knew she had to be in pain, but Sol was going to see the embers in her eyes, and she had to bluff enough to convince him he had no choice but to surrender.

She gave a shallow nod, gritting her teeth against the scream that threatened to rip from her throat when he hauled her to her feet. He helped her limp halfway to Sol before letting go.

"*Beg,*" Morgen said around the hand Sol had tightened around his throat. He didn't see her yet.

Sol hissed in fury. "You worthless fucking—"

When she spoke, she forced herself to steady her voice, letting every note of her rage coat the words. "You should probably listen to him if you'd like to live, Sol."

Sol stiffened, his hand slackening. Morgen gasped—for air or at the sight of her behind Sol, she was not sure. The god of Light whirled, and Morgen coughed roughly, blood staining his lips. She could already see the embers starting to build again in his eyes. She just needed to hold on a little longer.

"You can't be…" Sol trailed off and shook his head. "This is impossible."

She shrugged casually, hoping she masked that just lifting her shoulder sent an agonizing bolt pain down her arm. "Evidently not." She tilted her head. "You know, as a payment for your 'help', I was considering letting you pick what happens to you. I'm curious to see what happens if I mix my nytfire and Morgen's lightning. Or, if you'd prefer humiliation over pain, you could get on your knees, proclaim your loyalty to us, and pray I'm still in a forgiving mood when you're done kissing my feet."

Morgen laughed, his voice catching on the air. His eyes

were wide and shining, and she winked at him, half for show and half because she needed to let him know she was really here.

Sol, on the other hand, did not find her words funny. "You little bitch—"

"Or." She cut him off. "I was thinking we could chain you up in some unmarked cave. Cut your throat, burn out your eyes, maybe take a few fingers, and then heal it all with the embers. If the lesson doesn't sink in the first time, we could always repeat the process. I have eternity, and I plan to take my second chance at life very seriously, which includes keeping you in line."

"I will *not*," Sol snapped, but she could see the fear creeping into his icy-blue eyes.

Morgen pushed to his feet, and Sol stiffened, his eyes flicking between the two of them.

"Neither of you are fit to rule," he said, his hands curling into fists, but his wavering voice gave away his unease.

"Neither was Kronos," Morgen said in a low voice. "You knew that, though, right? It didn't take you long to realize your mistake in giving him so much power, but you did nothing about it. And when Sora and Vane died to clean up your mess, you stepped in and acted like some savior." He laughed, his voice stronger now. "Did you really think *you* could be king, Sol? That's what you want, right?"

Sol's nostrils flared. "Nyx may have been the first to this world, but it would be a lifeless wasteland if not for me."

"Maybe," she said. "But I learned some things about your 'old friend' when it tried to take over." She paused, searching her uncle's eyes. "You were created from a dream,

Sol. Nyx was formed from the very darkness within its soul. You act as if you have power over her, but you are merely her absence; a figment of imagination from an ancient creator you very quickly forgot."

Sol frowned. "The void is not a creator. It is nothing."

Nya smiled, letting him think the edge to her tone was borne of cruelty and not the internal agony threatening to weaken her knees and send her crumpling to the ground. "I was told it prefers its true name. *Neachith an Soaghail.*"

Sol flinched as the ancient language flowed from her tongue.

"World Eater," Morgen murmured, glancing at her. He raised a brow. "Took a liking to you in the end, did it?"

She looked squarely at Sol. "I suppose it did. Creatures of darkness have few morals, but we do tend to understand each other."

"It tried to kill you," Sol sneered in an attempt to demean her again. "You should be more afraid of it than me."

"Are you afraid?" she said softly. A bolt of lightning struck the ground next to her, and she made a vague mental note to praise Morgen later for its impeccable timing. She hardly had the strength to stand, much less explore any of the new magic the embers granted her, but Sol didn't need to know that.

The god didn't reply, his throat working. He was obviously still trying to find a way out of his own mess.

A chill spider-walked up her spine when Thanatos approached. "It's over, Sol," he said smoothly. "Back down."

"Fighting Nyx's battles again, are you, dog?" Sol sneered. "Why am I not surprised?"

"No," Thanatos replied, his irises darkening. "I just wanted to be the one to insult you. I told you your scheming would someday catch up to you, and that day has finally come." He glanced at Nya and Morgen and smiled. The sight of it was mildly terrifying. "I would advise you bow for your new king and queen before getting the fuck out of here before they change their minds about granting you a speck of mercy."

Sol remained silent and unmoving. Nya clenched her jaw so tight, it ached. Finally, he said, "I get to remain on the council."

Morgen narrowed his eyes. "You're hardly in a position to bargain with us."

Sol glared at him, and though Nya didn't want to relent, she also wasn't sure how much longer she could manage to keep up her charade without passing out. She glanced at Morgen and blinked once before she gritted out, "I will consider your request."

"Now go," Morgen growled.

Sol didn't leave right away, but she didn't care anymore. She turned, motioning Morgen to follow with a tilt of her head. She didn't trust herself to speak without crying.

"You're pathetic," Sol spat when Morgen joined her. "*You* are the heir, not her."

Morgen stopped walking, a hand on her back. She took a shallow breath and spoke down the pathway, *Please just keep walking.*

"I'm not the heir anymore. I'm your king," Morgen barked without turning. "And *she* is your queen. Leave." *You're in pain. You have been this whole time, haven't you?*

She dug her nails in his arm. *Just pretend until he's gone. If he suspects weakness, he might not give in.*

Morgen glanced at her but obeyed, subtly supporting her as they walked. Sol still hadn't left, but she trusted Thanatos to keep an eye on him for now. There was a bend in the cliff formation ahead, where Anabeth, her parents, and Carus lingered, and Morgen led her towards it, out of Sol's sight.

We're almost there.

A small whimper finally clawed up her throat as they made it around the bend. From the clearing they had left behind, Thanatos said loudly, "And don't come back."

She wondered if it was for her benefit, so she knew Sol was gone. Whether he was or not, though, she truly didn't have it in her to think past the pain anymore. Her legs collapsed beneath her, and Morgen caught her, easing them both to the ground.

"You're alright," he said calmly, even though she could feel his hand shaking as he smoothed back her hair. "Just breathe, Nya. That's it."

Shudder after shudder wracked her body, each wave of pain bringing with it a wave of burning that felt like fire was blazing under her skin and dissolving her bones.

Blurred figures approached, but she trusted Morgen to keep her safe.

"What's happening to her?"

Her parents?

"It's the embers, isn't it?" Another figure knelt. Carus, she thought vaguely.

She shut her eyes. "I'm f–f-fine," she tried to say, but her words were fractured and slow.

"Not very convincing, sweetheart." Carus sighed. "Any idea how long this will last?"

Morgen took a breath near her ear. "I'm not sure."

"Can you do anything for her?"

"I don't think—" His voice broke off. "No, I don't think so."

"It's like when you're injured, and they heal you? But amplified?"

Nya tried to clamp her jaw shut, but the pain had moved to her head, and it felt like her *eyes* were burning. She thought she might have screamed, thought Morgen was murmuring in her ear, that he started to shake nearly as much as she was…

"She's about to lose consciousness."

"Thank the fucking Fates."

TWENTY-SEVEN

NYA DREAMT OF A LITTLE GIRL. She knew she was dreaming, because the child kept reminding her, insisting in a raspy voice that she was aware this was not real.

"Yes, I know," she assured the girl for the third time.

Finally, the girl relaxed. She smiled and her eyes twinkled. *"Good. What is my name, Nya?"*

Nya paused. For the first time since the dream had begun, she noticed the child's appearance: brown eyes speckled with amber, fawn-hued skin, and brick-colored hair, the strands framing her face shining bright silver. She was very small, perhaps only five or six years old.

"Who are you?" Nya whispered. Her voice echoed in the empty space around them.

The girl blinked, and shadows stirred in her irises. *"You promised you would not forget."* She reached for Nya but did not touch her. *"What is my name?"*

Suddenly, Nya did not have to think about her response. *"Ithesoa."*

The little girl sighed contentedly and took a step back. *"I had to make sure you remembered. Thank you, Nya."*

Nya reached for the girl, but when she stretched out her fingers, they only brushed against a familiar, empty void.

CHAPTER
TWENTY-EIGHT

The strangest part of the last fifty years is waking up and remembering she is really gone. Before, I always knew the worst could come to pass. It was likely, even, with a king like Kronos. But we all fooled ourselves into thinking we could defy the fates. Even me. Look at where that got us.
—*Lady Anabeth, Royal Scribe's Apprentice, D'anna*

SHE WAS UNCOMFORTABLY warm and covered in a sheen of sweat when she opened her eyes. Heavy blankets were wrapped around and draped over her. The flickering of flames blurred in the warped field of her vision. Someone was silhouetted by the hearth, their back to her, but when she tried to speak to them, she merely coughed, tasting copper in the back of her throat.

The figure turned, and she recognized Carus' eyes staring back at her.

"Nya." His voice was hushed and hoarse, and he appeared to have been rendered frozen in shock, the fire poker hanging limply in his hand.

She tried to speak again, and when all that came out was more coughing, he cleared his throat, setting the poker against the edge of the hearth and handing her a glass of water from a low table to the right of it. She accepted it, chugged over half of it, then glanced around, trying to place her surroundings.

They must be in Nyx and Thanatos' house again. She was lying on a couch someone had obviously dragged from its usual spot to sit directly in front of the fireplace. Had she been cold? She could hardly believe that, given how feverish she felt now.

She attempted to shove the blankets away but winced at the sharp ache in her muscles and joints. "Where is everyone?" she managed to croak.

Carus furrowed his brow. "You're feeling warm?" he asked, not acknowledging her question.

"Yes. Too warm, I think."

"Right," he muttered. "They said that might happen next."

"Was I cold?"

He grimaced. "Ah… Yes."

She coughed again, choking at the wet tang of blood in the back of her throat. Darkness encapsulated her vision completely before consciousness returned with an agonizing vengeance. A door flew open, the sound of wood cracking against the wall exploding in her over-sensitive ears.

She felt herself fall forward. Carus swore, and strong arms caught her before she could hit the floor. A sudden bolt of electricity lanced up her back, and she was vaguely aware she was screaming, clawing at the arms around her.

"You didn't need to come back," Carus panted against

her ear, and she tried to reply, not understanding what he meant. "I had it covered."

Morgen spoke just as her muscles went limp. "I should have never left."

"She was sleeping until five minutes ago!"

She needed to tell them she was *burning*. The blaze was overcoming her from within, fissuring her skull and ravaging her muscles and bones. She was sure she would be ash soon, but her lips would not move properly to form any words.

Fingers brushed against her forehead, and Morgen swore. "Start a cold bath. Now."

Carus didn't argue further, and she thought he might have left. Strong arms hooked under her legs and back, lifting her, and she braced for more pain. Although she was still burning up, the touch was almost soothing to the throb.

Morgen?

His chest expanded against her with a sigh. He carried her to the edge of the room, away from the heat of the fire. "I'm sorry, I shouldn't have left. Carus insisted I go back and explain things to the others."

The others? Did he mean his army?

She didn't think she had spoken aloud, but he replied, "Yes."

She wasn't angry. She understood why he needed to address them, to let them know there wasn't going to be a war anymore, though she had no idea where his forces would go now.

"With us," he answered her thoughts again, voice low and quiet, as if he knew not to add to the pain in her head. "I assured them they will all have a place if they want it."

With them? But where…

Oh.

Sol. The void. The embers.

"I would advise you to bow for your new king and queen," Thanatos had said.

She forced her eyes open, wincing, even in the dim light. Morgen frowned at her, the embers pulsating softly in his irises.

"I understand why Carus wanted me to go," he said, brow creased. "But I shouldn't have listened. You weren't sleeping, not really. It's bad, isn't it? The pain?"

She tried to speak again, and he shushed her, brushing his thumb against her mouth.

"Hush, I know it is." He leaned his forehead gently against hers. "I'm sorry, Nya. I don't know how long this will last."

She thought she might have passed out again. The next thing she remembered, there was ice all around her, and someone was stroking her hair, then braiding it. Consciousness slipped away after that.

The low hum of voices coaxed her from sleep next. Her head felt clearer, and it was not so difficult to open her eyes. But when she saw her parents sitting a few paces away and she tried to speak, she coughed. Their attention immediately zeroed in on her.

"Here," Morgen said next to her. He helped her sit then handed her a cool glass of water.

She took it and drank half, then handed it back to him, taking stock of her surroundings. She was in the same room as before, though the couch was not in front of the hearth anymore.

"How are you feeling?" Morgen asked. He looked exhausted. His eyes were rimmed in red, and dark, purple-hued shadows sat underneath them.

She rubbed her temple, trying to banish the lingering ache there. "Fine, I think. Better than before."

He nodded, though the tension on his face did not fade. She glanced at her parents, searching for any sign of injury. She was aware they had been hurt—that *she* had hurt them—but recalling the memories was like viewing them through a warped glass.

"I didn't…" she tried to say, but her throat constricted, her eyes burning with shame. "Are you both okay?"

Her father's mouth twitched, although he did not look like he was laughing. It was her mother who stood first, squeezing her father's arm then crossing the room and kneeling in front of Nya.

She reached out a hand, and Nya stared at her for a long minute before she took it, her fingers trembling. "Other than being worried about you, we're now fine, Nya," she said, reaching out to stroke her cheek with her other hand. "You've been in and out for some time."

Nya's lips quivered. "But I hurt you. I could have—" She cut herself off, unable to speak the horrible truth aloud. The void could have killed them easily.

Her mother tapped her nose. "I do not know that darkness so well, my love, not in the same way as you. But I do know its call, and I can only imagine the immeasurable will it must have taken to resist it the way you did."

A tear slid down Nya's cheek. "It was so lonely. It just

wanted to be seen and understood, but no one could, not until me."

A shadow flickered across her mother's eyes, a brief whisper of that very same darkness. "I can only imagine," she whispered. "It is a lonely thing indeed to be feared without understanding."

They stared at each other, both heirs of Death and Night, with little choice in the power they had inherited. For the first time, Nya thought she really understood her mother's wish to leave Arcadia behind all those years ago. In the quiet of the thick forest in Mise, no one feared them. She had not been raised in a bubble or a cage, but perhaps the one place where she could live without the shadow of her legacy. Mortals and gods alike feared their family's power, but her parents had given her the gift of growing up without the heavy weight of their judgement.

"Will you go back home?" she asked with a new sense of understanding, completely unclouded by any past judgement.

"Not yet," her mother said, tucking a loose strand of hair behind Nya's ear. She smiled, tilting her head to the side. "We'll stay for a time, at least."

Nya glanced back at her father, and he raised a brow. "Don't look at me as if I'd disagree."

She chewed on her lip and felt Morgen shift beside her. *Don't do that. You'll hurt yourself further.*

She glanced at him. *Relax. I'm fine.*

As much as I'd like to believe you, I know you're not. Don't think I can't tell. You need more rest.

"Are we being kicked out?" her father asked, and she jumped.

"No," she said at the same moment Morgen grunted, "Yes."

Her mother laughed softly. "You should take a bedroom now that your temperature has stopped fluctuating. It will be more comfortable."

Nya's brow creased. "My temperature?"

The room fell silent until Morgen explained, "You've been cycling between feverish and nearly hypothermic. That, and the pain I know you're feeling, is all a result of the embers. They're not…easy on a body, especially not one with any amount of mortal blood. I was ill often as a child with similar ailments."

She pressed a hand to the center of her chest. "So it's true," she murmured, searching for a confirmation not from anyone in the room, but from within herself, and…

Yes. There it was, pulsing within the burning darkness that made up the fabric of her and Morgen's souls; a fluttering flicker of light and warmth, humming and alive.

The embers.

It shouldn't have been possible, and yet she could not deny the truth of their presence. She had survived, albeit a little worse for wear.

Apparently, Morgen really did sense that last part, because he insisted, "You need to rest."

Her mother glanced at him briefly and nodded. "He's right. Sleep, Nya, love. We'll be here."

She stood, and her father did too. He patted her cheek with a tight smile before they both left.

Once the door shut softly behind them, she asked Morgen, "They're really alright?"

Morgen's jaw was tight and his body was tense, even as

he assured her, "Yes. Once I was able, I sped up their healing."

"They just seemed—"

"They have been worried and annoyingly prone to hovering."

Her brows rose. He almost sounded upset.

"They do that sometimes," she said, catching his gaze. "They *are* my parents."

His answering *harrumph* was little more than a low puff of air.

She smiled incredulously. "Morgen—"

"Everyone needs to just leave. Or leave some space at the very least."

He ran a hand over his face, shaking his head. He stood, and she watched his aggravated pacing with parted lips.

"No one but me needs to be here right now, and although I don't worry about your parents harming you, the same cannot be said for any of the principals. Janis can impersonate anyone, and I don't believe for a second that Sol is no longer a threat. And then Carus insists he needs *me* to go to the Gods' Aisle, and the second I come back, you're awake and your temperature is dangerously high, and he's not doing anything about it. Not to mention the distance didn't help your pain, even for an hour, and—"

"Morgen," she cut in, and he halted, his back to her. "It's alright."

He let out a ragged breath. "It's not. You were dying, and I…I couldn't do *anything.* It wasn't working, and I'm afraid it still won't."

His admission sank like a stone in the quiet of the sitting room. Her chest ached with the weight of them, though not because she was not afraid they were true. Deep down, she knew the worst had already come to pass. If the embers were going to kill her, it would have already happened.

"Come here," she murmured, holding out a hand.

He faced her but paused when their gazes met, looking unsure. His expression was tight, but there was a vulnerability in his eyes that made him look younger than usual.

She didn't lower her hand, waiting for all the time he needed. He let out a slow breath, and some of the tension eased from his shoulders. Once he sat next to her, she took his hand and silently pressed it to her sternum. With her palm spread over the top of his, she felt every part of them sync—the embers, their heartbeats, even the threads in their *soul*. Morgen's breath caught, and she met his widening eyes.

See? You didn't hurt me. You saved my life, Morgen.

A single tear slid down his cheek as he stared at her, followed by another, then another, until he dropped his head to her shoulder, his entire body wracked with silent sobs. Her eyes widened, but she held him tightly as the weight of years crashed down on him.

Not so long ago, she had told him he was a monster, and he had agreed, without hesitation, because he had truly believed it. Perhaps all the poison spewed from Kronos' mouth when Morgen was a child could have been a self-fulfilling prophecy, but the truth was, he had never let the corruption come to pass. He defied the doomed destiny fate had secured for him, just as she had defied hers.

They held each other in silence for a long time. It took a while, but he eventually stopped trembling, and his breathing slowed, gently caressing the place where his lips touched her collarbone. When he lifted his head to look at her, the embers and even the ether in his eyes were dim, hidden behind the natural brown of his irises. She could never mistake him for fully mortal, but for just a moment, he looked less than godly. He looked content.

"I meant what I said," he said, voice rough. "You should rest more."

She didn't argue, only asked, "Will you come with me?"

His hand slid to the nape of her neck, and he pressed his lips to her brow. "I follow wherever you are."

He scooped her up, shushing her protests as carried her out of the room and down the hall. By the time they entered the dim bedroom and he set her down atop the covers, she was already asleep.

TWENTY-NINE

I dream in such vibrant color, the world often feels dull in comparison. But watching Sora and Vane during the marriage ceremony makes me wonder if the strength of colors are simply held in feelings. The cavern, though dimly lit, was teeming with color and light, cradled perhaps in the emotions themselves. It gives me hope for the future.
—Anabeth, demi-god daughter of Juno, goddess of Fate

LATE IN THE NIGHT, Morgen startled so abruptly, she nearly fell off the bed in alarm.

"Morgen," Nya whispered, reaching for him.

He sat up, running a hand roughly through his hair. He must have been sleeping too; she wasn't the only one haunted by nightmares.

She took his hand, pressing her lips to the inside of his wrist. "You're alright."

He took a slow, shuddering breath. "I know."

"Was it bad? The dream?"

He paused then cleared his throat twice. "I didn't lie when I said the palace exists where it does for a reason."

She didn't understand what he was trying to tell her at first, but when he didn't explain further, she realized he meant that, in order to rule Arcadia, they would need to return there, to the place of all his childhood nightmares. She had no doubt all but one of the scars visible on his skin had been given to him there. Kronos, in his infinite creative torture, had found ways to make them last, despite the embers.

"I'm sorry," she said, curling against his side. "I wish you didn't have to go back there."

He tugged her closer and wrapped his arms around her, breathing evenly again. "I wish I didn't either," he whispered into her hair.

"I'll be with you."

"I wish you didn't have to see it, or be forced to rule and stay—"

"Morgen."

"—with me."

She shook her head, searching his expression. "Do you really still think I don't want to be with you now?"

He looked away. "I did force you into this. If you need some space for a while, I won't—"

But he cut himself off, inhaling sharply when she brushed her lips against the curve of his neck, just shy of the binding scar. She did it again, moving closer to the spot she knew would make him lose control.

"Nya," he said, voice strangled. "You're still—"

"I'm fine," she murmured against his heated skin. "You really need to stop making assumptions about how I feel."

"Are you sure?" he pushed. His hands slid up to her face,

cupping her cheeks as she shifted to straddle his lap. "You're not in pain anymore?"

Her lips tugged with a small smile, and she leaned her forehead against his. "Are you never not in a little bit of pain?"

His thumbs brushed absentmindedly over the curve of her cheekbones. "I was hoping that wouldn't be the case for you, since you have less mortal blood, but…yes. The embers always wear a little bit."

"Okay." She smiled fully now, pressing the heel of her palm against his heartbeat. "So, I'm in pain, but it's normal pain."

"I just want to make sure—" He began but cut himself off with a surprised groan as she rolled her hips against his.

"Trust me," she breathed, nipping at his mouth.

He slid a hand behind her neck, tangling his long fingers in her hair. "Only you," he murmured before kissing her.

Neither of them took it further than that for a while, though she was hyperaware he was completely hard beneath her. When he started to figure out if he pushed his hips into hers at certain angles, she whimpered and shivered, he began to do it more and more, until she was a trembling mess on top of him.

"If I touch you right now," he said roughly, kissing along the curve of her neck and sucking on the binding scar, "I think you'll come within seconds."

She didn't tell him he probably didn't even need to do that, because it was already happening. He fisted his hand in the fabric of her long tunic, pumping his hips and swearing under his breath as she panted, her forehead pressed against his shoulder.

"Did you come?" she murmured sometime later, nipping at his jaw, her eyes half-lidded and her mind hazy.

He moaned softly when she tugged on his ear with her teeth and tipped his head back. His cheeks flushed in the dim light of the gas lamp on the bedside table, his voice thick when he rasped, "Yeah. But don't you dare consider this done."

She laughed softly, brushing the tip of her nose against his. "You do know that's a little risky, right?"

"Risky how?" he muttered, kissing her to punctuate the words.

"Risky, as in…" She gasped as he gently flipped her so her back was pressed against the mattress. "If you're trying to prevent children."

He didn't freeze or shut down like she expected him to. He stayed where he was, stroking his fingers against her cheek, but his gaze wandered. He seemed a little distracted, though not upset.

"Morgen?"

His lips twitched in a smile that never quite formed, and then he cleared his throat and met her eyes. "You remember what I said, about why I was against that?"

"Yes, because of the embers…" Except she trailed off when she realized what he must have considered too.

The reason he didn't want children wasn't because he didn't *want* them, but because he was terrified of what would happen to her if she was pregnant with his child. He had vowed to never let such a thing happen, because he thought the embers would kill her. But she had the embers held within her now too. She had already technically survived the process that killed his mother and all the others.

"Do you understand what I'm saying?"

She nodded, eyes widening and burning with rising emotion.

"This doesn't mean I expect that of you. I would *never* ask you to have children if it was something you didn't want. You know that, right?"

"I know," she whispered with a trembling smile.

Her entire life had been ruled by fates she had no say in. When she was young, she hadn't been able to put her fear of love into words. But as she grew, she'd realized her idea of giving herself to someone in that way was tied directly to pain. Tragedy ran in her bloodline; the Fates had long decided for her that to love was a fatal thing. It could still happen, but when it did, it would destroy her—and it had. She was not the same, and something inside her was forever broken by what had happened. But perhaps that was just what was needed to end the cycle. Morgen had defied the Fates when he gave her the embers. She felt the truth of that in every breath she took, just a little more strained than before. But she was alive, and he was no longer cursed by the fear Kronos had never let him forget or deny: that he would destroy anything he loved.

They had choices now, not tragic destinies.

"Hey," he said softly, his brow creased. "I didn't mean you had to make any sort of decision right now."

She laughed, her voice breaking. "I know, and I won't, because I already know what I want. I just never had the luxury of being able to admit it, even to myself."

His lips parted, but he didn't speak. She could tell he didn't want to say anything that might push her one way or another.

"You can relax," she whispered, kissing him. "For now. Because I've always wanted a big family."

He laughed abruptly, pulling back to look at her. "Are you serious?"

"Completely. I used to be terrified Varax would randomly send you flashes of all our babies I was imagining. And then you'd ask, and I'd have to pretend it had nothing to do with you, but the lie would be very easy to pick up on because they all had your eyes—"

"Nya," he said, laughing and brushing his thumbs down her tear-damp cheeks. "That would have terrified me."

She grinned. "I know."

He sighed, still laughing softly as he dropped his forehead against hers and shut his eyes. "Just promise me something, will you?"

She nodded against him. "I'm not going to die in childbirth. I'm fairly certain the embers would make that very difficult."

"I wasn't going to say that, but thank you for reminding me of that terrifying notion."

"Oh… What were you going to say?"

He kissed her, slowly and deeply, and she almost forgot she was waiting for him to speak until he gently pulled away.

"Promise me to make sure I actually do my duty, by force if you need to. Even though I know you'll probably be much better at it than I will, ruling Arcadia is supposed to be my burden. A part of me would love to watch you put everyone in their place, and once we have children, it will be tempting to say fuck it and hand off being king to someone else. But I shouldn't hide from the responsibility, not anymore."

"And the embers," she muttered, arching her back as he kissed down across her collarbone. "Can't forget the importance of those."

"Mm, yeah, those," he said, entirely uncaring and completely distracted as his lips skimmed her breasts.

She bit her lip, and when he noticed, a low sound escaped him. He pressed his thumb over her mouth then appeared to reconsider before instead scolding her with a nipping tug of his teeth.

"Morgen?"

He pulled back just enough to look at her. His irises were a deep amber-gold, eclipsed by the dark spread of his pupils, and his expression was hungry but open. He wasn't trying to hide anything from her, not anymore.

"Yes, Nya?"

"I love you."

The gold of his eyes flared bright, and his lips twitched. He nudged his nose against hers. "I really thought you would never let me say it."

She kissed him, but he stopped her. He laughed shakily, nothing but warmth in his eyes when he told her, "I have never loved anything in my entire life. Nothing except for you. I love you so much, I sometimes think it will break me. It nearly did, and I don't even care."

A tear slipped down her cheek, and he kissed it away. His lips were salty when they met hers.

She had never wanted anything more than to imagine a future with him without fearing the cost. She could, now, she realized, and it was enough to make her chest ache with joy.

"Let's make some heirs," she said, meaning to joke but failing when her voice broke.

He didn't flinch or shy away at her words or the unfet-
tered emotion in voice. He only smiled and agreed before
kissing her again.

CHAPTER

THIRTY

Sora,

I am returning to Cion, to be with her in her final days. After her time has passed, I will not force you or Nya to relive the pain of the past by seeing me. I will haunt the memories for you both, so you may forget and finally live in peace, as you have always wished. As you deserve.
—Ana

A FEW WEEKS LATER, for the first time ever, Nya stepped into the palace where the former king of the gods, Kronos, once ruled. This was the place where her parents suffered unimaginable horror and loss, where countless mortal women lost their lives, and where Morgen had been tortured and abused by a father who was supposed to have loved and protected him above all others.

The interior of the palace was underwhelming. A little tacky. Too much gold in all the wrong places.

She lifted her chin high at the ridiculous, gaudy décor, and Morgen's hand tightened where it wrapped around hers. He had paused at the threshold of the main entrance, then again at the enormous arch signaling they were entering the throne room, the curved doors thrown open to welcome them. She stopped with him both times, allowing him every pause he needed.

Carus trailed behind them with a small group of guards from Morgen's army. Some of them had left now that the threat of conflict was diminished, but most had remained. Today, they would line the throne room as she and Morgen were crowned king and queen of Arcadia.

"They fixed the ceiling," Morgen muttered, his eyes sweeping upwards to the glass dome.

Nya furrowed her brow. "What?"

His eyes stayed fixed above. "Your mother and Thessilnn destroyed it when they came after your father. She blew out the stained glass on the walls too, though I see Sol altered the panels when they repaired them." He cleared his throat, finally looking away. "It's strange to see it all intact again."

Nya tightened her grip on his hand, more for her sake than his now. Sometimes, when he spoke of that day, she felt like she was hearing about strangers, not her parents. She vowed silently, then and there, to herself and all others, that she would never let anyone live in such fear again.

"Morgen," Carus said from behind them. "You two should probably get ready."

Morgen didn't reply at first. His throat worked, and then he gave a curt nod and turned swiftly, letting go of Nya's hand. She watched, lips pinched, as he strode out of the throne room.

Carus glanced at her. He looked sad. "Give him time, Nya. I think…this is much more difficult for him than either of us can fully comprehend."

"I know that," she said. "But he doesn't need to bear it alone either."

She didn't wait for his response before hurrying after Morgen.

She caught up to him at the bottom of a grand marble stairwell that led to a large open balcony. Morgen was staring past the stairs, down a small hallway that branched off to the left. His fingers were wrapped so tightly around the polished wood banister, his knuckles were white, his eyes wide in an old terror as they fixed on the spot.

"Was that it?" she asked quietly, stopping next to him. "Your room? Down that hall?"

He inhaled sharply, and his breath shook on the exhale. "It was, yes."

"Do you want to look? Or would it be better not to?"

He tore his gaze from the hall, and when he looked at her, she found his eyes were dull but shining with unshed tears. "Can you come with me?"

Her heart broke at the broken vulnerability in his voice, but she didn't let it show on her face. He didn't need her to be upset for him right now. He just needed her to be there.

She took his hand again. *Whenever you're ready.*

I'm afraid. Logically, I know he won't be there, but it feels… It's hard to convince myself he won't be lurking around some corner.

"I know," she whispered, pressing her palm to her cheek.

He stared at her for a stretch of time, and she didn't move, letting him take whatever he needed from her. Eventually, he nodded curtly, more to himself than her, she thought, then turned down the hallway.

She didn't have much experience at all with palaces, but she imagined this was what a servant's hall would look like.

Small, simple, conveniently hidden from the main splendor without being too far from reach.

He stopped at a slightly ajar door midway down the hall. The wood was splintered and burned in several places. She held his hand tightly, and he nudged the door with his foot. It swung open, creaking on its hinges, to reveal a small room, with only a bed and a roughly hewn chest of drawers. Dust floated through the air, illuminated by the dim stream of light coming in from a small, dirty window above the bed.

Morgen swallowed audibly then let go of her hand and walked slowly towards the bed. She pressed a hand to her chest to steady herself as she watched him kneel, peering underneath the bed. It was so small, the sheets tucked neatly into the thin mattress.

Morgen reached under the bed and pulled out a small wooden box. When he opened it, she came closer, watching him ghost his fingers over the objects within. They were simple, ordinary things: a cream-colored kerchief, two pieces of inked parchment, a crumbling autumn leaf, a tiny brass pendant crudely formed into the shape of a dragon.

"Kindnesses," he murmured before shutting the box again.

Her eyes burned, and this time, she could not stop the tears that fell silently down her cheeks. The objects in the box were mementos, just like the ones from her he'd kept in his room in the Gods' Aisle. But these objects represented the only moments of kindness or warmth he had been given as a child here.

"The people who gave me these are long dead," he said, sliding the box back under the bed. "It never took long for

Kronos to sniff out those who were extending too much sympathy my way." He glanced back at her, noting the tears. "Please don't tell me you're sorry. I don't think I can take any pity right now."

Her brow rose at his blank expression. She wiped the tears away and knelt next to him. "Give me a little more credit than that, Morgen."

She shut her eyes briefly, attempting to *try* and calm the embers rising to further bolster her emotions. It had been a feat she'd been working on with him these past weeks, but she was still not as controlled as she would have liked. "Of course I'm sad for you, and for them, and I'm angry all that had to happen. It would be impossible for me not to feel those things." She shook her head slightly. "But I don't pity you."

He exhaled, and his entire body slackened. He pressed his forehead to her shoulder and breathed deeply. "I'm sorry," he said, voice muffled. "It was instinct to expect that. This place is just… It's unbalancing my mind, being here."

She wrapped her arms around him, holding him tightly. "I wish we didn't have to come back here."

"Me too."

"The decor is obscenely ugly. Who allowed that much gold? It's garish. We'll have to tear everything out and start completely from scratch if we want to make it bearable."

He lifted his head, staring at her with an unreadable expression before a surprised laugh burst out. "The decor?" he said, still chucking. "*That's* what you're worried about?"

Her lips twitched, and she shrugged. "We have to start somewhere."

They both knew it was more than that without saying.

She wanted to make this place as far from the horror-filled halls he remembered as possible, to erase memories of Kronos so he and anyone else who had suffered at the former king's hands did not see him here.

Morgen pressed his palms to her face, nudging his nose against hers. "I love you," he said, and then, before she could reply, he kissed her gently.

"So rude, not letting me reply," she said when he broke away, but the words were too soft to even be teasing, especially when she added, "I love you too."

His smile was small and fleeting, but she took the victory regardless. He stood, offering her a hand. "Shall we?"

She took it, sweeping one more glance around the room. "We shall."

Hardly an hour into the evening, Nya decided she *hated* small talk. She'd never had to endure much of it before, given her secluded childhood, and even at the temple where she had served in D'anna, the sisters had only even spoken when necessary.

During the reception that followed the lengthy coronation ceremony, no one seemed to be saying what they really meant. Each polite inquiry had a double meaning, and almost every interaction felt coated in forced flattery.

She wasn't alone in her feelings; Morgen didn't seem to be enjoying himself much at all either. She could see the strain in every 'smile' he gave, if she could even call his expression that. A handful of painful hours into the party, Carus interrupted a stilted conversation with a 'friend' of

Thanatos' who Nya was fairly certain was actually terrified of the Death god.

"Your Majesties," he said with a bow, smirking when Morgen glared at him. "There's someone who wishes to speak to you both in the gardens. I can escort you there."

"We better go then," Nya said, forcing herself to sound apologetic.

Neither of them waited for the demi-god they'd been speaking to, and Carus trailed them as they escaped out of the ballroom. Double glass doors opened into the hedge maze garden, and Nya took a deep inhale of the cool evening air as soon as they stepped outside.

"You two looked like you could use a second," Carus said, striding ahead of them to a circular courtyard containing a gurgling fountain in the shape of a dragon and three stone benches. It was lined with a garden of white roses, some of the patches glowing in the night air.

Nya slumped onto one of the benches, a hand on her middle. Her gown spilled around her, the fabric brushing against the smooth white stones plastered together in strange patterns on the ground. Anabeth had been the one to procure the monstrosity of silver and dove gray tulle, gathered into a corseted bodice that had been laced far too tight for Nya's comfort.

She pressed a hand to her constricted stomach, and Carus eyed the dress warily. "Can you breathe in that thing?"

She rubbed her ribs, wincing. "Hardly."

She carefully untangled the iron circlet from her hair. It was a twin to Morgen's, stars hammered delicately into its shining surface—the crown her mother would have worn if she had actually wed Kronos.

She rubbed at her scalp. "No one told me being a queen would be so uncomfortable."

"You can wear whatever damned clothes you like," Morgen grumbled. "Don't let anyone tell you there's a 'proper' way."

"And if they do," Carus added, "just ask them where following the 'proper way' got them."

Her lips twitched. "Noted."

Footsteps crunched the gravel, and all three of them turned to see her parents approaching from down a shadowed pathway of the garden. Nya got to her aching feet as they neared.

"Are you leaving?" she asked, ignoring the way her chest tightened as she spoke.

Her mother nodded, smiling sadly. Her eyes shone with tears when she touched Nya's cheek with cool fingertips. "Not forever. We'll be back often, I'm sure."

"Don't feel guilty for needing to go. I understand now," she whispered.

Her mother pulled her into a tight hug. "My brave, brave girl," she whispered into her hair. "I love you more than all the stars combined."

Nya clung to her, squeezing her eyes shut and memorizing the comforting scent of jasmine and night air that always clung to her. "I love you, Mama."

When they finally parted, Nya threw her arms around her father, who held her tight before sighing and gently pulling away from her.

"Do you still remember how to throw a punch?" he asked, his expression completely serious.

She laughed even as her eyes burned with tears. "Of course."

"Good." He tapped her nose. "If he ever gives you trouble…" His gaze flicked back to Morgen, and he raised his hand, curled into a fist. "Punch first, ask questions later. And call for Thessilnn or Heles if you ever need anything."

"I'll be fine." She took a deep breath. "You can stop worrying."

He patted her cheek. "Not possible."

"What if I make a complete mess of ruling Arcadia?"

"Also not possible," he said, smiling and adding, "I love you. We'll be back soon, alright?"

She sniffled. "I love you too."

Both her parents hugged her one last time before they turned to Carus. She left them alone to say their goodbyes, following Morgen deeper into the hedge maze.

They walked in silence for a while. An owl hooted nearby, and foliage rustled in a light breeze. In many regards, Arcadia was not so different from the mortal realm. Still, there was an undercurrent of magic she had never felt in Mise, or even D'anna. Mortals were the only source of magic beyond Arcadia's borders, but here, the magic lived within the land itself, stabilized now thanks to the embers humming warmly in her chest.

"You really know how to punch someone?"

She smirked. "Are you afraid of me now?"

Morgen snorted. "No. I was just curious if it was merely an empty threat."

She swatted at him and exclaimed in mock rage, "Rude!"

He chuckled, some of the tension that had gathered in his face over the course of the day easing. She tipped her head back, staring at the expanse of star-speckled sky above them.

"It came to me again," she said quietly. "In a dream, while I was recovering."

Morgen stopped walking. "What did it want?"

She glanced at him. It had grown cold enough that their breath clouded the air, but she didn't mind. "It took the form of a child," she told him. "A young girl. All it wanted was to make sure I remembered its true name."

"Did you?" he asked hoarsely.

"Of course. But there was a reason it appeared the way it did in the dream."

"What do you mean?"

She sighed softly and took his hand in hers, pressing it to her flat stomach. When she looked at him, his eyes were wide, aglow with blazing amber-gold.

"She looked like us, whoever she was," she said quietly. "And someday, we will give her that name, so this world will not forget it again."

She knew her words frightened him, and she knew why. He did not understand in the way she did and never would, but neither of them spoke further about it for now. She lifted her eyes to the night sky once more, and he joined her this time. Two dragons flew overhead; one dark as midnight, the other the same milky shade as the full moon. Varax followed before looping back a few minutes later, an escort and a farewell for now.

The stars sputtered and flickered, as if wishing Night and Death's daughter goodbye for now. Nya's mouth lifted when she saw it, her smile growing when the expanse of the midnight sky paused before lighting up once more—an acknowledgment to her too, the one who had finally seen it for what it was.

Not a monster or a hero. Not evil nor good. Simply an existence.

"Nya," Morgen murmured, hand still pressed to her stomach. "You're cold. We should go back inside."

She finally lowered her gaze from the stars, and it was Morgen who caught sight of the bright-red comet streaking above.

"Good luck?" she asked him.

He shrugged, but his voice held a hint of surprise when he told her, "In Arcadia, red is the color of honor and sacred things. I suppose…some might say to see a comet such as that the night of our coronation is approval of the Fates themselves."

"I see." She paused. "I suppose you're right. We should return."

He kissed her cheek then took her hand as they walked. They returned to the ridiculous party, new gods blessed by the very void from which the world had been made.

CHAPTER 31
SEVEN YEARS AND ELEVEN MONTHS LATER

"Fucking Fates, they're here early," Carus groaned as he spotted the small group of gods lingering in the courtyard below them.

"Carus," Morgen said, shaking his head with a long-suffering sigh. "How many times do I need to remind you—"

Carus waved him off, rolling his eyes. "Yes, yes, no expletives around the tiny godlings."

Nya snorted, accepting a flower petal from tiny, sticky hands. "And yet you never seem to remember."

Carus' eyes twinkled, and he knelt as Thia held out a petal to him. "Thia," he said seriously. "What is my name?"

Her tiny brow creased. "What Cari want?"

Morgen barked out a laugh, and Carus tipped his head back before he patiently reminded her, "Carus, Thia. My name is Carus."

She frowned but didn't reply, returning to her pile of petals, raptly focused on selecting another.

"I don't even know why I try," Carus muttered, watching her with a rueful smile as she toddled over to Morgen.

"Thank you, darling," Morgen said when Thia slapped an entire handful of petals into his hand. He glanced at Carus and added, "She isn't even two, Carus. She's actually speaking incredibly well for her—"

"Blah, blah, yes, proud parent speech," Carus said, waving his hand just as Rhiann practically tripped over his own feet running into the room.

"Mama, they're here!" he said, jumping up and down, faint streaks of gold sparking in his blue eyes.

While Thia was like a tiny replica of Nya, Rhiann was mostly his grandmother's lookalike, with large blue eyes and a round nose. His magic seemed mostly fire-based so far, though, which had proved to be a bit of a disaster; several temper tantrums had resulted in burns that healed quickly but always detoured into a long session of tears.

"Should you really be going to council meetings right now?" Carus asked Nya, brow raised.

She rolled her eyes as she started to push herself off the chair. "Right, of course. Because letting Morgen lead the council meetings is *such* a good idea."

Morgen strode over, taking her hand and helping her up. "You're so mean to me," he said, though his tone was fond.

"I'm not mean, I'm just correct, and everyone here knows it."

Rhiann snickered, and Carus flicked his nose. "You have no respect, tiny," he said.

"I grew three inches this year!" Rhiann insisted, screeching as Carus ruffled his hair.

Morgen huffed, shaking his head, but said to Nya in a low voice, "He brings up a good point, Nya."

"I will be fine," she said, softening her tone and touching his cheek. "I'll be downstairs, over the border."

He took a breath, placing a hand over her rounded belly. "Sol will be there today."

"I'm aware. I was the one who ordered him to come to this meeting, something *you* could have protested if you wanted to."

"It is time he shows up," he grumbled, absentmindedly swiping his thumb back and forth. "I just wish it was not necessary right now."

"I would say you could just come with me if you're that worried, but I'm afraid you might kill him for…I don't know, speaking? And as much as I'd love to let you, that would be a horrible diplomatic decision. Not to mention, I'm not sure I trust Carus to keep Rhiann from burning the entire palace down."

He sighed, dropping to his knees and pressing a kiss to her belly. "You are right, as usual. Just…maybe sit far away from him. As far as possible."

Thia shrieked suddenly, running past them with something in her hands, and Rhiann screamed, "Thia, that is *my* book!"

Morgen pressed his forehead against her for a moment, then stood and said calmly, "Thia, darling, please give your brother his book back. I'll find you one with pictures instead."

Thia paused mid-motion, her hands still outstretched towards the chair she was attempting to scale. "Big lizzas?"

"Yes, love, the one with dragons," he said, scooping her

up and subtly handing Rhiann the book. "Though, I'm afraid if you keep referring to Varax as a big lizard, her goodwill may soon run out."

Nya smiled and took the opportunity to slip from the room. When she stepped into the hallway, Morgen said down the pathway, *Promise to be alert and let me know right away if anything seems amiss?*

I promise. Stop worrying.

No promises. I love you.

Her lips twitched, and she rested a hand on her belly. *I love you.*

A slight ache spread up her back as she walked to the small room where she typically held council meetings, but she ignored it. It was probably just one of the many daily reminders from the embers of their presence.

Despite telling Morgen not to worry, her pulse sped up, and cold fear washed over her when she entered the room to see Sol sitting at the table next to Bella and across from Janis. It was nearing eight years since the last time she had been this close to him, but Vulcan had recently informed her Sol had been pushing his luck when it came to his network of spies and personal guards. The last thing she needed was for him to feel like he could get away with any sort of insubordination. The council usually ran more like a democracy, but that courtesy did not extend to him after what he'd done.

"Hello, Nya," he said in that same deep, smooth voice she remembered as soon as he saw her. "You've made quite the name for yourself, all while producing a whole brood of heirs, it seems."

Bella slapped a hand over her face and muttered, "Great start, Sol."

Nya merely smiled and replied coolly, "It's amazing, isn't it? Although, I must say, being a capable, level-headed ruler has been surprisingly easy for me. Perhaps it's because I don't have bull-headed gods like you breathing threats down my neck all the time, or maybe it's even just my lack of a cock. Unfortunately, the world may never know."

Thanatos grinned—a rather terrifying expression—and both Vulcan and Janis choked as they tried to suppress laughs. Nyx and Juno merely sat down, as if she had commented on the weather or the choice of wine at the table, and Bella still hadn't removed her hands from her face.

Sol, on the other hand, looked furious. Nya ignored him, settling with minor difficulty at the head of the table.

"On that note, Sol, I called you here to remind you—" She cleared her throat but plowed on despite the sudden telltale start of labor pains. "To remind you staying in line is not optional. You still have a place on this council and your life, both of which I am sure Morgen and I would be happy to rescind if you cannot manage to keep from meddling and sending your spies here."

Sol sneered at her. "And where is Morgen? Playing house, as usual, I imagine. Bella informed me he's often absent from these meetings."

"Some of us have a better head for diplomacy," she said, subtly pressing a hand to her belly beneath the table. "But I would be happy to ask him here if you'd like, though I will warn you, he's still quite angry about your prior actions, and I can't guarantee he won't harm you."

"Are you insinuating he could not even keep himself from, say, ripping my heart out? And you all say he isn't like Kronos."

"Spine," Vulcan supplied.

Sol balked. "What?"

Vulcan smirked. "I said, 'spine', which is probably more likely to be the body part you'd be missing if Morgen came down here and saw you insulting Nya."

"Alright, enough," Nya cut in. "Does anything have any pressing issues they would like to bring forward?"

Janis rested his chin on steepled fingers. "Don't we usually end with that?"

"Yes," Nya said, swallowing a groan. "But this meeting will be rather short, so I want to make sure no one has any immediate concerns."

Bella scowled. "The last time we had a 'short' meeting, it was a complete waste of time. Could you perhaps just reschedule it next time if that's going to be the case?"

"I was not planning on…" She gripped the edge of the table, hissing through her teeth. "Planning on cutting it —short."

"Nya, are you alright?" Juno asked, her brow creased.

"Fine," she bit out. "Any concerns?"

Thanatos raised a hand. "Just one question: shall I kick Sol out now, or would you prefer I wait?"

Sol gaped. "I haven't even been here for five minutes!"

Morgen.

Less than ten seconds passed before he replied. *What's wrong?*

I need you to come here right now, and I need you to stay calm.

"I demand an explanation!" Sol shouted, standing in his

chair at the same moment Morgen materialized through a portal next to her.

She grabbed his arm and hissed, "Calm," before he could move towards Sol.

He realized what was happening before she even needed to say it and barked, "The meeting is over, everyone out. Now!"

She was fairly certain most of the principals understood the reason for the sudden end to the meeting, but Sol, unsurprisingly, did not. Thankfully, before he could say or do anything else that might stoke Morgen's temper, Bella said, "You really want to leave now, Sol, unless you'd like to learn what happens when you try to push Morgen's buttons while his wife is in labor."

Sol's nostrils flared, and he shot a glare at Nya, scowled, then promptly disappeared through a portal. As soon as he was gone, the tension in the room eased, and Nyx asked, "Do you need anything?"

Nya shook her head, gritting out, "We have very capable midwives."

"Whom we are going to request come to the palace right now," Morgen said, glancing pointedly at Vulcan, who muttered, "Fine, yes, I'm on it," and hurried out of the room.

Bella and Janis disappeared without Nya noticing, and Juno touched Nyx's arm. "We should go. Send word later."

Morgen nodded distractedly, and they disappeared with Thanatos.

"Alright," Morgen said once they were gone. "Let's have this baby."

She blew out a shaky breath. "A sentence I never thought I'd hear you say ten years ago."

He chuckled, slowly easing her up. "Yet, here I am, saying it for the third time."

She let out a breathy laugh that ended in a wince.

Do try to keep the pathway closed my way until the babe has arrived, Varax said. *Someone opened it up last time for a few hours, and I cannot communicate the level of anxiety it created in me.*

Morgen kissed Nya's hand. *How do you think I feel, Varax?*

I would prefer not to consider it.

A short three hours later, Nya stared at the tiny, mewling baby in her arms. Morgen was positioned behind her on the bed, and he let out a breathy laugh as the baby grabbed at his pinky.

"She has long fingers," he murmured.

Nya nodded. "They aren't small and stubby like Rhiann or Thia's were when they were born. She has your hands, I think. And your eyes and mouth. Really, she doesn't look like me much at all."

"She has your nose," he said softly. "But everything else...I think you're right."

"I know I'm right."

The baby had fallen asleep, hand curled around his finger. Nya took a deep breath and said quietly, "Morgen, I think it's time."

He stiffened slightly. "I don't know."

"It won't hurt her. You know I wouldn't do anything to hurt her. But *she* is who I saw in the dream. I knew it the

328

moment I laid eyes on her, and I promised I wouldn't forget her name."

"You haven't. Isn't that enough?"

Nya took a deep breath. She had known this was going to be hard for Morgen, when the time came to give one of their children the name the void had given her in a dream. He still feared the creature who had tried to take her and their world with it. She didn't blame him; she would fear it too if she was anyone else, if she hadn't experienced what she had. But she meant it when she told him it wouldn't hurt her or their baby. Naming her daughter for the void was simply a reminder it was not alone, a way for its name to forever be remembered in this world.

"Ithesoa," she whispered, gently adjusting the soft baby blanket. "Your name is Ithesoa."

She had never said it aloud, never even told Morgen the exact name she had been given in the dream, but as he heard it, he sucked in a surprised breath.

"See?" she said, glancing back at him. "It's her."

His throat worked as he said hoarsely, "Yeah, it is."

She leaned against him, and Varax let out an audible breath down the pathway.

I am proud of you both, you know, she said. *I was told by many of my kind that choosing your soul was a mistake, that Fate had already made its choice, and I was damning myself along with you. I always hoped to prove them wrong, and you know how vain I am. It would have been too bad had they been right.*

Nya glanced at Morgen, who was smiling faintly and shaking his head slightly so as to not wake the sleeping baby in her arms. His eyes were still on Nya when he replied, *I'm glad you were so hellbent on being right, Varax. I suppose you were wise enough to see what we could not before.*

And what is that? Varax asked, sounding vaguely amused.

That we cannot choose where Fate makes our beginning, but we can certainly push against its hand in the end.

Nya nodded, and Morgen kissed her head as she added, *There are some things stronger than Fate.*

It was a while later, when Morgen was carefully handing Rhiann the baby and Thia sat on Carus' lap, that Varax replied.

My kind all told me your reign would be the harbinger of the end. Now, they say it is the beginning of something new. Something better.

Nya's lips twitched, and she met Morgen's eyes from across the room. He smiled too, before Rhiann tugged at his sleeve.

She had felt the doom of her fate as long as she could remember. Now, she only felt peace at the thought of the years stretched far ahead.

Acknowledgments

Thank you to MK at Azala Press for all the hard work you've put into creating such a wonderful community of authors, and also to Sam for your dedication to keeping the ship running! Thanks to Alexa at the Fiction Fix and also to everyone in the Azala family; I admire every one of you and am so happy we can share in each other's wins and joys. To my husband, Ryan, for being my person, and showing me how gentle and kind love can be. We would *definitely* share a dragon and she would definitely be SO annoyed with us.

Finally, to my wonderful readers. I truly wouldn't be able to do this without you, and I hope you were able to laugh, roll your eyes, and cry just as much as I did while following Nya and Morgen's story. We'll wrap up our adventures in Arcadia soon by going back in time to where it all began, with a certain goddess of night and her mischievous consort…

9 781969 444210